A Trick of Mirrors

A Trick of Mirrors

The Ladies' Wagering Whist Society, Book 4

Meredith Bond

ISBN: 978-1-7372086-2-4

Cover Art by QuarterbackTB,

https://qtbdesign.wixsite.com/qtbdesign

Logo by Anjali Banerji

Edited by The Editing Hall,

http://theeditinghall.com

Published by Anessa Books,
For more information please visit
http://anessabooks.com

DRAMATIS PERSONAE

Christianne Ayres (previously Lady Norman): Founding member of the Ladies' Wagering Whist Society

Lydia Welles née Sheffield: member of the Ladies' Wagering Whist Society

Diana Crowther, Lady Colburne née Hemshawe: member of the Ladies' Wagering Whist Society

Claire Tyne, Lady Blakemore: member of the Ladies' Wagering Whist Society

Alys Russell, Duchess of Kendell: member of the Ladies' Wagering Whist Society

Mrs. Penelope Aldridge: member of the Ladies' Wagering Whist Society

Cynthia Montley, Lady Sorrell: member of the Ladies' Wagering Whist Society

Ellen Aston, Lady Moreton: member of the Ladies' Wagering Whist Society

Joshua Powell, Lord Wickford: owner Powell's Club for Gentlemen

Tina Bronley, Duchess of Warwick née Rowan: Christianne's natural daughter

Robert Bronley, Duke of Warwick: Tina's husband

Lady Margaret Bronley: Warwick's sister

Liam Ayres, Lord Ayres: Christianne's husband and Tina's father

John Welles, Lord Welles: Lydia's husband

Andrew Crowther, Lord Colburne: Diana's husband

Beatrice & Isabelle Kendrick: Lady

Blakemore's nieces

Edward Pike, Lord Conway: Bel's romantic interest

Paul Adler, Lord St. Vincent: Bee's romantic interest

Elizabeth Adler, Lady St. Vincent: Paul's young step-mother

Chapter One

~March 22, 1807~

Beatrice Kendrick crouched on the floor of the carriage as it moved through the streets of London. It wasn't easy to keep her balance in the moving vehicle and pull on the maid's cloak at the same time, but somehow, she managed. She pulled up the hood covering her telltale red hair and ducked her head down so no one could see her face, identical to her sister's, who was sitting and staring out the window. They moved ever closer to their aunt's Mayfair home where they would be staying for the Season.

Bee carefully sat back on the seat next to her maid, Annie, making sure to keep her head down, so her hood wouldn't be dislodged. They couldn't risk anyone even getting a glimpse of her.

As planned, Bee arranged herself so she couldn't be seen when the door to the carriage opened outside of Lord and Lady Blakemore's home. Her sister Bel and Annie got down, making a huge fuss over the beauty of the house and the number of footmen pouring out of the house to take in all of Bel's luggage.

The door to the coach opened again, causing Bee to hold her breath and scrunch down even farther into the tiniest ball against the side.

"Ach, ye don't need to check inside the carriage," Bee heard the coachman scold someone. "Miss Kendrick only had a luncheon basket in there with her, and I'll bring it round to the kitchen meself."

The door closed again, and Bee allowed herself to breathe. If she were caught now, their entire plan would be jeopardized. Months of arguing back and forth between her and Bel, weeks of Bee trying to convince her sister that she did, in fact, need to be there with her in London and that, no, simply relaying information by mail about the men she met would not be enough. Days of swearing to her sister that she truly had no desire to subvert Bel's debut into society for her own ends. She was going to happily enter society on her own the following year just as their parents had planned, but there was absolutely no way that Bee was going to allow her sister, with her cavalier attitude toward rules and proper behavior when she got an idea in her head, to come to London on her own.

Bee loved her twin sister, but they could not risk Bel getting into scrapes the way she did when they went out to parties and assemblies at home. She had to find a husband this season, so Bee could be presented next year. Their parents had been very clear that they could only afford to present one girl at a time. But no amount of love could change the fact that Bel was, well, flighty and not always the best judge of character.

It had taken months for Bee to show her sister this truth and weeks for her to agree that maybe it would be best if Bee were there to actually meet the men she might consider marrying. And now the time was at hand for them to put this plan into action, and it was vital that no one knew *both* twins were there. Bee could not risk getting caught. God only knew if they would get this opportunity again, were she to be found now.

The carriage jolted forward as John Coachman started toward the back of the house. Bee almost toppled off the seat but caught herself just in time. They had planned for him to park the carriage at the back of the house and leave it there for a few minutes. John would then make a scene bringing the luncheon basket into the kitchen so Bee could sneak inside behind him. Annie would be on the lookout for her upstairs so she could guide Bee to Bel's room.

This was going to be the trickiest part of their plan. Bee took in a deep breath and tried to calm her pounding heart.

The carriage stopped again, and Bee could hear John talking to the horses. He was so funny. He always talked to them as if they could understand every word he said. When they were little, Bee and Bel truly believed the animals could understand him because they always did exactly what John told them to do.

The door opened once again, and John popped his head into the carriage. "All clear," he said, giving Bee a broad, toothy smile. He grabbed the basket and helped her down.

"You're wonderful, have I told you that recently?" Bee asked, returning his smile.

"Ye told me when I agreed to this havey-cavey plan o'yers," he told her. "Ready?"

She took in a deep breath and let it out slowly. "Yes. Let's go."

She followed in his shadow through the garden

gate and to the back door of the house where, they presumed, the kitchen was. It was a question as to whether the door opened directly into the kitchen, in which case John would drop the basket, causing a ruckus . If it opened into a hallway, Bee could easily find the servants' stair and sneak up.

He opened the door and then paused to peer inside. He gave a shake of his head, letting Bee know that he was about to make a mess, and she had to move fast and find the back stairs.

John took two steps into the kitchen and then deliberately tripped over a chair, sending the picnic basket and all its contents flying across the large room. Two maids screeched as they were hit by flying debris, the cook started screaming, and a footman shouted as he was covered with the messiest food the girls could find to leave in the basket just for this. Bee resisted the urge to watch John's excellent acting skills—a privilege she'd been witness to before—and moved quickly for a door that lay open just enough to see that it led to the stairs. She slipped through on silent slippered feet, ignoring the curses and shouts behind her, and ran up to the first floor where she imagined Bel's room would be.

A voice higher up the stair called out quietly for her, and she continued up to the second floor where Annie was waiting.

"The room is here, quickly now," the maid said, gently pushing her down the hall and toward an open door. "Luckily, there's a separate dressing room. You'll be able hide in there whenever anyone comes into the room."

Bee gave a nod, not daring to speak aloud until she was safely ensconced in the room. Once inside the dressing room with the door closed behind them, she finally took in a deep breath and threw off Annie's stifling cloak.

"Ha..." She sighed. "We made it!" She took in a few more breaths just for good measure. She didn't think she'd actually breathed for a good five minutes, and her heart was still pounding.

Annie giggled and shook her head. "You made it."

"Yes. Now we only have three more months of hiding to manage, but I'm in."

Annie dropped her head into her hands.

Bee rubbed the dear woman's back. "It'll be all right, Annie. We'll get into a routine, and it will all be fine. Don't you worry."

Annie looked up, her forehead creased with worry. "I don't know how, but if you say so, Miss Bee."

"Come, I'll help you unpack while we wait for Bel."

~*~

They'd arrived! Finally, after days cooped up in that nasty old travelling carriage with no one except Bee and Annie, Bel felt like she could breathe again.

She hopped down from the carriage and paused to take in a deep breath of London air. It was nothing like the air at home. At home everything smelled of hay, soil, and animals. Here in the city, it was all humanity. Of course, there was still the smell of the horses, but more than anything, Bel felt as if she could smell the sheer number of people all around her. The street where her aunt lived was quiet, but still, the city around her hummed with energy. She could feel it, and it sent a thrill of excitement up her spine.

She was in London for her season! She could barely wait to get started.

The door to the well-appointed house in front of her opened, and two footmen in livery spilled out, immediately moving toward the carriage to take Bel's trunks into the house. An older woman wearing a plain black gown with a white cap followed, pausing to curtsy to Bel before approaching her.

"Miss Kendrick, welcome to Blackholm House. I'm Mrs. Sully, the housekeeper. Please, if you would follow me."

Oh, yes, she was most definitely going to like living here, Bel thought with another frisson of excitement. At home, they barely got by with a very limited staff—a cook and housekeeper, a daily, and one footman—but here there were so many people to see to everything.

She took in a very satisfied breath and followed Mrs. Sully past the white marble pillars on either side of the black door, adorned with an impressive brass knocker in the shape of a lion's head, and into the house.

She paused to take in the luxury. The black and white tile floor. A ceiling that soared above painted sky blue. It was complete with clouds, a golden sun on one side, and cherubs adorning the corners. The housekeeper had stopped two steps up an impressive curving staircase with a black iron-work balustrade, waiting for her.

Bel suddenly remembered her sister and knew she had one thing to do, just one.

It had been drilled into her from the time they'd entered the city. She'd tried to look out the window to see where she was going to be living for the next few months, but Bee had been so insistent and annoying. Bel had finally given in and turned to acknowledge her sister. She'd assured Bee that she would, in fact, remember her instructions—and then in the excitement and splendor she'd almost forgotten!

"I'd like to be taken directly to my aunt, if you please," Bel said in her most commanding voice. In truth, she wasn't used to speaking to unfamiliar servants, and this woman intimidated her just a little.

"Yes, Miss, of course. As soon as you've freshened up from your journey—"

"No, thank you, we stopped at an inn just outside of London less than an hour ago," Bel said, interrupting the housekeeper. "I'd like to see Lady Blakemore now if she is available."

"Oh. Very well, Miss. If you would follow me, then, Lady Blakemore is in her private parlor." Mrs. Sully continued up the stairs.

Bel followed.

The housekeeper opened the second door from the stair and Bel followed her into a bright room with cream silk-covered walls. "Miss Kendrick, my lady," the housekeeper announced.

Lady Blakemore was sitting on a lovely flowered sofa with an embroidery frame in her hand and a sewing bag at her feet. She looked so very much like Bel's mother, she had to stop and take a second look. Her face was a touch rounder, but she had the same high cheekbones and pert nose. Her eyes were the same hazel as Bel's own, only her hair was a faded gray-blonde like her mother's, whereas Bel's hair was deep red like her father's. The lady's gown matched the blue flowers of the sofa perfectly as if she had chosen it specifically for that reason. She looked up with a surprised but welcoming smile.

Setting aside her stitching, she stood as Bel curtsied and then held out her hands to her niece. "Welcome, my dear Isabel, welcome to London."

Before Bel could say a word, there was shouting that sounded like it came from the bowels of the house—perhaps the kitchen. There must have been a whole host of people all screaming for them to hear. Lady Blakemore took a step toward the door, perhaps to go see what the commotion was about. Bel jumped into action and grabbed her aunt's hands.

"Thank you so much, Aunt Claire, for allowing me to come visit you," she said over the noise. "I can't tell you how much I'm looking forward to making my debut. I have been positively dreaming of this day for the entirety of the past year," she said with as much enthusiasm as she could muster.

Lady Blakemore was clearly torn, wanting to see what the problem was in the kitchen and needing to be polite to her niece. She kept looking over her shoulder toward the door, even as she tried to smile and be warm and welcoming.

"And we have been so looking forward to your arrival! I can't imagine what that noise is," she said, looking anxiously toward the door.

"But you are lucky to have so many staff members and so well-trained, I'm certain. Why, we have merely four servants at Bender Hall. Yet, the moment I arrived there were *two* footmen to take my things inside as well as your most efficient housekeeper, Mrs. Sully, to greet me," Bel gushed.

It worked. Her aunt turned back to her and

lifted her chin. "But of course, my dear. This is London, where appearances must be kept and well... We do have the means to maintain a proper staff—that is not to say anything against your dear Papa..."

"No, naturally, I understand. Mama reminded me any number of times how fortunate you were to have won the affection of Lord Blakemore when you were brought out into society. She hopes that I may do half as well as you."

Chapter Two

"I expect you to do as well, if not better, I'm sure," Lady Blakemore said. Bel could tell from the strain showing through her aunt's eyes how difficult a conversation this was for her. One did *not* discuss such things. Bel knew that, and if it weren't for her need to keep her aunt's attention on her rather than on her sister, who was probably even now sneaking in through the kitchen and up to her room, she would never have had the nerve.

"Do you, indeed?" Bel gave a little giggle. "I pray you are right! I would like nothing more than to live in such a beautiful home with a large staff. I don't know what sort of dowry Papa was able to manage for me. Do you think I might... And well, that is to say nothing of the prospect of falling love. Did you, dear Aunt, fall in love like Mama did? Oh! Or is that too personal a question to ask?" She put a hand to her mouth and widened her eyes. She truly did *not* wish to offend her aunt in any way.

Lady Blakemore's lips pursed, but the corners of her mouth lifted into a smile. "It is indeed a personal question, and if I were anyone other than your aunt... However, I understand you have been raised in a small society where such topics may not be out of bounds. Mine was not a love-match like your mother's, however, Blakemore and I are very attached to one another. One need not fall madly in love like your parents did to make a good marriage. Please do keep that in mind."

"Yes, ma'am, although… Is it very bad of me to *want* a love-match, do you think?" She now spoke from her heart for she wanted nothing more than to fall deeply, madly in love like her parents had. Bel saw their love every day in the way they looked at each other. She wanted a man to look at her the way her father looked at her mother, even after twenty years of marriage. She hoped she could find someone to smile at her in just that way.

Her aunt seemed to take pity on her as she gave Bel a true, understanding smile. "It's not bad at all, I just don't know that you should get your hopes up. Your mother has specifically said in her letters that she would like you to make a match this season so they may bring out your sister next year. Sadly, as you know, your parents simply cannot afford to have you both out at the same time."

"I know." Tears pierced Bel's eyes. "There is nothing I wanted more than to be brought out with Bee, but…"

"I understand. Naturally, the two of you are very close." Lady Blakemore gave Bel's hands a squeeze before letting them go.

The commotion downstairs had died down. Bel hoped her sister was now safely hidden away, and she could relax some.

"We are, indeed, very close," Bel agreed as she followed her aunt to the sofa to sit down.

"However, you will, I'm certain, manage without her these next few months. In fact, you'll probably be so busy you'll hardly have a moment to miss her," Lady Blakemore said, resuming her seat.

"I will take your word for it, my lady. And, oh, I am so looking forward to all the parties and balls, drives in the park, and outings to the theatre. Mama told me all about the wonderful things she did when she made her debut," Bel said with a giggle. "She said there would be *many* gentlemen to dance and speak with. And of course, I so look forward to making new friends among the ladies as well. Oh, and clothes! Please do tell me we'll be able to go shopping? Mama said I would have money to buy some new gowns." Bel could have gone on and on with all she was looking forward to, but Lady Blakemore smiled and shook her head.

"You must contain your excitement, my dear. It is very sweet but so very provincial. I do hope your Mama has taught you what is appropriate conversation and what is not?"

"Yes, indeed," Bel said. "She said that you were extremely, um, particular when it came to one's behavior, and I would need to absolutely be on my best behavior at all times."

Her aunt gave a little laugh. "Why do I have a feeling your mother used a different word than 'particular'? Difficult, perhaps? Horrid?"

Bel bit her lower lip. "I should not say," she whispered.

Her aunt gave her a look from under her eyelashes. That, coupled with a little smile, had Bel giggling. "I believe the exact word she used was 'hard-nosed'," she admitted.

Aunt Claire laughed, much to Bel's relief. "Yes. Well, I suppose that is deserved. I *am* rather hard-nosed, or as you so politely put it, 'particular' when it comes to a young lady's behavior. I have a reputation to maintain, Isabel. I am known for keeping to the rules and expecting others to do the same. When we leave this house or have guests in, I expect you to be a model young lady, is that understood?”

“Yes, ma’am,” Bel said, nodding. This was nothing new or surprising. Her mother had told her as much.

“You are to be careful of your conversation at all times, no matter with whom you are speaking. When you open your mouth, you not only represent yourself but our entire family. And just as importantly, that includes your sister. If you are rude or unkind, society will expect Beatrice to be the same. You are the one forging this road. If you behave well and say just the right thing, you will have an easy time of it and smooth the way for Beatrice to follow, do you understand?”

“Yes, ma’am.”

“For example, you must not respond with ‘yes, ma’am’ but ‘yes, my lady’ or ‘yes, Aunt.’”

“Yes, ma’—my lady.”

Her aunt nodded. “Very good. You’ll get used to it.”

“I do expect I will, but you will please excuse me the first few times I make a mistake, Aunt?” Bel asked, hoping her aunt wasn’t actually as hard-nosed as her mother had said.

“I shall. And that was very well said.” Aunt Claire nodded approvingly. Bel did her best not to bounce in joy or clap her hands as she normally would have done at home. Instead, she continued to sit demurely with her hands clasped in her lap and simply allowed her happiness to shine from her eyes.

“Your enthusiasm, when displayed just so, will

be appreciated," her aunt said.

"Thank you, ma'—my lady. I am doing my best. It's not easy to hide my feelings. I'm not used to doing so."

"I understand, but a lady is always demure."

Bel opened her mouth to say that she wasn't sure if she would always be able to hide her feelings, but just then a maid appeared carrying a tea tray. Now for the real test, Bel realized. Could she pour tea and serve it with grace? Well, at least, in that she knew she would excel. And by now Bee must be well hidden away.

~*~

Edward Pike, Viscount Conway, followed the butler up the stairs, and waited while he was announced before walking into the drawing room of his sister's stately London home.

"Conway!" Elizabeth practically screeched.

He didn't even have time to bow before he was nearly thrown backward as Elizabeth hurled herself into his arms. He was forced to take a step back but managed to keep them both on their feet. Laughing, he pulled her tight and gave her a good squeeze before letting her go and pushing her away to get a good look at his little sister.

Her rich, brown hair was piled attractively atop her head and her brilliant blue eyes—exactly like his own—were beginning to have a light starburst of lines at the corners. The deep violet dress she wore brought out the pink in her cheeks and lips and was quite flattering.

"You look well. Older, but not in a bad way," he said critically, looking her up and down.

She gasped. "Older! You should know better than to comment on a lady's age."

"Oh, come now, you're what? Seven? Eight and twenty, now?"

She frowned at him. "You know very well I am to turn thirty next year. I am precisely eleven months younger than you."

He chuckled. "Yes, I know, but truly you hardly look older than the girls just making their come out."

Her lips turned up into a smile. "That's much better. It's a complete lie, but it's the right thing to say." She took another step back and said, "And let me look at you."

He held his arms out and turned in a slow circle so she could admire him from all sides. "Old is what I am but not quite decrepit, yet."

"Not at all." She paused as she examined him. "Thinner," she determined, putting a hand to her chin.

He shrugged. "It's what happens when you don't eat so much for a while."

"Why haven't you been eating?" she asked, the frown returning to her face as she dropped her hands to her sides.

"Come now, Elizabeth, you know why."

"Do you not eat when you are sad?" she asked gently.

"No, as a matter of fact, I don't. I'm afraid I haven't had much of an appetite for some time."

"I'm so sorry, Edward. Come, sit down."

He followed her to the stylish gold damask sofa. She took his hands as they sat next to each other. "Tell me."

His eyes burned for a second before he blinked to clear them. It had been too long. He shouldn't still be feeling this way—or so he'd been telling himself for the past six months or more. He tried to put on a brave smile, but he wasn't sure it worked. "The end was... She lingered...and in such pain," he whispered, his voice not quite working right.

"Oh, Edward, I am so sorry." Her beautifully expressive brow creased in sorrow. She'd always been so empathetic. He appreciated that about his sister. "Was it cancer? Did the doctor's say?"

He could only nod; his throat had closed as it always did whenever he thought of his dearest Angelica.

"You were together for so long. What was it, three years, four?"

"Five," he managed.

"But you never married..."

"No. But now, of course, I wish for all the world we had." He sighed. "How I wish I had let her know how much I loved her. I mean, I told her, but marrying her... It would have meant so much more."

"It certainly would have been more of a statement, but what would society have thought?" Elizabeth asked, getting straight to the heart of the matter—the one thing that had kept him from making his arrangement with Angelica formal.

"I should have... I should have been strong enough to ignore them. But I wasn't. I allowed other people to dictate my actions, and she died never..."

"It's all right, my love. I'm certain she knew how much you cared for her." She gave his hands a squeeze.

"I hope so."

"I know you, Conway. I know that you would have made her feel loved and cherished whether you were married or not."

Conway caressed the back of his sister's hand with his thumb.

"Have you been able to sing? To even go to the theatre since then?"

He could only shake his head. Just the thought of going back to where he and Angelica had spent so much of their lives made him nauseated. "I couldn't," he whispered. He cleared his throat.

"I mourned for her... I could do nothing for the longest time." He paused and looked down at his hands. "For months, I could barely get myself out of the house. After that, I did nothing but wander the city. I thought of coming back sooner, but I wanted to stay close to her. I felt her there...in Venice. It was hard to leave but finally..." He sighed and looked back up at her. "Finally, I realized that I had to. I needed to come back."

"Of course you did! My goodness! You've got to start your life over, and you're *going* to. Being here is wonderful and you are going to be a new man in no time. You mark my words. We're going to go out to parties and to the theatre and engage in all manner of activities. You will be so busy you won't have time to even think of her."

"No, it's too soon."

"It is more than past time. It's been two years, Conway. You are not only going to re-enter society, my dearest, you are going to dance and have fun and, perhaps, even meet a wonderful young lady who will make you happy."

He could only laugh at her optimism. "Oh, how I've missed you," he said from his heart. He pulled her into another hug. But as they separated again, he said, "But you haven't told me how *you* are doing. Has it been difficult since your husband died? You must miss him terribly."

She gave him a sad little smile. "We were never in love, you know that. He married me because I was young."

"I'm sorry, but now you have Matthew," Conway said, giving her a warm smile and hoping to see her smile return as well. "How is he? He's...what, three years old now?"

Elizabeth laughed. "Four!"

"Four? Really? Already?"

"Yes. I'd call for him, but he's napping just now," she said.

"No, no, don't disturb him. I'm sure I'll see him later."

"Yes, you will. Most definitely. I can't wait to introduce him to his uncle."

"But he does have an heir, doesn't he? There's an older child as well, from St. Vincent's first wife, no? I seem to remember you writing about your stepson," Conway asked.

"Yes, although Paul is hardly a child. He is, however, a sweetheart. I don't know how I would have gotten through all of this without his support."

"Is he here in town with you?"

"Yes. Happily, I convinced him to come. Everything is going to become quite wonderful again, I can feel it."

"You and your feelings," he said, laughing. "Very well. We'll see."

"You will give it a try—re-entering society?" she confirmed.

He sighed, knowing that to argue with Elizabeth would be futile. She would simply keep pestering him until he agreed to do things her way. "Very well. I'll try."

~*~

Claire was enjoying a brandy with her husband that evening before bed as they always did. It was a lovely tradition they'd started on their wedding night and had never stopped. Initially, Blakemore had suggested the drink to calm Claire's nerves when faced with the prospect of what was to come—such an innocent, naïve thing she'd been. It had worked so well, they'd continued doing it every night. For the past seventeen years, they'd enjoyed the time together just relaxing and talking about their day.

Now, Blakemore sat back in his favorite chair by the fireplace, cradling his glass in his hand. He wore his breeches and shirt but was barefoot and allowed his collar to hang open, revealing the blond hair that sprinkled across his chest. "So, what do you think?"

Claire finished swallowing the sip of liquor she'd just taken. She, herself, was completely ready for bed. She wore her dressing gown, and her hair had been braided for the night. She toyed with the ribbon holding the end of her braid together as it lay in her lap. "I'm sorry to say Isabel is exactly like her mother was at that age."

"Is she *that* silly of a girl? I don't know that I got that impression," her husband said, narrowing his pale blue eyes, clearly thinking about her niece further. They'd met at dinner.

"She seemed so to me, although, I have to admit she is more capable of holding an intelligent conversation than Lily ever was. It must be her father's influence."

"I do rather like Kendrick," Blakemore said, relaxing his forehead again.

"Yes, despite the fact that he is so enamored with my sister, he is quite a reasonable, thoughtful man—quite intelligent."

Blakemore chuckled. "Indeed."

"Well, tomorrow I will take Bel, as she likes to be called, to the modiste. The Duchess of Warwick will join us."

"Excellent. I'm certain she'll be a good influence on the girl."

"Precisely. She also has an impeccable eye for fashion. One could not go wrong eliciting her opinions."

"And then you'll begin taking her to parties?"

"Yes. We'll get a gown or two to start her off, just so she has something to wear to the first couple of events—they usually have something half finished that they will simply adjust to her."

"Do you think she'll take? Are silly girls in fashion?" he asked with a little laugh.

Claire couldn't help but giggle. "They are always in fashion. I don't quite understand it myself, but men seem to enjoy a girl who has very little brain of her own."

Blakemore really laughed at that. "There is a certain type who does, yes." His eyes twinkled suggestively. "I, myself, never was. I prefer clever women like you." He set aside his drink and stood.

Claire laughed but allowed him to help her to her feet. "Oh, Blakemore—"

He didn't give her the opportunity to finish her sentence before he caught her lips with his own. He pulled her against him, his hard wall of muscle now slightly softened with age but still masculine enough to send tingles of pleasure straight down to Claire's toes. There was no more talk after that, and the rest of their drinks were left abandoned by the fire.

Chapter Three

~March 23~

The following morning, Bel insisted Bee take her place at breakfast and meet their aunt. She hadn't been out of their room for nearly a full day, so she was happy to comply. She did her best not to make it too obvious that she was looking around the house for the first time. Luckily, she knew Bel wouldn't have known where the breakfast room was either, so she had no qualms about asking a footman to direct her.

Her aunt and uncle were both in the room when she entered. She paused in the doorway to give them a curtsy, hoping that wasn't too formal of her for first thing in the morning. But the instinct was there since this was actually the first time she was meeting them.

"Good morning," she said, coming forward. She accepted a plate from the footman and proceeded to fill it with eggs, ham, and potatoes. She, herself, wasn't so keen on a large breakfast, but she knew that Bel was, and since she was supposed to *be* her sister, she felt she needed to do as she did.

"I trust you slept well, Bel?" her aunt said with a welcoming smile.

"I did, thank you." Bee sat down with her breakfast.

"Do you take tea or chocolate, Miss?" the footman asked, placing a cup next to her plate.

Bel loved chocolate, it was a special treat they were allowed every so often, but this was already going to be a much heavier breakfast than she was used to. Her sister would just have to manage without it. "Tea, thank you," she told him.

"I'm glad to see you aren't like one of those simpering misses who eat nothing," her uncle said with a laugh.

Bee had the grace to flush slightly, but she laughed and said, "No, Uncle. I'm afraid I enjoy my meals perhaps too much."

"By the looks of you, I wouldn't say that. No, no, you enjoy your breakfast," he said, giving her a wink.

She knew he meant it kindly, so she gave a very Bel-like giggle and proceeded to eat as if she were truly hungry.

"I have great plans for us today," Aunt Claire said, giving her a broad smile.

With her mouth full, Bee could only look quizzically at her aunt.

"As soon as you have finished eating, we will pick up the Duchess of Warwick and go to my modiste. Yesterday you said you were looking forward to getting some new dresses, and I believe your mother said in her last letter that you were in need of a few walking dresses and ball gowns."

"Oh, yes! I *have* been looking forward to shopping with you and am indeed in need of some gowns for my time here in London. I'm afraid our provincial dressmaker, while a wonderfully sweet woman... Well, she just doesn't have the panache that a London modiste would," Bee agreed with all the enthusiasm of her sister.

"Precisely. I wouldn't want you looking like you just came in from the countryside. And the duchess has an excellent eye for fashion. I don't know if you know her story, but before she married the duke, she was a modiste herself."

Bee choked on her food and had to quickly take a sip of her tea to clear her throat. "I'm sorry. Did you say the duchess was a *modiste*?"

"Yes. Her parents are peers, of course, but she was raised by a foster family in a little village and thought to become a modiste here in London—she's very talented. But then she met the duke, and they fell in love. He was broad-minded enough to not care about her background, so naturally, if he doesn't care, neither does society," Lady Blakemore explained.

"How *very* unusual," Bee could only say as she sat there dumbfounded by this story. She suddenly remembered that she was supposed to be Bel and added, "And how *romantic*, my goodness! For a modiste from a little village to marry a *duke*..." She gave a dramatic sigh. "I can only hope I find a love like that."

Her aunt smiled at her with a touch of condescension. "Happily, your bloodlines are impeccable. But, yes, I'm sure every girl dreams of falling in love and having the feeling reciprocated."

"I wouldn't count on it though, my gel," her uncle said, bringing a touch of reality to the conversation. "What's most important is that you find a fellow with a fine income, of good standing and family—and do so within the season—so that your sister can follow in your footsteps next year."

"Yes, my lord," Bee said, sobering immediately. His words reminded her of the importance of what she and her sister were doing—making sure that Bel found herself a good husband. That was, after all, why Bee had come along. Bel just wasn't good at being practical. She would want to fall in love and have a wonderful romance, but for Bee to be able to make her come out the following season, Bel *had* to marry this year. Who knew how long it took to find someone to love?

"And so, when you are ready, we will be off to the modiste," her aunt said, bringing them back to the main point.

Bee nodded and reapplied herself to her meal. Her stomach clenched in protest to what she was putting into it, but she forced herself to finish just about everything on her plate, knowing it was what her sister would have done.

What worried her, however, was how she and Bel were going to trade places before they actually left for the modiste's. If Bee knew her sister—and she most definitely did—she would want to be the one to choose her dresses. Bee and Bel had very, very different tastes. Bel loved finery, frills, and fanciness; Bee preferred quiet elegance in her dresses with as few embellishments as possible. It wasn't going to be easy wearing Bel's dresses if Bee went out in her sister's place, but Bel would probably object even more strongly if she had to wear dresses of Bee's choosing.

Somehow, Bee had to create an excuse to go back to her room, before they left the house, so she and Bel could quickly trade places.

As she finished her meal, however, her aunt stood and motioned for the footman. "Please tell Miss Bel's maid to fetch her pelisse for her. I wish to leave immediately. Already we're going to be a little late to pick up the duchess."

"Oh, that's all right, Aunt. I'll go up and fetch it," Bee said, jumping to her feet.

Her aunt looked at her oddly. Frowning, she said, "But that's what servants are for, child. I know you're not used to having so many around, but you should leave the running to them while you finish your tea."

Bee had no choice but to resume her seat. "Yes, ma'am. I am not, er, quite used to there being so many people at hand." It was true, but it was embarrassing to admit as much and made it impossible for Bel to be the one to go to the modiste. She was *not* going to be happy, but sadly, there was nothing Bee could do about it.

~*~

Half an hour later, Bee, her aunt, and the Duchess of Warwick entered the modiste's shop. Bee had to work hard to keep her jaw from dropping at the fantastic array of material, lace, feathers, and ribbons. The sweet little seamstress's shop in Revesby was nothing to this. Even more wonderful was the duchess, who immediately took charge. She was so beautiful; Bee felt a little intimidated in her presence. Her bright green eyes were very striking, and she was so small and delicate-looking. Bee wasn't exactly large, but she felt like a giant next to Tina.

Despite her small stature, Tina was very much a duchess in the way she took command of the entire situation. Before Bee knew it, she was being shown fashion plates and asked whether she wanted a train on her walking dress or preferred to have one without. "Without," she said immediately. Her sister popped into her mind and her conscience nagged at her, so she added hesitantly, "And perhaps the other with? I'm to have two, aren't I?"

The duchess, who had asked Bee to call by her first name, Tina, nodded. "Of course."

"And perhaps on the one without the train, we could add a flounce? Or some lace?" Bee asked. "Just so it's not quite so simple," she added with a Bel-like giggle. She had to remember she was Bel. She had to act silly like Bel did, giggle, and be brighter and livelier. Bel had better appreciate her efforts, Bee thought, as she watched Tina immediately turn to pick out some lace to add to the bottom of the dress.

It took another half an hour to go through fashion plates, picking out just the right styles to flatter Bee's form. Tina was both insistent and helpful in this. Once the styles were chosen, they had to choose fabric for each one, requiring a good number of trips from the back of the shop to the front window so Tina could hold up material to Bee's face to be sure it went with her coloring. All Bee could think about was how lucky it was that she and Bel were exactly the same in that way.

Finally, once all the materials and lace were chosen, the modiste's assistant took Bee to the back to take her measurements. Tina, however, once again stepped in. Pulling a measuring tape from her reticule, she said kindly to the assistant, "This is so much easier with two people. Why don't I measure and you note everything down, if you would?"

The girl didn't seem to have a problem with this and dutifully wrote down all the numbers Tina dictated to her. She was very precise, measuring every part of Bee's person. When they were finished, another assistant came forward with a mostly finished dress for Bee to try. Once again, Tina took command of the pinning and re-pinning of the dress, making sure it fit just right.

"I appreciate you time, Tina," Bee said, standing absolutely still as pins were adjusted and the material twitched just so.

"Oh, not at all," the duchess said, looking around from Bee's side. "This is actually fun for me. I know it can't be particularly enjoyable for you, but you've been wonderfully patient."

Bee gave a giggle—a true one this time. "I have to admit, it hasn't been all that easy standing still for so long, but I know it'll be worth it in the end."

"That it will," Tina said with a smile. "Are you looking forward to your first ball?"

"With some trepidation," Bee answered honestly. Bel was very excited. She couldn't wait to finally get out in society, to meet people, to dance, to talk, and sip lemonade. Bee, however, was much more nervous. She worried about who her sister would meet, what she would say that might give her away as inexperienced, and what sort of gentlemen would be attracted to her and her silly, giggly ways. She wanted only the best for her sister; it was why she'd come.

"Try going to your first ball when already half of society knows you in a completely different way," Tina said with a little laugh.

"What do you mean?" Bee asked, looking down as the duchess knelt in front of her to fix the hem of the dress.

"I don't know if your aunt told you that I was a modiste before I married my duke."

"Yes, she did. I didn't hear the whole story, but it's sounds incredible."

"It is, rather. Many women in society knew me as a modiste the first time I went to a ball as a guest. So, no matter how nervous you get at your first ball, just think of me," she said with another laugh.

"My goodness! You must have been terrified," Bee said, understanding immediately what Tina was trying to say.

"I was. But I held my head up high and simply behaved as if I belonged there. You *do* belong there, so know that, be confident in yourself, and you'll do just fine."

Bee's heart went out to this young woman. Her advice was kind and supportive and so true. Even better, it was exactly what any young woman facing her first ball needed to hear.

Chapter Four

Paul St. Vincent found his step-mother in her drawing room that afternoon going through a pile of mail.

"You seem to be quite popular," he said, allowing a broad smile to hover on his lips as he came forward into the room.

"Oh! St. Vincent you startled me," she said, looking up suddenly.

He sat on the chair opposite her. "And what happened to you calling me by my given name? My father dies and now I'm St. Vincent. You called me Paul when we were at Vinley Hill."

Elizabeth gave a little laugh and a shrug. "I just thought it would be more appropriate while we were in town. Everything is more relaxed in the countryside."

"It's true, but while we're alone I'd prefer it, if you don't mind."

"Not at all." She put down the small knife in her hand with which she was opening letters. "And what are you up to today, Paul?"

"I was going for a ride in the park, actually. Would you care to join me?"

"I would, thank you. It'll be good to get out."

"Yes. That *is* why we are here, isn't it? To get back out into society?" he said, almost wishing it weren't true. He didn't relish being in the marriage mart, but both he and Elizabeth had agreed it was necessary.

Now that his father was gone, Paul had to marry and produce an heir. The problem was, he'd learned well from his father—love didn't exist outside of children's stories. The best Paul could hope for was a girl who wasn't too silly. He'd prefer one who could hold an intelligent conversation, but he didn't know if such a creature existed among the *ton*. He'd soon find out, but first he needed to get his home situation settled.

"I have to admit, I'm rather looking forward to it," Elizabeth said, looking down at the piles of invitations on the sofa next to her with a small smile hovering on her lips.

Paul laughed. "And it looks like you'll have plenty of opportunity as well."

Her smile broadened. "Yes, indeed!"

Paul fidgeted like a child in his seat for a moment. What he was about to say wasn't going to be easy, but he felt it necessary. "I was, er, wondering if maybe I shouldn't find myself some rooms."

Elizabeth had lifted one invitation to look at the one below it, but at his words she looked up at him again. "What do you mean? This is your home. Why would you need rooms elsewhere?"

"Just, er, to give you some privacy, should you need it."

His step-mother narrowed her eyes. "I'm not planning on needing such privacy. If you do, I'm sure I could find other accommodations."

"No!" He quickly softened his tone. "No, not at all. I would never kick you out of your home—and this house is as much yours as it is mine."

"Well, technically it's entirely yours," she began.

"Legally, perhaps, but I feel that it is yours and I like it that way."

Her expression softened. "Thank you. But there is no need for you to live anywhere else. In fact..." She paused and fiddled with the paper in her hand, folding it and unfolding it. "I appreciate your presence here."

"Oh?"

Her gaze slid away. "I imagine you heard of my reputation before I married your father."

He nodded.

"It wasn't of my doing, you should know that. It was..." She paused again and winced as if she'd suddenly felt a pain behind her eyes. "I'm afraid I was the victim of a vindictive young woman. I was silly enough to go to her for advice, disclosing private information I thought she'd be intelligent enough to keep to herself. I didn't realize how badly she wanted me gone from society, but I quickly found out when the rumors started."

She looked directly at him. "This young woman gave me false information, which led me into a great deal of trouble and men getting the wrong idea about me. One man's lies concerning my behavior led to others making similar claims. There was nothing I could do or say to stop them. Eventually, my mother and I had no choice but to leave town. I am older and wiser now and determined to correct the situation, to rebuild my reputation. I don't want to be known as... as *that* sort of woman."

Paul realized his jaw had fallen open a touch. "I... I'd heard the talk, naturally. Friends told me about it when my father agreed to marry you. So, what you're saying is it *wasn't* true? You didn't allow—"

"I didn't allow anyone up my skirts!" she interrupted him. "In fact, the whole thing started *because* I refused one gentleman's advances." She stood and began pacing in front of the fireplace. "Lord Brentley, may his soul rot down below, started the rumors because I refused to allow him liberties with my person. I had confided in some girls my own age, who said it was normal to allow men to touch and kiss you, but when I followed their advice and allowed this, I..."

Tears streamed down her face. She shook her head. "They told everyone that I'd allowed Lord Brentley to...and... He confirmed their rumors. Somehow other men began to say they *too* had taken liberties and that I was no longer innocent." A sob slipped out just before she buried her face in her hands.

Paul couldn't stand it. He jumped up and pulled her into his arms. "Oh, Elizabeth, I am so sorry."

He hated the fact that such horrid people existed in society, and it was sweet young women like Elizabeth who were punished for nothing more than their own innocence. If he had been there... Well, there wouldn't have been anything he could have done. He admitted that to himself, but it didn't make him feel any better about what Elizabeth had gone through. Oddly enough, it did raise his father in his eyes. He had married the ruined girl.

She held onto him. After a minute, Paul didn't hear any sobs, but she didn't seem to be breathing either. He could only imagine she was holding her breath until her tears abated. When she did finally breathe again, she said, "St. Vincent was so good. He never accused me... He never blamed me... He never said a...a word."

Paul didn't have the heart to tell her that his father wouldn't have said anything because it was the sort of behavior he *expected* from beautiful women like Elizabeth. He had thought all women shallow, pleasure-seeking creatures, and he didn't care.

Paul wasn't certain his father was right. He'd met a number of women with more depth than his father ever gave them credit for. In fact, Elizabeth was one. She was a good, caring person. And clearly, she'd been very wronged, not only by Paul's father but by a good number of the so-called gentlemen and ladies of the *ton*.

"I would wring each and every one of their necks if I could," Paul said gently.

Elizabeth gave a hiccoughing laugh and pulled away. "You are too good."

"No, but I love you like a sister, and I can't stand the thought of anyone ruining your reputation in that way," he said, pulling out his handkerchief and giving it to her.

She took it and delicately wiped at her eyes. "I am so lucky to have you, Paul. I know we're too close in age to be like mother and son, but I love you too, yes, like a brother." She gave a little laugh.

"That is one nice thing about my father having married someone so much younger than him," he said, using his thumb to catch a tear from her cheek. She immediately wiped the rest of them away.

"Yes."

"And I will do everything in my power to make sure your reputation is revived in the *right* way," he said. He then looked at the pile of invitations. "But perhaps it already is?"

She too looked in that direction. "I don't have nearly as many invitations as perhaps I should, and I think a great many of them aren't to the right sort of party."

"Oh, dear. Well, it's of no matter. I've got quite a stack of my own, and they are all to the right sort of parties," he admitted.

"I should expect so. You are an eligible bachelor."

"A sought-after commodity, you mean," he corrected her with a laugh.

"Well, yes. You're handsome, wealthy, and an earl. Everyone will be wanting you to attend their functions."

"And marry their daughter," he added.

She laughed. "I think you can only marry one."

"But which one?"

She sat on the sofa now that they were onto an easier topic of conversation. "That will be up to you. You'll need to find the right girl. The one who stirs your heart."

"I'm not entirely certain I have a heart. I think my father might have beaten it out of me when I was younger."

"Oh, I don't believe that for a second," Elizabeth said, settling herself back between the piles of letters and invitations.

"Well, at least he taught me that there was no use in having one. He didn't believe in love. You know that better than anyone."

She sighed. "Yes, but he was wrong, and you should know it."

He could only smile at her sadly. He truly didn't know what to think. Never in his life had he actually seen anyone who was in love, or if they thought they were, it wasn't reciprocated. No, his father wasn't a perfect man. He wasn't right on a lot of things, but Paul had a suspicion he was correct on this. Love was something that only existed in stories. "In any case, I will do my best to find someone with whom I will be able to live comfortably, that's all I require. It will be wonderful if she is interesting and, or intelligent. That's all I want."

"And pretty. She needs to be very pretty," Elizabeth said, smiling at him.

He was happy to see her smile once again, so he laughed and agreed. "That would be a bonus."

"I'll find someone for you, don't you fear," she said, the twinkle returning to her eyes.

"Oh dear, I think that in itself is something to be afraid of," he said laughing.

"And there is to be no more talk of you moving out, agreed?"

He gave a decisive nod. "Agreed."

~March 25~

Claire walked into her good friend Christianne's drawing room and smiled. No, even more than that, she relaxed. She could feel her shoulders drop and her stomach unclench. The season had officially started, and the ladies of the Wagering Whist Society had returned.

Not everyone was present just yet, but they were coming, and that knowledge made everything better.

"Lady Blakemore!" It was Lydia Sheffield... No, as of last summer, she was the Viscountess Welles. She ran up to Claire, gave a quick curtsy, and threw her arms around her. The girl always did have too much exuberance, Claire thought with a laugh. If she had thought for a minute that marriage would calm that, she was immediately made aware it was not so. If anything, the girl was even *more* enthusiastic, giggling, and happy.

"Lady Welles, it is good to see that marriage is treating you right," Claire said, disentangling herself gently from the girl's grip.

"Oh, yes, my lady. John and I are so very happy," she said with a broad grin.

"And what of our other newlywed, Lady Colburne?" Claire asked, looking around for her.

"Diana should be here soon. I saw her yesterday, and she specifically said how much she was looking forward to our first meeting of the season," Lady Welles said.

"Excellent. I look forward to seeing her again." She took in Mrs. Aldridge and Lady Moreton standing with Lady Sorrell waiting their turn to greet her.

"It is good to see you all again," she said, giving them all a nod.

Lady Moreton laughed. "It's good to see you too, my lady, although happily, it hasn't been too long since we saw each other at Warwick for Tina's wedding."

"It is true, but I hope the intervening months have been restful?" Claire asked.

"Indeed," Lady Moreton said.

"I am greatly looking forward to the start of the season," Mrs. Aldridge said, bending down and giving her little King Charles Spaniel a bite of cake from the plate in her hand. Claire suspected the expectation of the treat was what had kept the little dog from jumping on Claire the moment she'd entered the room.

"I think we all are," Claire agreed.

"Claire, how wonderful to see you," Christianne said, joining them.

"And you. How are your wedding preparations going?" Claire asked her good friend.

Her lips twitched as if she were trying to temper her smile, but Claire could feel the happiness radiating off her. "Everything is going very well."

"It's going to be the event of the season!" Lady Welles said, joining them.

"Well..." Christianne, soon to be the new Lady Ayres, demurred.

"It most certainly is. I am sure everyone will be talking about it at Lady Bradmore's ball tomorrow," Claire said.

"Oh, are you going?" Lady Welles asked.

"Yes, of course," Claire began. Lady Colburne and the Duchess of Kendell arrived before Claire could continue. After they were properly greeted, Christianne called for everyone to sit down with their tea so she could start the meeting.

As soon as the newcomers had been served and everyone was settled in their seats, Christianne began. "Welcome to the 1807 Season of the Ladies' Wagering Whist Society!"

There was a round of applause and laughter.

"Before we begin to play, let us take a moment to go over the exciting events since last season and what we may have to look forward to in this one." She paused to look at Ladies Welles and Colburne. "We've had two of our members marry."

Another brief round of applause followed with giggles and appropriate blushing of the two ladies in question.

"My daughter, Tina, is now married to Warwick," she said with her own smile of true happiness.

"And my father is now married to John's mother," Lady Welles added.

"Oh, yes?" Christianne asked, turning toward her.

"They had a very small, private ceremony—just immediate family," Lady Welles said.

"How lovely and very appropriate," the duchess nodded approvingly.

"And what do we have to look forward to this season?" Christianne asked, looking around at the women.

Chapter Five

"**W**arwick's sister, Lady Margaret, is now staying with me and needs to be married this year in order to fulfill the dictates of her father's will," the duchess put forward.

"Really?" Lady Moreton looked with curiosity at the duchess.

"Yes. Sadly, her father insisted she marry by the time she was twenty or else she would lose her inheritance. Since Warwick is now rather pre-occupied with his new wife, and Tina with learning how to be a duchess, we felt it would be easier if I took over chaperoning the girl. And of course, it's much easier for her to just stay with me," the duchess said.

"And it must be so lovely to have company. Lady Margaret is such a sweet girl," Mrs. Aldridge said, reaching down to pet her dog, who had the unfortunate name of Duchess. It was generally a well-behaved creature, but for obvious reasons, the Duchess of Kendell couldn't stand the animal. Mrs. Aldridge almost never went without Duchess, so she was always present at their meetings, much to the Duchess of Kendell's dismay.

The duchess looked at her oddly for a second, perhaps startled that the woman had spoken such good sense. The two of them had not gotten along at all last year. Hopefully, this was a sign that things would be better going forward. "All that you say is true, Mrs. Aldridge," the duchess nodded.

At Mrs. Aldridge's smile, Claire shared a look of optimism with Christianne.

"And you have news as well, don't you, Lady Blakemore?" Christianne asked.

Claire snapped her attention back and said, "Oh, yes. My niece, Isabel Kendrick, has come for the season. I have been tasked with seeing her married this year so her twin sister may have her debut next year. Their parents, er, didn't want the two girls coming out at the same time."

"Are they identical twins?" Lady Colburne asked.

"Yes. They are what's called mirror twins. One is right-handed, one left—just like looking into a mirror," Claire explained.

"Oh, what fun! Are there other differences or similarities?" Lady Welles asked, clasping her hands together.

"Well, one is quite bookish and intelligent while the other..."

"Is not?" Lady Sorrell asked with a smile.

Claire sighed. "Bel, as my niece likes to be called, is rather silly. She is enthusiastic and outgoing, while Beatrice is quieter. Bel loves being social, however, so I'm certain she will do very well this season."

"So, it is Isabel who you have with you?" Christianne asked. Claire had told her about the girls off and on throughout the years that they'd known each other.

"Yes. Their parents thought it better to send the more outgoing one first to smooth the way for the quieter one next year," Claire said.

"That does make a great deal of sense," the duchess said.

"Yes. It's just…" Claire paused, uncertain as to how much to say in public about her concerns for her niece.

"Is there a problem?" Lady Moreton asked.

"No, not really. I only hope Bel is not *quite* so much like her mother. I hope she has a little more common sense than my sister did at her age, that's all."

"I'm sure she will do very well," Lady Welles said.

"I would appreciate any assistance you might give her," Claire said to the girl. Perhaps if Bel saw someone as giggly as she was, and yet well-behaved and with a good head on her shoulders as Lady Welles did, she would learn from her.

"I would be happy to guide her," Lady Welles said.

"I think we all will be more than willing to help in any way," Mrs. Aldridge added.

"Thank you. Tina has already been kind enough to come with us to the modiste's yesterday and help choose Bel's new gowns," Claire mentioned.

"Oh, did she?" Christianne asked. Clearly, she hadn't spoken to her daughter recently.

"Yes. She was so very helpful. She has such a wonderful eye for fashion and colors," Claire said.

"And for what is flattering," the duchess added.

"Yes," Claire agreed.

"So, you see, all will be well. You won't be in this alone, Claire," Christianne said making Claire feel so much more comfortable. With the help of the Ladies' Wagering Whist Society, this season was going to be a great deal easier than if she were trying to manage Bel alone, that was for certain.

~*~

Claire just didn't know what she would do without her good friends, she thought as she stepped into her house after her Whist Society meeting.

As she paused to take off her gloves and remove her hat, the most beautiful music wafted across her senses. She stopped with a glove half-on, half-off as a feeling a joy rushed through her. The piano piece was light and playful. Notes hopped and skipped around like a line of dancers.

A maid stood next to her, waiting to take the items up to her room, but Claire turned to her and asked, "Who is that playing the pianoforte?"

"That's Miss Kendrick, my lady. She's been practicing for the past hour or so. I hope it's all right. She asked permission, but you weren't here so we didn't see—"

"No, no, it's perfectly fine," Claire interrupted her. "It's quite lovely."

"Yes, my lady. I have to say, we've all been enjoying the music. I think the maids have even been cleaning the house more quickly and with more gusto since she started," the woman said with a smile.

Claire finished pulling off her glove and handed them to the maid. She headed straight to the most unused room in the house, the music room.

Bel was sitting at the pianoforte, her fingers

dancing across the keyboard. Claire could only stop and watch. There was such happiness coming from the girl. She was absolutely transformed from an ordinary, pretty, young lady to one who radiated with life and energy.

The piece came to an end with another hop and a skip, and Claire found herself applauding madly.

The girl jumped.

"I beg your pardon. I didn't mean to startled you," Claire said, coming farther into the room.

"Oh, no. I beg *your* pardon, Aunt. I just hadn't realized you were there."

"Well, no, I don't imagine you would have, you were so caught up in the music," Claire said.

Bel gave a little giggle but then widened her eyes. "I do hope you don't mind. I do so love to play, and I haven't had a chance since I arrived."

"Not at all. It was lovely. You play very well."

"Oh, thank you." The girl gave a little curtsy.

"I hadn't realized you were so talented."

A smile graced her lips. "Mama always said Bee had the brains, but I had the talent." She laughed and shrugged.

Claire nodded. "It is very good you each have something at which you excel. I am very happy to know what your special ability is, and you may practice any time you wish."

~March 26~

When Bel checked herself in the mirror for the third time, Bee finally let out a groan. She'd been wondering when her sister would finally lose her patience. She knew it would happen sooner or later, but Bel just couldn't help it. She'd never looked so good in her life. Not only that, but she *had* to look her best.

She was going to her first ball!

"Bel, save the dancing for the party," Bee groaned.

"Ball, Bee, it's a ball. It's not a party, it's not an assembly, it's a *ball*," Bel said, catching her sister's reflection in the mirror and speaking to that rather than turning around to look at her directly.

"All right," Bee sighed. "*Ball*, save your dancing for the ball. You're going to tire yourself out before you even leave the house."

Bel laughed. "As if I could possibly do so! I have more energy than a puppy. Do you remember when Tiger had puppies and that one—what did we call him?"

"Lightning," her sister supplied.

"Yes! Lightning. He didn't stop running around that one afternoon for hours." Bel laughed as she remembered the dog's antics. He'd been so funny. She'd been sorry her father had given all the puppies from that litter away. They'd been so cute and cuddly.

"I remember," Bee said with a small smile hovering on her lips.

"Well, that's exactly how I feel, so don't—" A knock on the door interrupted her. Bee ran for the dressing room and just managed to close the door as Aunt Claire came in the other.

"Are you ready, Bel? It's time for us to go. Oh, don't you look lovely!" her aunt said, coming into the room.

Bel could feel her heart racing. That had been close! They really had to start locking the door to their room. She forced a smile onto her face.

"Thank you. I think, I think I'm ready." The moment she said it, nerves hit her stomach. She put a hand to it and rubbed lightly, not wanting to crease her dress.

"Are you all right? Is your stomach upset from dinner?" her aunt asked.

"No, no, dinner was fine. I think it's just... I guess I'm a little nervous, that's all," she admitted.

Her aunt gave her a reassuring smile. "You are going to be fine, no, better than fine. You will probably even be considered one of the diamonds of the season."

Bel's breath caught in her throat. "Do you think so?"

Aunt Claire nodded. "I do. But we need to go."

"Right." Bel turned around to get her shawl, but it wasn't on her bed where she'd expected it to be. Hadn't Bee taken it out earlier? Oh, yes, she'd placed it around her own shoulders to see how the pale pink color went with the dress she was wearing.

"I, um, I need my shawl, just a moment." Bel opened the door to her dressing room as little as possible in order to slip in without her aunt seeing what—or who—was inside. Before she could go into the room, however, a hand popped out holding her shawl and fan. "Oh!" she said, jumping back as the items nearly hit her in the face.

She grabbed them and the door closed again quickly. Turning back to her aunt she gave a little laugh. "My maid is so shy."

Aunt Claire was frowning at her in a confused way, but she gave a little shrug before turning to head out the door. "So long as she does a good job."

"Yes, yes, she does," Bel said, following in her wake.

The ballroom was filled with girls looking as nervous as Bel felt, and gentlemen standing around in small groups laughing and talking. A few men were speaking with young ladies, but for the most part, the girls simply stood along the walls with their chaperones. A small group of women stood off to one corner talking as they looked around, taking stock of who else was there.

"It's early yet," Lady Blakemore said with a sniff as they entered the room. "I'm sure more people will be here soon."

The room looked to be quite full to Bel's inexperienced eyes, so she said nothing.

Her aunt led her over to the group of ladies who'd been watching the room. "Good evening, ladies," Aunt Claire said, a smile lighting up her face.

"Good evening, Lady Blakemore," a younger woman said amidst the replies from the others. She was very pretty and had an air of worldliness about her, though, that made Bel feel more provincial than ever.

"May I present my niece, Miss Isabel Kendrick?" her aunt said, turning toward her.

Bel curtsied as her aunt introduced each lady in turn. "Lady Moreton, Lady Sorrell, Lady Norman, and Lady Colburne." She looked to Lady Sorrell, a paler lady with brown hair that seemed to be making a weak attempt at staying curled. "Is Lady Welles not here yet?"

"No, but I'm sure she will be soon. She rarely comes late," Lady Sorrell said with a smile for Bel.

"Lady Colburne and Lady Welles are just a year

older than you," Aunt Claire explained. "They both came out last season and were married within the last year."

"Oh. Congratulations!" Bel said, looking at the petite woman with bright blue eyes—Lady Colburne, she thought. Her rich auburn hair had been pulled up into a complicated coiffure giving her an almost elfin look.

"Thank you. My husband was supposed to come this evening, but he got called away to an emergency at the last minute. I'm still hoping he'll arrive before too long," Lady Colburne said.

"Lord Colburne is a well-respected physician," Bel's aunt explained.

"Really? How fascinating!" She'd never heard of a nobleman who was also a physician. What an extraordinary group of friends her aunt had!

"Good evening, ladies," a happy voice said from behind them. Bel turned around and found herself being eyed critically by a young, woman with light brown hair, wearing a very unusual gown. It had a white underdress with pretty scalloped edges and an over-dress of a light pink silk that just seemed to flow around her. Bel was sure she was turning green with envy at such a beautiful ensemble. On the other hand, she didn't like the way the lady was looking at her, despite the bright smile on her face.

"Oh, Bel, you look wonderful in that gown, just as I knew you would!" the woman said.

CHAPTER SIX

Bel nearly gasped at the woman's use of her given name and presumption of informality, but then wondered if this wasn't someone Bee had met when she'd gone out to the modiste's. Just in case, Bel immediately pulled her lips up into a smile. "I'm so glad you think so!" she said.

"Duchess, you look stunning," another lady said with a giggle as she approached from their other side. Her bright green eyes shown out of a delicately rounded face. "But when ever do you not?" She was accompanied by a slender gentleman wearing a very understated but elegant gray suit.

Bel smiled and very nearly laughed. Thank goodness she'd held her tongue! The woman who'd looked critically at her had to be Tina, the duchess modiste who Bee had told her about. She refocused her attention on the newcomers.

"Truly, Your Grace, you've got to tell us where you got your inspiration for that gown," Lady Sorrell said, returning to the matter at hand.

"I saw it in a fashion magazine from Italy," the duchess said with a laugh. "It was so different, you know I just had to make it!"

"You will be the talk of the ball!" the new woman said, giggling.

"Goodness, I hope not! I think Miss Kendrick should hold that honor. It is her first ball, after all," the duchess said kindly.

"Oh no, I just hope to have the opportunity to dance," Bel said quickly.

"Bel, allow me to introduce you to Lord and Lady Welles," Aunt Claire said before turning toward the couple. "This is my niece, Miss Kendrick."

"Lady Blakemore told us all about you yesterday at our meeting," Lady Welles said with a bright smile. "I am so happy you're in town this season. I know that we'll become good friends in no time."

Bel couldn't help but smile and feel happy to meet other women her own age, even if they were already married. But she wasn't sure she knew what Lady Welles was talking about. She looked to her aunt. "What meeting was that?"

"The Ladies' Wagering Whist Society. We are all members," Lady Blakemore said.

"Except me," the duchess said with a laugh.

"We would need to find another three people—" Lady Moreton started.

"Oh no, it's fine! I didn't mean anything by my comment, honestly," the lady said with a laugh.

Bel remember her aunt saying something about a society meeting when she'd gone out the previous afternoon. It did seem to be quite wonderful to have all these friends at hand. Bel felt a twinge of sadness. Her aunt had so many friends, but Bel had no one here. Never had she missed her sister more! Thank goodness she was waiting for her at her aunt's home and not all the way back in Lincolnshire. Just that knowledge alone made her feel better.

"Good evening, ladies," a new voice said from just behind Bel.

All the women curtsied. "Good evening, Your Grace," a number of them said.

"Oh, Lady Margaret! How wonderful to see you again. I do hope you enjoyed the rest of your holidays," Lady Welles said, turning to the younger woman who was accompanying the older lady they'd all called 'Your Grace.'

Goodness, Bel thought, this was truly an esteemed group! Two duchesses and Lady Margaret was clearly the daughter of either a duchess or a marquess. Never had she met so many titled people. Well, she supposed she'd better get used to it—this was *London society*!

"I'm very happy to see you this evening, Duchess," Lady Blakemore said.

The slightly rotund woman raised one blonde eyebrow. Despite her age—probably the same or a little older than Bel's aunt—she had no gray or silver in her hair and her brown eyes seemed to peer critically around at everyone and everything. "And I you, Lady Blakemore, but is there a reason for your happiness?" she asked with a slightly imperious tone.

"Yes. We both have young charges this season, and I do hope that the girls can become friends," Bel's aunt said, clearly not at all cowed by the woman. Bel, herself, had to force herself not to step back and hide behind her aunt.

"Ah, yes. Is this your niece?" the duchess asked.

"Yes. May I present Miss Isabel Kendrick?" Lady Blakemore said as Bel dipped into her lowest curtsy.

The duchess nodded approvingly. "It is a pleasure, Miss Kendrick. And this is my good friend, Lady Margaret."

Bel curtsied again as Lady Margaret bobbed a small curtsy her way. "I'm very pleased to meet you. Is this also your first season, Lady Margaret?" Bel asked.

"Er, no. It's my second, actually," the girl said. Her voice, like the rest of her, was quiet and understated. It was odd. Bel had always imagined that people were as imposing as their titles, but clearly Lady Margaret wasn't. She was just a slip of a girl, and while she was certainly pretty enough, she was also very unassuming with watery blue eyes and brown hair pulled into a rather simple chignon.

"Oh, but that's wonderful," Bel said as she was overcome with the urge to just put her arm around Lady Margaret and comfort her. She looked so nervous that Bel immediately forgot her own fears. "You'll be able to show me how to go on. I've been hoping to meet other girls my age to share this experience with."

She eyed Lady Welles, Tina, and Lady Colburne who were standing nearby talking amongst themselves. "I am looking forward to getting to know others, of course, but having someone in the same situation is very comforting," she finished, looking back at Lady Margaret.

Lady Margaret gave her a warm smile. "I know exactly what you mean. Last season, I couldn't have done a thing without Tina's support—not that she was in the same situation as me for most of the season, but she was there, nearby and throughout. Diana and Lydia, um, Lady Colburne and Lady

Welles were also quite wonderful, although I didn't get to know them quite as well as I'd have liked."

"So, Tina was with you? I'm afraid I don't quite understand," Bel said, trying to understand the relationship between the two women.

"Yes. At first, she was my modiste, and now she's my sister-in-law," Lady Margaret explained.

"Oh! So, your brother is…" Bel searched her mind for the name of the duke who married Tina. Bee had told her and so had her aunt, but there were so many new names she was getting them all mixed up in her head.

"Warwick," Lady Margaret supplied for her.

"Yes, of course. Thank you." Bel laughed. "There are simply too many new names."

Lady Margaret smiled. "I know. I know *exactly* how you feel."

"All right, ladies, Bel and Lady Margaret are never going to be asked to dance if they are surrounded by us. I think it would be best if we stood off to the side a touch so they can be seen," Lady Welles said, taking control of the situation.

"You are so very right, Lydia," Lady Colburne said. She moved a few paces back and away. The other ladies followed her, each nodding their agreement.

Lady Margaret gave Bel a little nod as she and her chaperone, the duchess, moved off in another direction so she could have the opportunity to be asked to dance as well.

Bel suddenly felt bereft of the camaraderie and support of the other women. At least she still had her aunt by her side. She took in a deep breath and turned to survey the ballroom. A large number of people had come while she'd been pre-occupied with her aunt's friends. It was now so full that it was a wonder there would be space in the center of the room for dancing.

There were a great many more gentlemen too. One particularly handsome man in a black coat with a deep red waistcoat caught her eye. He wasn't very tall but looked more solid, even a little intimidating, in how broad his chest and shoulders were. As she watched, he was approached by two women, each with a younger lady in tow. His smile looked almost painful as he bowed and nodded to the women. He spoke to them for a moment and then moved on.

As Bel watched, he did the same thing four more times. Each time he was approached by an older lady, introduced to her younger companion, and then extracted himself from them as quickly as possible. It would have been amusing if it didn't seem to be so very sad. He was clearly avoiding people, but why? And why would a gentleman come to a ball and then evade all the young ladies present?

"Aunt, do you know who that gentleman is over there. The broad one in the black coat with black hair?" Bel asked.

Her aunt looked in the direction she was looking. "The one with the red waistcoat?"

"Yes."

"No. I don't believe I've ever seen him before," her aunt said, sounding rather surprised. She stood and watched him as well for a moment before turning back to Bel. "He seems to be rather set on not getting caught by any young ladies making their debut."

"Yes, he does."

"Don't stare, my dear," her aunt warned.

Bel immediately turned her head away. "Of course. How silly of me!" She gave an embarrassed little giggle.

When she turned back to her aunt, she found two older ladies approaching them with determination. "Lady Blakemore," the first lady said. She had white-blond hair, very fair skin, and such pale green eyes the entire effect was a little disturbing. The fact that she wore a deep gray gown just emphasized the lack of color in her person.

The second lady was extremely rotund, but was more ordinary-looking with brown hair, brown eyes, and drooping cheeks common in older-ladies.

"Lady Findlater. Lady Wrexley. Good evening," Aunt Claire said, not sounding very happy to be greeting the women. There was a distinct lack of excitement in her voice and her eyes, unlike when she had met her friends from her Whist Society, Bel noted. "May I introduce my niece, Miss Isabel Kendrick?"

Bel curtsied and gave both ladies a polite smile.

"Miss Kendrick is your younger sister's child?" Lady Findlater asked, ignoring Bel altogether.

"Yes," Lady Blakemore responded.

"Well, let's hope she does better than your sister did," the lady said. She then turned and walked away, her friend accompanying her like a puppy.

"Who was that?" Bel whispered.

"Someone you should avoid at all costs," her aunt said quietly. "She is one of the most notorious gossips in society. You want to be sure to keep from her notice, or you may find the number of invitations you receive greatly diminished."

"Goodness!"

Another lady with dark brown hair in a beautiful purple silk gown was approaching them so no more was said. The gentleman on her arm looked quite large and imposing, and after being unnerved by Lady Findlater and her companion, Bel wasn't so sure she was up to meeting him. She knew she had no choice in the matter, however, and so did her best to look happy and welcoming.

He was much taller than the man she'd been watching. In fact, he was taller than anyone she'd ever seen. His brown hair and eyes were pleasant enough, but his sharp cheekbones made Bel think him harsh. No sweet gentleman would have such a sharply defined face.

"Good evening, Lady Blakemore. How lovely to see you again," the woman said, a polite smile gracing her pretty bow lips.

"Why, Lady St. Vincent, what a surprise!" her aunt said, sounding much happier. Lady St. Vincent was clearly closer to a friend, Bel thought. Lady Blakemore indicated Bel. "May I present my niece, Miss Isabel Kendrick?"

Bel took her cue to curtsy.

Lady St. Vincent turned to the gentleman with her. "And you remember my stepson, Lord St. Vincent?"

The man with her was her stepson? But he didn't look to be much younger than the lady. In fact, she didn't look old enough to have a son older than perhaps two. Of course, he was her *step*son so she must have married the man's father. That would make sense. While all this was going through

Bel's mind, the gentleman had turned to her and said something, but for the life of her she couldn't recall what he'd said.

At her silence, her aunt jumped in. "Yes, my niece has only just arrived in town."

"Yes, this is my first ball," Bel said quickly, realizing that he must have asked when she'd come to London.

"Where did you travel from?" he asked.

"Lincolnshire," Bel answered.

"Ah, some wonderful Roman ruins in the area." Lord St. Vincent's brown eyes brightened.

"Yes. My sister has dragged me to *quite* a few," Bel admitted.

"Are you not interested in history?" he asked.

"No, I'm afraid such studies never held my attention for very long. Bee had to be pulled away from her books, and sometimes the only way to get her outside was to go to the ruins." Bel laughed. "She would go on for hours about this settlement and that old king. I don't even remember all that she said." She gave a giggle to soften her words.

Lord St. Vincent's smile became more forced, Bel could tell. She worried that she'd said too much. She supposed she wasn't supposed to admit that she disliked history. On the other hand, if this gentleman was a historian, it was unlikely they would suit. Better to find out now rather than later.

The pair quickly found a reason to move on.

Bel turned to her aunt. "I'm so sorry. I said the wrong thing, didn't I?"

"Just as well. You should find someone you have more in common with," her aunt said kindly.

Chapter Seven

"And that is why I don't come to events like this," Paul said as soon as he and Elizabeth were out of earshot.

"I'm sorry. I know Lady Blakemore. She is such a stickler, so straightforward, and precise. I thought that whoever she sponsored would be the same. I suppose one can't choose nieces," Elizabeth said with a little laugh.

"No, I suppose not. But truly? She *hates* history. She seemed positively dim-witted." Paul tried not to sound as if he were complaining, even though that was exactly what he was doing. He hadn't wanted to come to this ball, but Elizabeth had insisted. It was almost as bad as going to Almack's—which he outright refused to attend. He would find a girl at a soiree or an intimate dinner party filled with people he knew and trusted. Not here. It was like opening day of the hunt, and these vixens were determined to run him to ground.

"We'll find you someone else, Paul, I promise." Elizabeth wove her arm through his.

"Fine. But no more young ladies just making their come out, please."

"Now, now, I'm certain you don't mean that. We just need to find the right one for you. I'm sure there must be some who are more to your liking.”

"Well, at least she didn't start spouting all that nonsense about falling in love like the last one," he said, relenting.

Elizabeth laughed. "She was a little much, I have to agree, but I believe in romantic love."

"But truly, love at first sight?" he asked, thinking about the nonsense the girl, Miss Pen-something-or other, was spouting.

"Some people believe in it," Elizabeth said in a non-committal way.

"You don't, do you?" Paul asked a little horrified.

She gave a little laugh. "I don't know. Personally, I've never experienced it, but that doesn't mean that it doesn't exist."

"That's ridiculous. There is no such thing as love at first sight—no such thing as love. Now, please, help me find a young woman who isn't going to moon over me."

"Why don't we try some wallflowers? Perhaps some of them are bluestockings in hiding," Elizabeth said, steering him toward the corner where the potted plants probably hid one or two young ladies.

~*~

Bel turned back to survey the ballroom after Lord and Lady St. Vincent walked away. Her gaze immediately latched onto that handsome man she'd seen before. He was still not speaking with anyone, despite the fact women were approaching him. He didn't seem to be impolite about it, but he also didn't talk to anyone for more than five minutes before moving on.

It was completely obvious to Bel as to why so many women were approaching him—she'd never seen a more handsome man. But why was *he* not speaking to anyone?

The more she watched him, the more determined she was to be the one to catch him and actually have a conversation. But how...

"Good evening, Lady Blakemore," a well-padded gentleman said as he approached, blocking Bel's view of the man she'd been watching.

"Why, Sir Reginald, I haven't seen you for ages. Were you away last season?" Lady Blakemore asked, acknowledging his bow.

"Yes. Sadly, my aunt passed on. We were quite close. She's lived with my father for the past ten years, keeping his house, acting as hostess when the need arose..."

"Oh, I am so sorry," Bel's aunt said. "But now you are returned to us and ready to engage in society and all its amusements?"

"Indeed, indeed," he said, turning a bright smile onto Bel. "And who have we here? No, don't tell me, you must be... No, my lady is much too young to be your mother, you must be..."

"You are absolutely ridiculous, my lord," Lady Blakemore said with a laugh. "This is my niece—my *younger* sister's daughter—Miss Isabel Kendrick."

"I don't believe it for a minute," he said to her aunt before making a leg before her. "The honor, Miss Kendrick, is all mine." He took her hand as she curtsied to him and placed the lightest kiss on the back of it. Bel could feel her cheeks heat immediately, and she couldn't stop the giggle that bubbled up her throat.

"How do you do? My condolences on your

loss," Bel said.

"Thank you." He tried to look sad for a moment, but it hardly lasted a breath before he said, "Would you care to dance, Miss Kendrick? I just can't stand moping about, and you don't look like the sort to do so either."

"I would love to, sir, thank you," she said, curtsying again. She quickly looked at her aunt and added, "If that's all right with you, Aunt Claire?"

"I suppose it couldn't hurt," the lady said. It wasn't a ringing endorsement, but it was permission, which is all that Bel needed.

She allowed Sir Reginald to lead her out for the first set.

Despite his generous size, the gentleman proved to be an enthusiastic dancer. He also kept up a witty repartee throughout the dance, making Bel giggle so much that her face was aching from all the smiling. He returned her to her aunt much in need of one of those famed glasses of lemonade.

Bel cooled down with her fan, wondering if she could ask permission to find where the refreshments were, when she spied the handsome gentleman from earlier. He was heading in *their* direction. "Aunt Claire," she said quietly, "there is that gentleman again. I swear he hasn't spoken for more than five minutes to anyone here."

Her aunt followed the line of Bel's vision, but before she could even say anything, Lady St. Vincent, whom they'd met earlier, joined him. Bel gave a little gasp. Either it was an unusual coincidence or the two of them were related in some way—they did look very much alike.

"Do you think you could ask Lady St. Vincent to introduce us?" Bel asked.

"I could, but I think you've got other admirers just at the moment," her aunt said with the slightest nod toward two very well-dressed men who were just about upon them.

Bel watched sadly as the handsome gentleman and Lady St. Vincent walked past behind the two gentleman she was supposed to be curtsying to.

"...Miss Kendrick," her aunt was saying.

Hearing her name, Bel snapped her attention back to her aunt and the gentlemen. She must have just been introduced, but she'd completely missed the names of the men. Bel curtsied anyway and gave them her best polite smile. "It's a pleasure," she murmured.

One of the men took her hand and bowed over it, placing a light kiss onto her glove. She gave a little giggle. Well, if they were going to be gallant, she supposed she could wait a little to meet the handsome friend of Lady St. Vincent's.

"When Rosebury told me that Lady Blakemore was sponsoring a young lady this season, I almost despaired. But then he told me that you were her niece, and I had to rejoice," the gentleman with black hair and pale blue eyes said. He gave her a toothy smile.

"Why would the fact that my aunt and I are related be a cause for such happiness?" Bel asked with a small tilt of her head.

"Why, because I knew that any relation of hers would be beautiful, like the lady herself," he said with a bow toward Lady Blakemore.

Bel's aunt let out a little huff of a laugh. "Doing it too brown, Mr. Hershawn."

"Oh, not at all," he protested.

"In either case, we can plainly see what you have here, my lady, is a diamond of the first water, and I would like to be the first to dance with her," the other man said.

"I'm terribly sorry, but you've already missed that opportunity. I just danced with Sir Reginald," Bel said with mockingly sad smile. Flirting was easy for her, and these gentlemen seemed to be experts as well.

The one her aunt had called Mr. Hershawn gasped and widened his eyes. "Sir Reggie? But why?"

Bel couldn't help but laugh. "Because he was kind enough to ask. And why shouldn't I dance with him? He's an extremely amusing gentleman."

"Amusing, yes. Intelligent, clever, or handsome? No," the other man said.

"Oh, now that's not quite fair, Rosebury," Mr. Hershawn objected. "He can be a perfectly nice chap, and he's not that bad to look at, is he?" He turned to Bel for her opinion.

"I will withhold my opinion on the matter and simply say that I had a very enjoyable dance with him," she said with a giggle.

"Very well done, my dear," Lady Blakemore said with a nod. "One does not disparage others and certainly not to other gentlemen." She looked sharply at the two men standing in front of them. "Now, which one of you is going to lead my niece out for the next set?"

Bel laughed. "That's awfully bold, Aunt."

"But absolutely right on the spot. It shall be me," Mr. Hershawn said quickly.

"Why you?" asked his friend, who Bel guessed

was Lord Rosebury.

"Because I saw her first and was the one who suggested we come over and introduce ourselves. If you're nice, perhaps she'll grant you the next dance," Mr. Hershawn said, putting out his arm for Bel to take.

She just giggled as she allowed the gentleman to lead her to the floor.

Even though she was a little warm after the dance, Bel was exceedingly pleased to see who her aunt was speaking with when she was returned to her side. Somehow, she had managed to catch the attention of Lady St. Vincent and her very handsome friend.

"Ah, here is my niece," Lady Blakemore said as she approached. "Lord Conway, may I present Miss Kendrick?"

Bel curtsied as her aunt explained, "Lord Conway is Lady St. Vincent's brother just returned from Italy."

Bel curtsied. "It is an honor, my lord." She looked up at him. "Italy sounds awfully exciting. How long were you traveling there?"

"I wasn't traveling. I have been living in Venice for the past six years," he said.

"Oh, how fascinating!" Bel received an odd look from her aunt. "I may not like history, but I do enjoy reading about foreign places," she explained to Lady Blakemore and Lady St. Vincent.

"I feel as though I've missed something," Lord Conway said, looking confused.

"What you're missing is your invitation to the young lady to dance," his sister informed him with a laugh.

At the unhappy expression on the man's face, Bel immediately felt bad for him. She hated being brow-beaten into doing things she didn't want to do by her sister too. "You need not feel compelled—"

"Don't be ridiculous, Conway loves to dance, and I saw you dancing in the last set. You looked like you were enjoying yourself immensely," Lady St. Vincent said.

Lord Conway put a brave smile on and bowed. "Miss Kendrick, I would be grateful if you would dance with me."

Bel curtsied and smiled warmly up at him. "Thank you, my lord, I would love to." She placed her hand in his and allowed him to lead her toward the assembling dancers. "So that you can get your sister off your back," she added quietly as they walked away.

An involuntary laugh tried to escape his lips, but he suppressed it well enough. His twitching lips told another story.

Happily, he wasn't as enthusiastic as her previous partner, which gave her the opportunity to say a word or two whenever the dance brought them together. "You wouldn't know who wrote this music, would you?" Bel asked. "It's not by Mozart." She had no idea whether Lord Conway knew the first thing about music, but it was worth asking.

The gentleman paused his movements and nearly had the lady next to him spin right past when he was supposed to have grabbed her hand. "No, it's not Mozart. I believe it's the new contredanse from Beethoven. Did my sister tell you I was a musician?"

"No! Are you?" Bel asked, suddenly even more fascinated by this incredible man.

"Well, I sing. My piano playing is just passable," he answered when he had a chance.

"Ah, then we complement each other, my lord. I play the pianoforte, but my singing is painful to anyone within earshot."

He laughed and spun away.

"I think you must be right that this is Beethoven, though," Bel said, curtsying as the dance ended. "It's not a piece I recognize, and I do try to keep up with newly released music as best I can."

"We can ask the musicians if you like," he offered.

"Oh yes, of course! What a splendid idea," she said, smiling up at him. He was so handsome!

He offered her his arm, and they moved through the crowd to the front of the room where a set of stairs led up to the musicians' loft.

He got the attention of the conductor at the top of the stairs. The man came toward them. "Could you tell us which piece you just played?"

"It is from the Scottish dances just published in Berlin, my lord. I have a cousin there who sends me all the latest music," the man said.

"It was excellent," Bel put in.

The man bowed, smiling at her. "I'm very happy you liked it, Miss."

"Oh yes, I do love Beethoven's music," she said. "Thank you."

He bowed to them as they turned around and went back down to the ballroom.

"Perhaps there were some pieces for pianoforte released along with the orchestral works," Lord Conway said.

"I'm hoping so. I'd love to have a new piece to work on," she said with a giggle. "I do love a musical challenge."

As Lord Conway escorted Bel across the room to her aunt, she could feel the stares of the other girls who'd tried to get his lordship to speak with them. She hadn't thought of it before, but she now realized that both dancing with the gentleman and spending even more time with him after the dance had ended might just do wonders for her reputation. She just prayed the other girls didn't dislike her for it. She hadn't made any friends yet, but she was hoping to do so before too long.

Chapter Eight

Edward had been so annoyed at Elizabeth for forcing him to attend this silly function and then not even paying any attention to him. She had spent most of the time on the arm of some fellow he didn't know and didn't care to know.

Entirely on his own, he'd had to fight off the matchmaking-mamas and their doe-eyed daughters. He'd been very proud of himself for managing to avoid them as well as he had until Elizabeth had shown up by his side.

He'd never realized how very controlling his sister was—well, no, that wasn't true. He'd always known how controlling she was; it was just that when they were young, he'd been bigger and older and had been able to bully her into submission. But she'd clearly grown up since then, and being a gentleman, he couldn't very well argue with his sister in public.

There had been no polite way to avoid her without making a scene, and she'd promised, *promised* not to introduce him to any simpering misses. Well, he had to give her that. She had not done so. No, she'd introduced him to the sweetest, most clever, beautiful girl in the room instead—and she was a *musician*. How was he supposed to fight that one?

Dancing with her had been a joy. She'd even made him laugh, something he hadn't done in far, far too long. Their little excursion up to the orchestra had been an amusing little aside. If he hadn't wanted to avoid the dagger-looks of every other matron in the room, he would have been happy to stay by Miss Kendrick's side and talk, but he'd already spent more time with her than he had anyone else. No, he'd had to excuse himself and make nice to some other girls or else he would never hear the end of it from Elizabeth.

~*~

Paul took in a deep breath of freedom and fresh air the moment he walked out of Lady Bradmore's ball. It had been hot and stuffy in there with too many people and too much perfume.

He'd done his duty. He'd danced with a couple of the less objectionable girls and then made good his escape as soon as he could. Now, he needed a drink. Male companionship wouldn't go amiss either. He wondered who he might find at Powell's.

He was in luck. Soon after he arrived, he spied his good friend Warwick in a corner talking with... My God, was that Crow? Could it possibly be that his two closest friends from school were here, together? Good things were about to happen; Paul could feel it.

"Well, well, well, look who's washed up on our shores," Paul said, sauntering over to his friends.

Crow stood up and grabbed Paul's outstretched hand. "Saint! Good to see you," his old friend said. It was clear Crow had aged a bit since they'd been in school together, but so had he.

"How are you, old man?" Paul asked with a laugh. He pulled up a chair and joined them.

"I'm doing well. My condolences on the loss of your father," Crow said.

"Yes, I was sorry to hear of it," Warwick added.

Paul waved it off. "Thank you. We weren't particularly close, but, well, the loss of one's only parent does have a bit of a sting to it."

"I can only imagine," Crow said.

"Lord and Lady Danby are well?" Paul asked.

"They are, thank you."

"Sadly, his brother was killed in a riding accident while you were mourning your father. You are now speaking with the Viscount Colburne," Warwick told him.

"Oh, I am sorry," Paul said, turning to Crow.

"Thank you. It is a double loss for me," his friend said with a wan smile. "Not only have I lost my brother, but, well, you know that being the heir was the last thing I ever wanted."

"Yes. I seem to recall you shoving it into our faces more than once that you had a freedom neither one of us had," Paul said, laughing.

"And now, here I am, well caught," Colburne said, raising his hands in the air as if in surrender.

"Not only that, but we've both been caught in the wonderful trap of matrimony," Warwick said.

"My God! Yes, I remember reading about yours, Warwick. It was, of course, in all the papers," Paul said. "And you too, Colburne?"

"I'd say that I was afraid so, but I'm truly not afraid at all. Rather happy about it, in fact," Colburne said, broadening his smile into one a true happiness.

"Now we've got to find a bride for you,"

Warwick said with a laugh.

Paul gave a chuckle. "I am extremely sorry to say you're right. I am, actually, on the lookout for a bride. Now that my father's gone, it's time..."

"We understand." Warwick patted his arm consolingly.

"I was just at the Bradmore's ball taking a look at this year's crop," Paul mentioned.

"No love at first sight?" Colburne asked, clearly joking.

Paul could only shake his head. "The nonsense that was spouted to me by more than one young lady was enough to curl my toes, I'll tell you. Love this and love that and, oh, for a romantic walk in the moonlight. My stomach was nearly churning."

His two friends just looked at each other, sharing some private joke.

Warwick put a hand on Paul's shoulder. "I'm very sorry to break this to you, but, well, we're converts."

Paul frowned. "What do you mean?"

Colburne gave a laugh. "We're both very much in love with our wives. *And* we'd be more than happy to help you find what we are now enjoying."

"You've got to be kidding me!" Paul couldn't believe his two best friends had been played this way. They had to have been tricked. Befuddled. Something!

"No, I'm sorry. I know we laughed at the thought of falling in love when we were school boys, but I can tell you, love is very real," Warwick said.

"And it will make you do some crazy things," Colburne added.

"Hah! Don't I know it!" Warwick agreed with a

loud laugh.

"Don't worry, Saint, we'll convince you of it too. We won't give up on you," Colburne said.

"I think I could use that drink now," Paul said, turning around to find a footman. His friends had become completely ridiculous.

~*~

Bee was dozing in the chair by the fireplace when Bel waltzed into the room, but she was wide awake within seconds. She'd tried so hard to stay awake for Bel, but it had gotten so late and still her sister hadn't returned. But now, finally, she was back and Bee could ask her all about her evening.

"Tell me everything and don't leave a single moment out," Bee said as their maid began to undress Bel.

"Ugh! I'm exhausted, Bee. Can't this wait until morning?" Bel whined.

"What? No! I've been waiting all night for you," Bee said.

Bel sighed heavily. "What do you want to know? I met people. I danced. I had some truly awful lemonade. What else is there?"

"Who did you meet? Who did you dance with? Why was the lemonade so awful? I want to know everything!"

Bel let her eyes drift closed. "I met Aunt Claire's friends, some very nice ladies." Her eyes suddenly popped open. "Oh, and I met Tina."

"Isn't she wonderful?" Bee asked, a smile coming to her face.

"She is! But I nearly did something truly awful," she said, stepping away from her maid, Annie.

"What?" Bee asked.

"I didn't know who she was! All I knew was that a strange woman approached me started calling me by my Christian name," Bel said.

Bee gasped. "You didn't say anything unkind, I hope?"

"No, I didn't." She smiled and then gave a little giggle. "I had the good sense to wait and see if she wasn't someone who you'd met, and indeed, it quickly became clear who she was."

"Oh, thank goodness!" Bee said, sagging with relief. "We cannot afford to make an enemy of her. She is so very kind."

"Yes, indeed, she was. But we're really going to have to be careful and tell each other everything about the people we meet or else we're going to give ourselves away."

"Yes!"

"Oh, I suppose *that's* why you're so eager to hear about my evening," her sister said, finally getting it.

"Well, that and because the whole reason I'm here is to help you find the right man to marry," Bee reminded her.

"Yes..." She was forced to stop talking as an enormous yawn overtook her. "But it *is* going to have to wait until tomorrow when I'm not quite so tired."

"At least give me a little bit tonight. First impressions are so important. Who else did you meet? Who did you dance with?" Bee asked.

Bel sighed and thought back. "First, I danced with Sir Reginald, who is a lot fun. Lud, I've never laughed so much! And then I danced with Mr.

Hershawn, who nearly came to blows with Lord Rosebury over who would escort me out," she said with a giggle. "Apparently, they always come together and are rarely seen without the other. I danced with Lord Conway, who was a dream and so sweet. After him, I met a number of other gentlemen." She paused to think. "Oh, and I met a very sweet gentleman named Lord Bertram. He started to ask me to dance, then seemed to get distracted by a girl hiding behind a plant."

"Oh?"

She shrugged and said, "He asked her instead and was so gentle and encouraging I'm glad he did. I'm sure I'll have another opportunity." She sat down at the dressing table to allow Annie to brush out her hair.

"Perhaps she was just shy," Bee suggested.

"Perhaps."

Bee wished that Bel were more forthcoming with details. She had no idea what her sister thought of any of the men who she'd danced with. She didn't know what they looked like or whether any of them might interest her sister enough so that she might want to marry them. On the other hand, she had only met them once and, presumably for a short time, so it was probably much too early to have formed any firm opinions.

"Was there anyone else of interest?" Bee asked.

"No," Bel said just before a huge yawn overtook her. "It was a wonderful evening, though. I am looking forward to meeting these people again." Annie placed her plait over her shoulder to let her know she was finished.

"Anyone in particular?" Bee had to ask.

But Bel was already sleepwalking toward their

bed. Bee didn't even think her eyes were open any longer. Clearly, she was not going to get any more information tonight.

CHAPTER NINE

~March 27~

Bel happily left her sister in their room the following afternoon and ran down to join her aunt in the drawing room. Lady Blakemore had let it be known to a great many people the previous evening that she would be "at home" that afternoon. As a well-respected member of society, she was expecting quite a crowd.

Only a quarter of an hour after she'd opened her home, fifteen people had already arrived. Some of them Bel had met the previous evening, and some were entirely new to her. Still, she eagerly waited for Lord Conway to come.

She spotted Lord Bertram and accidentally made eye contact. He immediately came forward, another young lady in tow. "Lord Bertram, how lovely to see you again," Bel said politely.

"And you, Miss Kendrick. May I present my good friend, Lady Blackglass?" he said, turning to the beautiful dark-haired woman by his side.

Bel curtsied. "How lovely to meet you, my lady. Were you at the ball last night as well?"

"No, sadly, I couldn't make it," she answered. Her voice was soft and husky.

"I had to drag her out with me today. Deirdre

has a tendency to hide in her study and avoid people," Lord Bertram said.

"I have an estate to run! In my family, a female can inherit the title and lands," she explained to Bel. "Sadly, my father passed on a few years ago, making me the marchioness."

"How very unusual! And what a large responsibility for someone so young," Bel said.

"Yes. It also makes it imperative that I marry, so my dearest friend is going to ensure that I get out and meet people," she said, turning a smile onto Lord Bertram.

"You are very lucky to have him," Bel said.

"Good afternoon, Miss Kendrick, Lady Blackglass, Lord Bertram," Lady Margaret said, giving them all a small curtsy.

"Good afternoon," the gentleman and lady said in unison.

Bel gave a little giggle, but the two of them didn't even crack a smile or look at each other. Perhaps they were used to such things, she thought with amusement.

"I saw you dancing at least once last night, my lady," Bel said, turning a smile onto her new friend. "I do hope you enjoyed yourself."

"Oh, yes. Mr. Hershawn was very kind," she said with a slight blush, suddenly finding the floor very interesting.

"And Rosebury was with him, I suppose?" Lady Blackglass asked.

A smile hovered on Lady Margaret's lips. "Naturally."

Lady Blackglass gave a little laugh. "Never one without the other."

Out of the corner of her eye, Bel spied Lord and Lady St. Vincent come into the room. Her conscience pricked her for how she had treated him and his love of history the previous evening. She knew he'd only been trying to make polite conversation, and she'd put a plug in it. It hadn't been kind.

"Please, excuse me," Bel said. "I just saw someone come in who I need to speak with." She made a straight line to Lord St. Vincent, who was just greeting her aunt.

"How lovely to see you again today," her aunt was saying.

"Thank you," he said. "Good afternoon, Miss Kendrick." He turned a polite smile toward her.

"Good afternoon, my lord." She looked to her aunt and then said to Lord St. Vincent, "Might we have a word?"

He looked at her aunt, unsure of whether she'd meant with her aunt or with him.

"I, er, I wanted to apologize for my behavior last night," Bel said quickly.

Both he and her aunt turned to pay closer attention to her. She suddenly felt very unsure of herself, but she knew this was the right thing to do, so she continued with a giggle of embarrassment. "It was so silly of me to stop you from discussing your interest in the history of Lincolnshire. I know the area is of great historical significance." She gave an honest laugh. "My sister is forever talking to me about it. But I'm afraid I adhere more closely to what my father calls 'carpe diem'."

"Seize the day," Lord St. Vincent translated.

"Precisely. I live for the moment and have little interest in the past, whether it was last year or a thousand years ago, I'm afraid."

He smiled and Bel immediately felt relieved he understood. It also occurred to her that Bee would probably get along with him very well. Why hadn't she thought of that before? Plans began formulating in Bel's mind.

"Well then, I promise not to tax you with discussions of the past any further," he said. "Perhaps we could find other topics to discuss."

"I would appreciate that," she said. "Have you traveled, my lord? I find foreign places very interesting." Her glance slipped over to her aunt to see what she thought of the topic.

The lady gave an approving nod before excusing herself and moving on to speak with her other guests.

"I'm afraid I haven't been beyond our shores, but I do hope, after the war, to be able to do some traveling," he said. "Is there some place you would especially like to see?"

Bel gave a relieved giggle. "I would love to see Paris and Rome. I have read about Egypt and India, but I don't know that I would care to travel so far."

He raised his eyebrows. "You are quite well informed."

She gave a little shrug. "While there may be a lot of history in Lincolnshire, there isn't a great deal to do. I've spent a good amount of time reading. But please, don't tell anyone!"

He gave a little laugh. "I understand. You wouldn't want to be thought to be a blue-stocking."

"No! My sister fully embraces the concept, but I would much rather be thought to be silly than bookish," she admitted.

~*~

Later that afternoon, after they'd said goodbye to the last of their guests, Bel was still sitting and staring at the door.

"Is there someone you are waiting for?" her aunt asked, surprisingly observant.

Bel startled a little and turned toward Lady Blakemore. "I had been hoping that Lord Conway would come," she admitted.

"You seemed to get along quite well with him last night."

"Yes. He's a very interesting man and so incredibly handsome," Bel said with a giggle.

"I also noticed that you were the only one with whom he spent a prolonged period of time. Even after your dance with him, he only said a word or two to each young lady he was introduced to."

Bel couldn't help but smile with pride. "Yes, I noticed that too."

Aunt Claire nodded her approval but said no more on the subject.

~*~

Edward staggered back with the hit to his shoulder. He was going to be bruised after this, but he couldn't have passed up the opportunity to see his old friend again. It had been years since he'd seen Giampiero Abelli.

They'd sung together for years at the opera in Venice until the man had left to find better paying work in London. Oddly, when Edward had contacted him, instead of accepting his invitation to dinner, Giampiero had insisted they come to Gentleman Jackson's and "enjoy" a round of boxing. It was deuced hard to have a conversation with someone who kept hitting you, though.

"Come now, Eduardo, you have gotten out of practice," Giampiero said, dancing around him, his wrapped fists circling in the air in front of Edward's face.

"I have. I cannot deny it. I haven't been in a ring since the last time I saw you," Edward agreed. He did his best to take a shot at his friend, but Giampiero was too fast for him. He dodged out of the way before Edward's fist even came close to landing.

"You will get old if you do not keep it up," his friend said, taking another shot at Edward's abdomen.

"Tell me how you've been doing. Are you finding steady work?" Edward asked, just managing to hit Giampiero's arm—he'd been aiming for his chest.

"I have. This is a wonderful town to work in. You are appreciated, unlike Venice where there are too many opera singers."

"Good, I'm glad to hear that. I'll come and see you sometime very soon."

"I will send tickets," Giampiero said.

"You don't need to. I've purchased a box for the season."

That made his friend pause. "*Sinceramente?*"

"Of course! How could I not?"

Giampiero shrugged but turned it into a blow to Edward's left shoulder. Edward staggered backward again.

"I heard about Angelica," Giampiero said. "I was never so sad when I hear of her passing."

Edward landed a punch to his friend's ribcage.

"I also heard you never left her side the entire

time she is ill," Giampiero added, taking a step back.

Edward followed with a left-right switch to his stomach—blows which landed so hard his friend doubled over for a moment, giving Edward an opening for an undercut to his shoulder.

"Ah, this is good," Giampiero said through clenched teeth.

Edward didn't pause but hit him again and again, forcing him back.

"It is still painful. I can see this," his friend said, trying and failing to block Edward's blows.

"Very. I loved her with all my heart. All my soul," Edward said, catching him in the stomach once again. "But I have to move on, Giampiero. I have to…to live my life again."

"Can you?" his friend asked, managing to land a blow of his own.

"I must. *I* did not die." Edward got another combination hit to Giampiero's side.

"No. You did not. But how can you just set aside the love of your life?"

"I haven't and I won't ever set her aside," Edward responded with another blow to Giampiero's shoulder. "But she's gone. She's been gone for over two years. I *have* to move on."

"If you must, you must."

Edward landed a particularly hard blow to Giampiero's solar plexus, forcing him to bend over coughing. Lowering his fists, Edward said, "I will always love Angelica. Never will she leave my heart. But I need to marry. I was hoping you would understand."

Giampiero could only nod as he tried to

breathe through the pain. "Remind me not to discuss Angelica with you when we are boxing," he croaked.

"Next time, hopefully, we'll be discussing whoever I have met."

Giampiero rubbed his stomach. "I can only hope your feelings for whoever that is won't be as strong."

Chapter Ten

~March 28~

The following day, Bel was taken to the modiste for a fitting. She was incredibly excited to see the gowns her sister had chosen for her and hoped beyond hope that they wouldn't all be plain and boring. Bee had a tendency to choose the most ordinary designs, but she'd promised Bel that she'd asked for lace and other frills, knowing how much she liked them. Knowing also that Tina had been there to help, gave Bel confidence that they would be flattering.

They stopped at Tina's home to pick her up on their way.

"You didn't need to come to the fitting, Tina," Bel said, as soon as they'd gotten under way once again.

"But I enjoy this! Truly, I do. And I want to make sure that they did a good job, and everything looks just the way it should," Tina said.

"Well, I certainly wouldn't want to deny you your fun," Bel said, laughing.

"I don't know what we would do without you," Lady Blakemore said, smiling at her friend. "Your taste is impeccable, and you know just how to make clothing most flattering to a person."

"Thank you, my lady. I do try," Tina said.

When they arrived at the shop, the duchess immediately took control. She had Bel in the dressing room stripped down to her stays in no time and was helping her put on the first gown—a walking dress. Strangely, Bel had to take in a breath in order for the dress to be buttoned up properly.

"It's too tight!" Tina said, surprised.

"We made it precisely to the measurements," the assistant said, trying to shift it across Bel's bosom to be sure it was in the right place.

Tina reached into her reticule and pulled out a measuring tape. "Lift your arms, please, Bel."

Bel complied and stood while Tina measured across her bust.

Tina paused, released the tape, and then put it back into place, measuring her once again. "That's—" She stopped and stood back for a moment, looking closely at Bel's form. Suddenly she turned and said to the assistant, "I'm sorry, but would you excuse us for a moment?"

The girl nodded, gave a little bob of a curtsy, and left the room.

"Am I mistaken or did your aunt say that you had an identical twin?" Tina asked, looking up at Bel.

Bel's eyes went wide, and her mouth suddenly went dry. "You are not mistaken, but she's in Oxford visiting a friend."

"Is she *really*?" Tina narrowed her eyes.

Bel didn't say a word.

"I measured you. I did so myself because I wanted to be sure that your clothing fit precisely. I can tell you either grew in the past three days, or you are not the same person I measured."

"I grew?"

"You are almost half an inch bigger. That's why this dress isn't fitting the way it should."

Bel's mouth dropped open. She hadn't known she was larger than her sister. It was true, she ate a bit more than Bee did, but she'd always thought that they were precisely the same size—they even shared clothing. Of course, none of their dresses were as form fitting as this one.

"You can't tell anyone!" she whispered. Bel grabbed Tina's hand. "Please, please swear you won't tell a soul! Bee is supposed to be in Oxford, but...but I *couldn't* have faced coming here alone. We've never been apart for very long. And *she* insisted because she's a much better judge of people than I am."

Tina took in a deep breath and closed her eyes for a moment. When she opened them again, she said, "Your aunt doesn't know?"

Bel shook her head.

"Where is...your sister staying, then?"

"Bee. Beatrice. She's staying in my room with me. Our maid knows, of course, and she sneaks food up to her, and sometimes Bee takes my place at meals or when I'm supposed to go out."

Tina nodded, understanding. "And so, she was the one who came to choose your dresses."

"Yes. Our aunt sprung the trip on her, making it impossible for us to switch places before they left."

"I see."

Bel looked at her pleadingly but stayed silent.

"Well then, we'd better... No, wait. Is she going

to be wearing these dresses too?"

"Yes, she probably will."

"All right, then. Let me think about this." She walked slowly around Bel, looking at the dress she was wearing. She then snapped her fingers. "I've got it!"

She turned and called the assistant back into the room. "I'd like hidden hooks put into the dress here," she said, indicating the side seam under the arms. "Miss Kendrick would like to be able to put on and take off her dress herself and she simply can't do so if there are buttons going up the back as they are now."

"Shall we remove the buttons and create a seam in the back?" the woman asked, walking around to look at the back of the dress.

"No, leave them there. They're pretty. Just add in the hidden hooks in the side."

The girl nodded and made some notes in her notebook. As she did so, Tina whispered to Bel, "We'll add in a second set of hooks for Bee so that it fits her the same as it fits you. No one will know the difference."

She then said in a normal volume, "We'll do the same for the other dresses. And we'll need to loosen all of them. It seems I made a mistake when I measured Miss Kendrick last time."

Bel mouthed a thank you while the assistant's focus was on her notes. Tina gave her a slight nod.

"And could we add a flounce to this?" Bel asked. "I do like a bit more to my dresses."

Tina laughed. "We can add a little more lace to the skirt, but I think *Miss Kendrick* will be happier if there isn't too much." She raised her eyebrows significantly.

Bel immediately understood that she was referring to the *other* Miss Kendrick. She gave a sigh. "Yes, I suppose you're right."

Tina giggled and they set to work adjusting the fit on all the gowns that had been ordered and making it so they could be adjusted to fit a little tighter or looser depending on which hooks were used.

Bee was reading when Bel came back up to their room after dinner. She stopped just inside the door, her hands on her hips.

"What?" Bee asked when her sister didn't move for nearly a minute.

"Come, it's time for you to get dressed," Bel said, finally moving again.

"What? Dressed?" Bee sat up on the bed.

"Yes, dressed." She turned to their maid who was just coming in from the dressing room, gown in hand. "Annie, Miss Bee will be going to out this evening. Have you finished putting the second row of hooks onto the dress that was delivered this afternoon?"

"Yes, Miss Bel, I just finished not ten minutes ago. I figured you'd want to wear it this evening."

"Not me, Bee is going to wear it," Bel said.

Annie looked at Bee, still sitting on the bed. She hadn't moved because she still didn't know what her sister was up to.

"I thought you loved the ball and were looking forward to the party this evening," Bee said.

"I did enjoy it, but you need to go and meet these people I've been telling you about. How else are you going to be able to judge their characters, which you so love doing?" Bel said, plopping down onto the bed.

Bee thought about it and realized Bel was right. She did have to meet these men face-to-face to assess how good they'd be for her sister. "And you won't mind missing a party?" she confirmed.

"I've been wanting to read that book by Maria Edgeworth that Aunt Claire gave me," she said, scooting back to sit next to Bee. She leaned back against the pillows and folded her arms.

Bee sat there for a moment trying to gauge how honest Bel was being. Was she just doing this to be nice or did she truly want Bee's opinion? Was she going to mope and groan when Bee returned and be upset because she'd missed the party?

"You'd better get dressed," Bel said, interrupting her thoughts. "Aunt Claire does not like to be late."

With a shrug, Bee closed her book and hopped off the bed. "And you're going to let me wear your new dress?"

"It would look odd if you didn't."

Bee had to agree.

With the new hooks Annie had put in, the dress fit her perfectly and looked stunning. It had a few more bows and fribbles than she normally liked, but it wasn't bad. She turned this way and that in the mirror. No, not bad at all. She swallowed a smile and then sat down to let Annie do her hair.

Annie was fast and soon she was heading downstairs and looking forward to her very first London society party!

An hour later, she had to clamp her jaw closed to keep her mouth from hanging open at all the beautiful people and lovely decorations gracing the incredibly opulent London townhouse of the Marquess of Danby. She'd nearly spoiled everything when she didn't greet the Marquess's daughter-in-law, Lady Colburne, as if she knew her. Bel had told her very briefly about each of the ladies of Aunt Claire's Wagering Whist Society, but actually meeting someone in person was very different from hearing a brief description of them.

"I'm so sorry, Lady Colburne, you will have to forgive me," Bee said, trying to giggle like her sister did. "I was so distracted the other night at the ball..."

"Of course you were!" the young woman said. "It was your first ball."

"My first foray into London *society*," Bee added for emphasis.

"Naturally. You probably don't remember half the people you met that evening." She was so kind.

"Thank you so much for understanding. Next time, for certain—"

"Next time, I hope it will be in a quieter environment with fewer distractions," the lady said. She cocked her head to one side and asked, "Do you ride, Miss Kendrick?"

"I do, but I haven't brought my horse with me to town," Bee said. Both she and Bel enjoyed riding about their father's estate and around the locality.

"I'm sure we could find a mount for you if you wish to ride," her aunt said. "Lady Colburne actually races horses."

Bee turned back to the lady. She was so petite and delicate-looking, it was hard to imagine her riding in a race.

"I do, but I promise I wouldn't try to race against you. I was just thinking of a ride in Hyde Park," Lady Colburne said with a laugh.

"Oh, yes, that sounds wonderful. I would love to go riding with you some afternoon." And then it suddenly struck Bee that she'd heard about how many people in society go for a drive or a walk in the park in the afternoons to see and be seen. "Oh! Do you mean along Rotten Row? That's what it's called, isn't it?" she asked.

Lady Colburne gave her a broad smile. "Yes, that's precisely what I mean. I was going to join Lydia—Lady Welles—and Lady Margaret tomorrow, perhaps you'd like to join us?"

Bee gasped. "I would like that best among all things!"

"Then we'll see you tomorrow," Lady Colburne said decisively.

Lady Blakemore gently guided Bee away from the lady and farther into the ballroom where there were a great many people. Once again, she had to hold back her gasps and surprise. She was sure her aunt would think her response strange, especially since she was sure Bel had done the same the other night at the first ball she'd gone to.

Impersonating her sister was going to be trying in so many ways.

"Ah, look, there is Lady St. Vincent and her brother," Lady Blakemore said.

Bee had no idea who either person was, but she recognized Lady St. Vincent's name as one Bel had mentioned so she asked, "May we go over and speak with them?"

"I was sure you would want to do so, considering the marked attention Lord Conway graced you with the other night," her aunt said with a smile.

Lord Conway? Oh, so this was the infamous Lord Conway, Bee thought to herself. All right, now things were most definitely going to get interesting.

"Good evening, Lady Blakemore," Lady St. Vincent said as they approached.

"Good evening." Bee's aunt nodded to them both. "Lord Conway."

"And how are you this evening, Miss Kendrick," Lord Conway asked, turning a bright smile onto Bee.

She could feel herself flush at his close attention and then remembered she was supposed to be Bel, so she added a giggle as she curtsied. "Very well, thank you, my lord." She turned to his companion, a beautiful woman who looked to be about five or six years older than herself. "Good evening, my lady."

Lady St. Vincent nodded. "That is a very fetching gown," she said kindly.

"Thank you." She added a giggle for good measure. "I was so lucky to have my aunt and a friend of hers help me choose designs for my new dresses."

"The Duchess of Warwick is a friend of mine," Lady Blakemore explained. "She has an excellent eye for fashion."

"How very nice. I'm afraid I'm still just coming out of mourning, but I think it's time I started wearing some newer, brighter dresses, don't you think?" she asked, turning to her brother.

"Undoubtedly," he agreed, "you do look particularly stunning in deep red."

"Or blue," Bee said, thinking about it. "A dark blue would bring out your eyes."

The lady smiled at her. "Thank you. Actually, blue is one of my favorite colors."

"Have you had a chance to find the music you were looking for, Miss Kendrick," Lord Conway asked.

Bee had no idea what music Bel might have been interested in, so she answered honestly, "No, I'm afraid I haven't yet had a chance to go to the store. We've been so busy with the modiste and morning calls," she said.

"If you wish to go to a particular store, and I'm not available, you simply need to inform the footman, and he'll arrange for your uncle's coachman to take you. Just be sure to bring your maid," her aunt said.

"Oh, thank you, Aunt Claire. That would be wonderful! I did so want to get..." she trailed off wondering what her sister had wanted.

"Some new pieces by Beethoven," Lord Conway put in helpfully.

Bee giggled as she knew Bel would. "Yes! Thank you, my lord. It was on the tip of my tongue."

"You did so admire the music we danced to the other night," he said. "And speaking of which, it sounds as if a quadrille is about to begin. Would you care to join?"

"Oh, I would love to, thank you," Bee said with another giggle. She allowed Lord Conway to take her hand and lead her onto the floor.

Chapter Eleven

He was an excellent dancer for such a large man. Bee was impressed. He even managed to hold a bit of a conversation with her as they moved through the steps. Sadly, Bee couldn't add much to the conversation as he seemed only to want to discuss music, and that was one topic Bee didn't know well enough. She took refuge in asking about the promenade in the park.

"I'm afraid I haven't been in a number of years, but the last time I went it was simply a way for people to see and be seen," he answered.

"So, one can glean quite a bit of information by who is out with whom?" she asked, knowing that it was something Bel loved. Bee's sister wasn't a terrible gossip, but she did like to know the latest on-dits.

"Oh, absolutely," Lord Conway laughed, just before they moved away from each other again.

"And you, my lord, do you enjoy the promenade?" Bee asked when they came together again.

He gave her a little smile. "I have been known to attend on occasion. You wouldn't happen to be hinting for an invitation, would you Miss Kendrick?"

Bee pretended shock at such a suggestion but then burst into giggles. Her sister would absolutely do such a thing. Hmmm, maybe Bee was better at pretending to be Bel than she'd imagined.

As the dance ended just then, Lord Conway bowed to her and took her hand. "Miss Kendrick, I would be honored if you would go driving in the park with me one afternoon."

Bee ducked her head shyly for a moment and then remembered that Lady Colburne had invited her to go out riding with her the following day. "I'm afraid it will have to be next week. I have another invitation to go riding in the park tomorrow."

"Oh?" he asked, curious. He narrowed his eyes at her, even as he tucked her hand into the crook of his arm, and they headed back toward her aunt. "You aren't trying to make me jealous, now are you?"

Bee laughed. "No, my lord, I would never do that. To tell the truth, it was Lady Colburne who issued the invitation. I believe I am to go riding with her and a couple of other young ladies."

"Oh, well then, that's all right. I will forgive you that."

"You are too kind," she said with another giggle.

He left her with her aunt and went off to be polite to other young ladies, but Bee didn't think he looked very enthusiastic about the idea. She gave a little smile as she thought of her sister with Lord Conway. On the other hand, there were a great number of gentlemen here. Many more than she'd imagined. How in the world was one to decide on who to marry? If she spoke with even half of the men, she would feel overwhelmed and confused.

Although, maybe they weren't all as sweet and clever as Lord Conway.

She was standing next to her aunt, looking in one direction, when a gentleman approached from the other. He was a larger man with straight brown hair that fell into his eyes. He made a grand leg to both her and her aunt. Bee thought him rather ridiculous, but managed to give a giggle because she was sure that her sister would have done so.

"Oooh, Miss Kendrick, you look absolutely stunning this evening," the man said.

"Why, thank you," she said, curtsying. "You are too kind."

"Absolutely not, but I must insist that you dance with me. We were quite the talk of the Bradmore ball after our performance the other night," he said.

Oh, my goodness, what did her sister do? Fear flashed through Bee's mind. "What? What did we do that caused—"

"I believe Sir Reginald is teasing you, my dear," Aunt Claire said repressively.

"Oh." Bee could breathe again.

"Very well, we might not have set tongues wagging, but that doesn't mean we can't do so tonight," he said with a giggle. "Come, please say you will dance with me again?"

Bee looked to her aunt, who gave her a small nod. "Very well, so long as you don't do anything that would cause a stir."

"I approve wholeheartedly," Lady Blakemore said. "Sir Reginald, you will please behave yourself."

The man sighed dramatically but smiled and

said, "Very well, my lady. Just being in Miss Kendrick's presence will have to be enough. So beautiful. So delightful," he said as he led her back onto the floor.

The gentleman kept up a constant stream of what Bee imagined Bel would call witty repartee. She dutifully laughed at his quips and attempted to answer with a few of her own, but she wasn't nearly as adept at such banter as her sister. The man seemed to be satisfied enough, however, so when he started to return her to her aunt, he said, "I do hope we have a great many more opportunities to see each other, Miss Kendrick. You are a joy!"

"Oh, why, thank you." For herself, she sincerely hoped that was not the case because there was just something too silly, too...too *much* about the man. Even though he was rather amusing for a short period of time, she didn't like him a great deal.

"Ah, Miss Kendrick, good evening," said a very tall, blond-haired man standing with Lady Blakemore.

"Good evening," Bee said. Her mind went absolutely blank for a moment as she took in this incredibly handsome man. He was wonderfully tall, and while Lord Conway filled out his coat extremely well, this gentleman made her feel almost overwhelmed by the strength of him. She suddenly realized she was staring at him like an idiot, so she quickly added, "It's lovely to see you again." And then prayed like an idiot that "she" had met him before.

"And you," he said. His voice was deep and sent tingles down to her toes. "Have you started any more fascinating books since yesterday?"

Bee widened her eyes at him. Bel had spoken to

him about books? But she hated reading—well, she hated reading anything that wasn't a novel. Every once in a while, she would pick up a book on travel and look through the pictures, but that was the extent of her reading habits.

"Oh! I promise, I haven't told a soul," he whispered just loud enough for her to hear.

"Thank goodness," Bee said with a giggle, wondering what her sister might have said to this man.

"So, what *are* you reading just now?"

"A History of Greece by William Mitford," she answered without thinking.

"A history? But you told me you hated histories," he said with surprise.

"I...I did?"

"Most emphatically. You told me you disliked history and especially the history of Lincolnshire, in no uncertain terms." He frowned as he seemed to think back to what she'd said—which was good since Bel hadn't told Bee a word about this. "But you did say that you enjoyed reading about foreign lands, so I suppose Greece counts in that way."

"Er...yes. Greece is definitely foreign. And, er, my uncle's library here isn't very extensive. I had very little to choose from." Well, that was honest. What was also honest was the fact that Bee was going to have a serious word with her sister on alienating handsome men!

"Ah, I understand. One must make do, I suppose," he said, his smile returning to his face.

"Yes," she said, giving a little giggle. Bee wasn't sure, but she thought all this giggling was giving her a headache.

"Well, I promised you no more discussion of the history of Lincolnshire, and I'm determined to keep to my promise."

"The history of Lincolnshire? Oh, but it has such a wonderful, rich history," she blurted before her tongue could catch up to her brain. But truly, the history of the area where she lived interested her beyond anything. She'd read every book she could find on the subject and had been to visit a great number of ruins, dragging poor Bel with her every time.

He frowned. "Yes, indeed, it does. But you made it more than clear to me yesterday that you had no interest in it."

"Oh." For a moment Bee wanted to curse her sister. How could she tell this fascinating man that she wasn't interested in history? How could she tell him that she wasn't interested in *anything* he wanted to discuss? He could talk about horse manure, and she would find it fascinating. "While that's true, there are a great many fascinating ruins not far from where we live, not to mention Lincolnshire Cathedral itself, which is just beautiful."

"I think I mentioned that to you myself," he said, raising one eyebrow.

"Oh, did you? I... I didn't recall." Ugh, now he was going to think her an idiot.

"Miss Kendrick, how lovely to see you!" Bee spun around, grateful for the interruption. She was even happier when she saw it was Tina who was the one approaching them. "Your Grace," Bee said, giving her a little curtsy.

"Oh, my goodness," Tina laughed. "No need for such formality with me!" She turned to Lord St.

Vincent. "I don't believe we've met."

Bee jumped in, "Duchess, may I present Lord St. Vincent? My lord, the Duchess of Warwick."

Tina gave a little curtsy while the gentleman bowed lower than he had for Bee. Status was a wonderful thing, she thought with a little internal laugh.

"It's a pleasure to meet you," he replied.

"The duchess was so kind as to see me properly outfitted for this evening," Bee said, giving her friend a smile.

"Really?"

Tina laughed. "I went with her to the modiste, that's all."

"And helped me choose this gown among others. She has the most incredible eye for fashion and can tell exactly how a dress will look on someone simply by looking at a picture." She turned to her friend. "I can't tell you how amazed I am at your ability."

"It's many years of experience and a good imagination."

"Well, if you chose what Miss Kendrick is wearing this evening, then it's clear that you are indeed the expert she claims because she is looking particularly lovely tonight. I, er, meant to mention it earlier," he said, his cheeks turning slightly pink.

Bee giggled. "It is of no matter, my lord. I don't expect a man to notice such things right off."

"They don't!" Tina agreed. "It took me nearly all of last season to convince my husband that he shouldn't wear brown. He has brown hair, brown eyes, and the only color he would wear was that same dreadful brown! You, my lord, clearly have the good sense to wear clothing that go with your coloring and isn't completely unremarkable."

"Thank you. It's not easy for someone as blond and fair as I am to find colors that don't emphasize how pale I am," he admitted with a little smile.

"I imagine it can be a touch challenging," Tina said.

"Perhaps some more time out in the sun, my lord?" Bee suggested.

"And then I turn beet-red," Lord St. Vincent laughed.

"Oh, dear!" Tina said.

"Well, the blue of your coat is quite flattering," Bee said, admiring his coat. His waistcoat was of a lighter blue and a very simple double-breasted design. He looked quite elegant. Bee appreciated the simplicity of his choices.

"I'm happy you approve," he said with a twinkle to his eye. He was teasing her, which was a wonderful turnabout from their earlier conversation. It had been entirely too serious—and dangerous—considering what Bel had already told the man about her interests, which were precisely the opposite of Bee's.

"And I think we finally have a topic that we can both agree upon and discuss without any confusion," Bee commented aloud.

Lord St. Vincent burst out laughing. "Yes, indeed, Miss Kendrick. And it only took us a quarter of an hour and the excellent assistance of the duchess to find it."

"Yes, thank you, Tina," Bee said, turning to her friend. The duchess looked a little confused but seemed happy to have assisted in something she didn't quite understand.

"But now, I will leave you ladies to your discussion of fashion and make good of an earlier promise. If you will please excuse me?" He bowed and strode off in the direction of another young lady who was looking anxiously about.

"He must have promised this dance to her," Bee said, watching him go.

"He is quite handsome. Who is he?" Tina asked.

"Lord St. Vincent? I don't know. Bel was the one who was properly introduced to him," Bee admitted. "I think I'm going to have to find my uncle's copy of Debrett's and remind myself of who's who."

"Oh, you're Bee!" Tina began to laugh behind her hand. "Without my measuring tape, I can't tell you apart."

Bee laughed. "Sorry, yes. And I did want to thank you so much for the wonderful idea of the hooks in this dress. It's perfect."

Tina looked it over critically. "Whoever sewed them in did an excellent job. I can't even see where they are."

"My maid Annie is wonderful with a needle," Bee agreed.

"Tina, how lovely to see you this evening," Lady Blakemore said, rejoining Bee. She'd been speaking with a friend a few feet away while Bee had been talking with Lord St. Vincent.

"And you, my lady. I was just commenting on how good that dress looks on Bel," Tina said, giving Bee a smile.

"It is thanks to you, I'm sure," Bee's aunt said.

"Oh no, it is her lovely figure. You don't know how lucky you are, Bel. A number of girls would give their eye-teeth to be slender like you."

"I may be thin, but I've got curves, which sadly isn't the fashion," Bee complained. She followed it up with a little giggle. "Being petite must be so much easier with the styles we wear now."

"Well, that's true. Diana can wear *anything* she wants," Tina said.

"Remind me who Diana is? I'm afraid I only know most people by their titles," Bee said, widening her eyes.

"Oh, I'm sorry. Lady Colburne's given name is Diana. Lady Welles is Lydia. We're all the same age and are good friends, so we just call each other by our Christian names. I'm sure you'll be invited to do so as well tomorrow—I hear you're going riding together."

"Oh, aren't you going to join us?"

"No. I'm afraid I never learned to ride. Warwick has promised to teach me, but he's so busy..."

"Why doesn't Lady Colburne do so?" Bee asked. "I hear she races horses. Surely if she can do that, she can teach you how to ride."

Tina gave Bee a smile. "That's a wonderful idea. I'll have to ask her."

Bee wondered whether she would get to go on the outing the following day or if Bel would go in her stead. She hoped she'd be able to do so; she truly did want to get to know all these ladies better. Having new friends was wonderful. On the other hand, it was very important for Bel to make friends as well, and since this was *her* season... Bee nearly sighed when she realized she probably should be the one to stay home. It was difficult to not exist.

~*~

"Well, well, you were speaking with Miss Kendrick for some time," Elizabeth commented to Paul after he returned his dance partner to her chaperone.

"I can't quite figure that girl out," he said, handing a glass of lemonade to his step-mother and taking one for himself. "One day she tells me she can't stand history, the next she says she's reading a history of Greece."

When Elizabeth looked at him curiously, he explained further. "Yesterday when I saw her at Lady Blakemore's at-home, she apologized for being so curt at the last ball we attended and explained that she just dislikes history. Then this evening when I was speaking with her, she *did* seem to like it. No, don't give me that look," he said quickly as Elizabeth frowned at him. "I can't figure it out either, that's what I'm saying."

"Either she does like it or she doesn't," Elizabeth said.

"That's what I would have thought, but she seems to change her mind by the day."

"Maybe she's just trying to get your attention."

"Yes, that's what I'm beginning to think. I can't imagine a girl as giggly and silly as Miss Kendrick is actually reading a history of Greece," he said before finishing his lemonade. He wanted more. The dancing and the crowd had made him hot. Trying to figure out the enigma that was Miss Kendrick was beginning to make him bothered. "I think I need to escape and head over to Powell's. You'll have to excuse me. I can only take this sort of thing for so long."

Elizabeth laughed. "At least you've got

someplace to escape. I can only go home."

"I'm sorry. I'd offer to bring you to Powell's, but I don't believe ladies are allowed."

"No, and I don't think I'd want to sit and have a drink with so many men," Elizabeth said, laughing.

Chapter Twelve

Claire sat back in her favorite chair by the fireplace, a glass of brandy in her hand. Even better was her most wonderful husband, who was sitting on his chair, which he'd pulled up close to hers, massaging her feet.

"I don't know why you insist on wearing those heeled slippers, my love. You always come home from a party with aching feet after you've done so," he said, digging his thumb into the center of her foot, eliciting a moan of pleasure from her.

"I always forget. I should probably just get rid of them," Claire agreed.

"You said that the last time you wore them, but then decided to only wear them at parties where you'd be sitting down most of the evening," he pointed out.

"Well, this time I am going to throw them away for certain. They are much too uncomfortable to be standing in all evening."

"True. Now, tell me how our girl is doing," he said, running his thumb down her arch.

"Not too badly," Claire admitted. "She has met a great number of men, naturally."

"Is she favoring any?"

"Three. Lord St. Vincent, who I do not feel will amount to anything. He is much too intellectual for her."

"I met him the other day at Powell's, and I have to agree, although he does keep excellent company. I believe he, the Duke of Warwick, and Lord Colburne all went to school together."

"Really?" Claire asked, lifting her head to look at her husband. He truly was a font of excellent information. While she was sitting up a little, she took a sip of her brandy.

"I saw the three of them in the reading room laughing and chatting," Blakemore said with a nod. "And who else has caught Bel's interest?"

"Lord Conway."

"I don't believe I know him."

That surprised Claire. She thought her husband knew everyone. "He's just arrived back in England after living in Italy for many years. I'm certain you'll meet him soon. Very nice fellow. A bit old for her, though."

"Oh?"

"Yes. He is Lady St. Vincent's older brother, and she's got to be eight and twenty if she's a day."

"Hmmm, yes."

"And sadly, Bel has also been rather keen on Sir Reginald. She danced with him at both Lady Bradmore's ball and again this evening."

"Oh, I don't think I'd encourage *that* alliance," Blakemore said immediately.

"No. I will have to inform Bel that while Sir Reginald is immensely amusing, she may only think of him as a friend. He is completely ineligible."

"Broke as a board," her husband agreed.

"Yes. And she doesn't exactly have the most generous dowry, so I'm not exactly certain why he's interested in *her*."

"Probably just having some fun. You know how he is."

"Yes. I think you may be right."

"But she should be aware of how things stand with him," Blakemore pointed out.

"I couldn't agree more, my love. I will discuss it with her tomorrow."

~*~

"Bel, how could you?" Bee asked, after arriving home from the ball.

"How could I what?" Bel mumbled from their bed where she'd been sleeping. She turned over to speak with her sister and flipped her long braid from around her neck.

"Well, first, how could you not tell me that Lord St. Vincent was absolutely the most handsome man on this earth? And secondly, how could you tell him that you *hated* history?" Bee threw herself down onto the bed next to her sister, despite the fact that Annie was standing by waiting to help her undress.

Bel sat up, now awake. "You think Lord St. Vincent is the most handsome man? *Really*?"

"What do you mean? Those cheek bones! That smile!"

"That fair skin? Those cheek bones?" Bel nearly screeched and then remembered she was supposed to be alone. She immediately lowered her voice. "Truly, you can't find someone so blond and fair attractive, and I'm sure anyone with cheeks so sharp has to be evil."

Bee sat up. "I disagree completely. I can and I do find him very handsome! He's wholesome looking. And what about history? I *love* history and you told him you hated it?"

"I do hate it!"

"How could you hate something so..." Bee took in a deep breath. It was an argument they'd had hundreds of times. She wasn't going to engage in it again now. "But he's so good-looking," she said, melting back onto her pillows.

Bel giggled. "I'm very happy you think so, and indeed, I did think that he was perfect for you."

"But this is your season, not mine," Bee sighed.

"You'll have yours next year and then you can tell him all about your passion for dried up, dusty, old ruins," Bel said.

"You try me, Bel, truly you do," Bee said, getting herself up in order to get changed for bed.

"Did you see Lord Conway?" Bel asked.

Bee smiled at her sister. "I did. And you may thank me now because I convinced him to take you for a drive in the park, dear sister."

Bel gasped and jumped to her knees and clasped her hands together in front of her chest. "You did?"

Bee laughed. "I did."

Bel leapt from the bed and threw her arms around her twin. "Thank you! Oh, thank you! A drive in the park! When?"

Bee laughed. "Next week. Tomorrow one of us is going riding with Ladies Wells, Colburne, and Margaret."

"Oooh, that sounds wonderful. What an excellent idea!"

"Actually, it was Lady Colburne's, but yes, I thought so as well."

Bel did a little dance around the room before hopping back into bed. "Driving in the park with Lord Conway," she sang quietly to herself.

Bee could only laugh at her silly, silly sister.

~*~

Edward did the best he could under the circumstances. He'd danced not only with the lovely Miss Kendrick, who seemed a little different this evening but still just as fascinating, but he'd also danced with two other young ladies. Elizabeth had better be proud of him.

Actually, *he* was. And so, he felt he deserved a break from female company for a little while. He decided to head to Powell's and take the owner of the gentleman's club, Lord Wickford, up on his offer of male companionship and excellent rum.

"Yes, sir, may I help you?" the majordomo at the door said, clearly not willing to let just anyone in.

"Lord Wickford invited me," Edward said.

They seemed to have been the magic words for the man smiled and stepped back to allow Edward into the club.

"If you would just wait here a moment, I'll inform him of your arrival. Your name please, sir?"

"Conway. Viscount Conway."

"Of course, my lord. Just one moment, if you will?" The majordomo raised a hand, and a footman came running up to them. He requested Lord Wickford's presence, and the fellow gave a nod and ran off to find him.

~*~

Happily, Edward didn't have to wait long. Wickford popped out of a door to their right and came forward, his hand outstretched in greeting.

Edward took it saying, "You suggested I come…"

"Yes, and I'm so glad you have! Please, let me show you around. I'll have my man send papers around tomorrow with your official membership agreement and so on," Wickford said, leading him into the room he'd just come from.

Edward laughed. "That sounds awfully official."

"It's just a formality, you understand. Must be seen to be exclusive, you know."

"Are you not?"

"Oh, no, we are. Most definitely. The agreement just adds an extra veneer." He paused inside the door to a gaming room. There were tables of men playing everything from vingt-et-un to whist to hazard. "If you are inclined to lose some money, this is the place to do it," he said, laughing.

"I assume there is some winning as well," Edward said, raising his eyebrows and turning a smile onto his new friend.

Wickford gave a shrug. "Naturally, but I don't like to think about that."

They both burst out laughing and then Wickford turned back around and led him into the room across the hall. "And here is our reading room for quiet contemplation, reading, and conversation."

"Very nice. Very relaxing." Edward turned around and looked at the door that had been closed behind them. "You must have excellent soundproofing. I can hardly hear the noise from the gaming room in here."

A smile slid onto Wickford's face. "Few people notice that. Yes, I have had the walls of both rooms padded on the inside to keep things quiet in here and contain some of the noise from the other room as well."

Edward nodded appreciatively. "Very nice. Well done."

"Thank you. There is a dining room toward the rear of the building if you'd care to have some dinner another night. But for now..." He raised a hand and called a footman over. "Now, for some of that rum I promised you, eh?"

"Absolutely," Edward nodded.

Another footman came into the room and headed straight for Wickford. A whisper in his ear and his host turned toward him. "I am terribly sorry. I'm afraid you're going to have to have that drink alone for at least a bit. I've got an issue I need to deal with."

"Of course! It can't be easy running a club of this size."

"There's always something," he said with a laugh before following the footman out the door.

Edward went farther into the room to find a couple of free seats when Wickford was able to spare him a moment. It wasn't easy, considering how full the club was. As he passed one group of men talking quietly together, he recognized a man he'd seen his sister with a number of times, but they'd never been in the same place at the same time to be introduced. He'd also seen Miss Kendrick speaking with him after their dance this very evening. Curiosity got the better of him and he stopped.

"I beg your pardon," he said, facing the man. "I'm Conway, and I don't believe we've had the pleasure."

The man stood and held his hand out. "St. Vincent."

"Ah! That explains it!" Edward said with a smile.

St. Vincent cocked his head to one side in curiosity. "Explains what?"

"Why I've seen you with my sister. I'm Elizabeth's older brother."

"Oh, of course! I should have known that." St. Vincent pumped his hand a little harder before letting go. "I can hardly believe we haven't been introduced before this."

"Elizabeth has mentioned that she wanted to do so any number of times..."

"Yes! But somehow, we've simply missed each other," St. Vincent said, completing his thought.

Edward laughed. "Yes. I can't quite figure out how, but well, I'm glad I saw you here this evening."

"As am I. Please join us." He indicated an empty chair next to one of the other men he'd been speaking with. "This is the Duke of Warwick and Viscount Colburne. We all went to school together," St. Vincent explained.

Edward shook each man's hand in turn and then sat down just as the footman with his drink came looking for him.

"Conway is..." St. Vincent paused to think about it and then gave a bark of a laughter. "Well, I suppose you're my uncle."

Edward laughed. "Good God, yes, I suppose so

since my sister was married to your father."

"These things can be deuced awkward when a man marries someone so much his junior," Colburne said good-naturedly.

"Indeed," St. Vincent agreed.

"My sister was exactly thirty years younger than St. Vincent," Edward said.

"My God! And your father agreed to the match?" Warwick asked Conway.

"Encouraged it," Edward said. "She was in a spot of trouble, and St. Vincent's offer came at precisely the right time. I'm afraid I wasn't around at the time."

"I've heard you've just returned from Italy, do I have that right?" the new Lord St. Vincent asked.

"Yes. I've been living in Venice for the past six years. Now that I've returned, my sister has decided it's time I marry," Edward said.

"She's quite the matchmaker," St. Vincent said with a laugh. "She's decided the same for me."

"What were you doing in Venice?" Colburne asked.

"Singing," Edward said, turning to the man. "I'm an opera singer—much to my family's embarrassment."

Colburne burst out laughing. "Welcome to black sheep club! I'm a physician. It took my saving a man's life for my father to recognize the value in having a son engage in such a lowly occupation."

"Really? Well, it sounds like you're a good man to know," Edward said with a laugh. "I can merely entertain the onlookers while you resuscitate."

The men all burst out laughing.

"Well played, Conway," Colburne said, bowing to him in his chair.

"I don't know which, of the two of you, has the more difficult position, the opera singer or the physician," Warwick said, still laughing.

"Neither is a respected occupation," St. Vincent agreed.

"At least I don't have my parents looking over my shoulder disapprovingly," Edward said.

"Touché," Colburne said. "And I *can* save lives."

"I think we should call it a draw," St. Vincent said.

"Friends?" Colburne asked, putting out his hand.

Edward took it very happily. "It is good to have friends, especially those with your expertise."

"Just so long as I can call on you to entertain at my wife's parties," Colburne said.

"It's a deal," Edward agreed.

Chapter Thirteen

Bee was disappointed when Bel put on her riding habit the following afternoon. She'd rather been hoping that her sister wouldn't want to go riding with their new friends. At home, Bel didn't particularly enjoy riding. Sadly, the prospect of riding with the ladies and developing her friendship with them was too enticing to pass up. It was for exactly that reason that Bee wanted to go as well.

It was Bel's season, Bee reminded herself. She should be grateful she had the opportunity to go Lady Darby's party at all. And Bel had also insisted that she attend Lady Sorrell's soiree a few days hence, as well.

"It's going to be a more intellectual sort of affair, from what I gather. No dancing, just a lot of people standing around talking about the events of the day. In other words, exactly your sort of affair," Bel had said as she'd turned this way and that in front of the mirror.

"It does indeed sound like fun," Bee had agreed. She reached out and placed Bel's hat on her head, then handed her the hat pin so it would stay in place as she rode. It was a very stylish hat, more like a small version of a man's tall hat than something made for a lady, and it was all the rage.

They'd actually had it made in Lincolnshire where a very clever milliner had seen a picture in a newspaper of a lady wearing such a hat and knew that Miss Bel would look stunning in it.

"So, you'll tell me all about your ride?" Bee asked, trying to keep the jealousy from her voice.

Bel gave her a quick peck on the cheek. "Promise!"

~*~

"I don't think we could have chosen a more lovely day," Lady Welles said soon after Bel had met her, Lady Margaret, and Lady Colburne at the gate to the park.

"Indeed. It's not even too cold," Lady Colburne agreed. She was on the most beautiful horse. Bel just couldn't help saying something.

"Lady Colburne, my aunt mentioned you race horses. That isn't your racing horse, is it?"

"Yes, it is, actually. I don't usually ride Nike in the park, but I haven't had a lot of opportunities to exercise her recently, so I thought I would take her out today," the lady said with a smile. "What I really need to do is to take her down to Epsom Downs and give her a good run."

"Oh, that sounds so exciting," Bel said wistfully.

"It sounds terrifying to me," Lady Margaret said with a little laugh.

"Have you raced, Miss Kendrick?" Lady Colburne asked.

"Me? Ha, no! I actually don't ride very often, but I just could not pass up the opportunity to come out with you this afternoon." Bee would be so proud of her for being open and honest.

"I also don't ride often, but for Diana I always make an exception," Lady Welles said with a laugh. "What one does for friends."

"You are too good to me, Lydia. Next time we come to the park, I promise we'll drive. Maybe Colburne will allow me to borrow his phaeton," Lady Colburne said with a little wiggle of her eyebrows. The other three women burst out laughing.

"So tell us how you're liking the season so far," Lady Welles said, turning to Bel as they rode slowly down Rotten Row.

"Oh, I'm enjoying myself even more than I had imagined," Bel said.

"Well, you are extremely lucky to have Lady Blakemore to bring you out. She knows absolutely everybody," Lady Margaret said.

"Yes, it's been wonderful," Bel agreed.

"She mentioned at our last meeting that you have a sister who will be making her debut next season?" Lady Welles asked.

"Yes Bee, er, Beatrice. We were both very disappointed that our parents decided not to bring us out together."

"But it must be nice to stretch out on your own. I've never had a sister, but I can imagine if you're always with them, it might be nice to do something entirely on your own," Lady Colburne said.

"I don't know, I couldn't imagine what I would have done were my brother not with me last season. And Tina was absolutely essential as well," Lady Margaret said wistfully.

"It *is* interesting. We've never been apart, and I have to admit I miss her terribly. On the other hand, it has given me the opportunity to make new friends, which is very nice," Bel said. In truth, she was grateful Bee was here with her, even though she wasn't able to join her when she went out. Just to have someone familiar, when she was otherwise surrounded by strangers, gave her a touch more confidence, which was funny because she'd always been the one to help Bee socially, not the other way around.

"Speaking of friends, you must call us by our given names," Lady Welles said with a broad smile.

"Yes! We decided long ago that it was silly of us to be on formal terms when we're the same age. The same goes for you," Lady Colburne said.

"Thank you, and of course you must call me by mine," Bel said.

"It's Isabel, isn't it?" Lady Welles said.

"Yes, but all my friends call me Bel."

"Bel it is," Diana said. "Now, you have to tell us who you have danced with and who you wish to dance with again."

"And who you absolutely do *not* want to dance with again," Lydia added with a laugh.

Bel happened to spy Lord St. Vincent just at that moment, driving by with Lady St. Vincent in an open carriage. "Well, there's one gentleman whose company I have enjoyed," she said, nodding in his direction. "I'm not entirely certain how much he's enjoyed mine, however."

"Who is that?" Margaret asked.

"That's Lord St. Vincent and his step-mother. They've just returned to London after a year in mourning for his father," Diana said.

"I don't know him either," Lydia said to

Margaret.

"Well, come, you should be introduced. We can't possibly have you, Margaret, unaware of one of the most interesting gentlemen of the season. You need to find a husband as well," Diana said.

Bel wasn't sure how things had ended between him and Bee the other evening. She thought her sister had said things had gone well once Tina had joined them and changed the subject of their conversation to fashion, but she also remembered that Bee was very upset because she believed he hadn't thought very well of her intellectual abilities. This didn't bother Bel at all. She didn't need or want people to think her smart, but for Bee it was extremely upsetting. Poor thing! Well, Bel would do her best to make him think well of her again, and Bee would follow that up at Lady Sorrell's soiree if she saw him there.

~*~

Paul was enjoying an afternoon out with Elizabeth. They hadn't actually spent very much time together over the past week. He wasn't entirely certain he could call a drive in the park spending time with her as they were constantly greeting others. Still, it was nice just to be with her.

He liked his step-mother and completely understood what had drawn his father to marry her. She was beautiful, charming, and very pleasant to be with. Now, if he could only find someone like that for himself.

Even as that thought passed through his mind, his eyes alighted on the beautiful Miss Kendrick. She was riding along the path with three other ladies and seemed to be heading directly for him.

"Good afternoon, Lord St. Vincent," Miss

Kendrick called out, slowing her horse to match the speed of his carriage.

"Good afternoon," he nodded.

"You remember my friend, Lady Colburne?" she asked, indicating a petite woman on an enormous thoroughbred horse.

"Yes, of course, my lady. Lovely to see you again," he said and nodded.

"And have you met Lady Welles?" Miss Kendrick continued.

"No. It's a pleasure." He smiled at the pretty brunette on Miss Kendrick's other side.

"And this is Lady Margaret," she finished, indicating the slender young lady on Lady Welles' other side.

He nodded his greeting to her as well.

"Lady St. Vincent it is delightful to see you again, as well," Miss Kendrick said, cutting off Paul's greeting to Lady Margaret.

"And you, Miss Kendrick. Lady Colburne, Lady Margaret, Lady Welles, very nice to see you all again," Elizabeth said, nodding at them all.

The women exchanged greetings and then Elizabeth said, "Lady Colburne, what a very impressive horse you have there."

"Thank you. I'm trying to give my Nike a little exercise, but I'm beginning to think this isn't really the place to do so," Lady Colburne said with a laugh.

"No, I can't imagine it is," Paul agreed. "And Miss Kendrick, may I say what a very pretty hat you have on?"

Miss Kendrick giggled. "Why, thank you, my lord."

"Is that something else the Duchess of Warwick assisted you with?" he asked, smiling.

"No. Actually, I got this in Lincolnshire before we came to London," Bel said.

"We?" Elizabeth asked, picking up on the same thing that had caught Paul's attention.

"Did I say 'we'?" Miss Kendrick laughed. Bright spots of pink suddenly glowed on her cheeks. "I meant me, er, before <I>I</I> came to London. I'm so used to saying 'we' because it's so rare that my sister isn't with me—and she and I bought the hat together."

"It must be so difficult for you to be here without her," Elizabeth said kindly.

"Yes, yes, it is, my lady," Miss Kendrick said. "Do you have a sister you are close to?"

"Me?" Elizabeth laughed. "No, just my brother. But we were very close as children. We're very close in age, so we spent a good amount of time together."

"Well, you are very lucky to have Lord Conway," Miss Kendrick said. Her color remained high, making Paul wonder why. The pink contrasted sharply with her otherwise creamy complexion and clashed with her bright red hair.

"Yes, I must agree," Elizabeth said as the driver of the carriage behind them shouted for Paul to move on. He had slowed his carriage to a halt as they'd talked, and the fellow behind them wasn't happy about it.

"I'll look forward to seeing you all at Lady Sorrell's soiree," he said as he gave his horse the go-ahead to continue.

"Yes, see you there!" Miss Kendrick called

after.

~*~

"She is a very sweet girl," Elizabeth said quietly as they drove on.

"She is, but as I mentioned last night, she confuses me."

Elizabeth chuckled. "Well, maybe you just need to get to know her better?"

"Perhaps," Paul said. There was definitely something funny about that girl, but he just couldn't put his finger on it. Maybe Elizabeth was right, though. Maybe he just needed to spend more time with her. Happily, he'd be seeing her again at Lady Sorrell's soiree.

"Lady St. Vincent!" a man's voice called out, jolting Paul from his thoughts. He looked to see who had called out and found a fellow standing up in his carriage as it passed going the other way.

"Who is that?" Paul asked, shocked at this fellow's behavior.

"Drive on," Elizabeth said, keeping her gaze straight ahead and completely ignoring the imbecile.

Paul did so, not even acknowledging the man.

"Oh, that's a fine a greeting," the fellow called after them. "Typical!" Paul heard him say more quietly after they'd passed.

After they'd gotten a little distance away from the man, Paul turned to his step-mother. "Now, would you care to tell me what that was about?"

Elizabeth pursed her lips together. "That was Lord Rogan and no friend of mine."

"Has he done something?" All of Paul's protective instincts jumped to the fore, making his fingertips tingle. He was ready to do absolutely anything for his step-mother.

"Not recently, and I'd like to keep it that way. I assure you, I plan on staying as far away from him as I can."

"Elizabeth, if you don't tell me what he did, I can't protect you from him," Paul pointed out.

She just shook her head. "It's over and done with and hopefully won't be dredged up from the past where it firmly belongs."

Paul sighed and relaxed again. It didn't look like he was going to get a straight answer, and since the fellow was well behind them, there didn't seem to be anything more he could do but leave it alone for now.

Chapter Fourteen

~March 31~

Bee was excited to be going out again. Even though it had only been a few days since she'd gone to the ball, she was looking forward to another chance to impress Lord St. Vincent. She'd really made a hash out of it last time, but this evening would be different.

Bel had discovered that Lady Sorrell's soirées were known for their excellent conversation. It was to be a more intellectual evening than one normally had at a party. In other words, it was an absolutely perfect opportunity to show off her intellect.

"But no talking about history!" Bel begged her for the fifth time as she was getting dressed.

"No, I think we've pretty much run that topic into the ground," Bee agreed.

"So, what are you going to talk about? What might impress him?" Bel asked, cocking her head to one side.

"I don't know," Bee whined, dropping her head back and looking up at the ceiling. She straightened her head, but still wrung her hands together. "There has to be some sort of topic you don't hate that I can discuss with him."

"Music?" Bel offered. It was the one topic that

thoroughly fascinated her.

"How about travel?" Bee offered. "You told him you were interested in travel, right?"

"Yes!" Bel gave a little jump of excitement. "I did. Of course, I was thinking about Lord Conway when I mentioned it, and the fact that he lived abroad for so many years."

Bee waved off the details. "That doesn't matter. You told Lord St. Vincent you were interested in travel, so I will discuss that topic with him."

"But he said he hasn't traveled outside of England," Bel pointed out.

"It doesn't matter. Neither have I, but I know a great deal about other countries. I've read about them. I'm certain he has as well." Now that her mind was made up, Bee was certain this was the right thing to do. Before Lady Blakemore could even send for her, Bee was downstairs ready and waiting to go.

Her aunt nodded approvingly at her dress and, Bee supposed, at her timeliness.

Lady Sorrell's home was beautiful. She had all the ground and first floors open to guests. It was a good thing; there were so many people that all the rooms were nearly full.

Lady Colburne and Lady Welles—no, Diana and Lydia, Bee had to remind herself—came up to her and her aunt soon after they arrived.

"Oh, Bel, is that one of the dresses you bought with Tina? It's lovely," Lydia said.

Bee gave a Bel-like giggle. "Oh, thank you. I do like this one, and Tina was so wonderful as to help me pick it out and get it made just right."

"She has helped all of us!" Diana said with a

laugh.

"So, tell me, how does this work? Is there a lecture or a particular topic we are supposed to be discussing? I've never been to a soirée before," Bee asked, widening her eyes.

Lydia gave a laugh. "No, you can discuss anything you wish. It's just that the conversation does tend more toward the academic or political rather than fashion or who danced with whom."

"Oh, all right," Bee said. She couldn't help but look around to see if Lord St. Vincent had arrived yet.

"Are you looking for anyone in particular?" Lydia asked with a giggle.

"Oh, no," Bee lied, embarrassed at having been caught out.

"Oh, come now, you can tell us," Diana said. "I haven't seen Lord St. Vincent yet," she added suggestively.

"Or is it Lord Conway you're interested in? I've heard that you made quite the impression on him when no one else could even get him to engage with them for more than five minutes," Lydia said.

"Ladies, I thought we were supposed to be having a more academic discussion," Lady Blakemore said repressively.

"Oh, well..." Lydia started with a giggle.

"The relative merits of a viscount over an earl?" Diana suggest with a giggle of her own.

Even Aunt Claire laughed at that. "How about the war with France?"

"Too depressing!" Lydia said immediately.

"All right. What do you think of the new Slave Trade Act?" Bee's aunt asked.

"Do you keep abreast of everything that's happening in Parliament, Lady Blakemore?" Diana asked.

"I try to stay informed," Lady Blakemore nodded. "And, of course, Lord Blakemore is quite active, so I hear about many things from him."

"How wonderful to have someone keep you so well informed," Bee said, before realizing that perhaps he'd been discussing the current events at dinner. She had yet to have dinner with her aunt and uncle, instead having a stolen meal up in her room with Annie.

Her aunt didn't seem to notice the misstep. "Yes, it is." She turned to the other ladies, "So, what do you think of slavery and this new law?"

"I think it's wonderful," Diana said immediately.

"I don't believe it goes quite far enough," Lydia said, surprising Bee with her knowledge of the subject. "It only abolished the *trade* of slaves, not slavery itself."

Since Bee knew very little about the new law, she felt at a distinct disadvantage. She'd always read the papers at home, but since coming to London she'd been concentrating solely on her sister's search for a husband. One thing was for certain, though, she was most definitely going to pursue a closer friendship with Lydia. The woman was amazing in her knowledge and intelligence. She was sweet and funny on top of that. She was exactly the sort of person Bee wanted to emulate.

"I beg your pardon?" a woman's voice rose angrily from nearby.

~*~

Paul turned to find Elizabeth as soon as he heard

her outraged cry. He'd been speaking with Lady Sorrell near the door to the drawing room. They'd only just arrived, but Elizabeth had gone immediately forward to speak with a friend of hers while he'd stayed to have a word with their hostess.

His step-mother was standing in the corner, not too far away. She looked like a cornered doe, her eyes wide, her face pale. He excused himself from Lady Sorrell and started toward her.

The man they'd seen in the park the other day was openly leering at Elizabeth. Paul held back for a moment to take stock of the situation. Elizabeth's eyes went from wide and scared to narrow and furious. He waited to see if she had things under control before barging forward. He didn't want to make a scene of something she could easily handle on her own.

"Oh, come now, Lady St. Vincent, you can't deny it, you *want* to join me. Come, let's talk about this in private. Just you and me." He chuckled, letting his laugh complete his meaning. His voice was quiet enough that if everyone had been talking as normal, he wouldn't have been overheard, but when Elizabeth had raised her voice, everyone had turned to see what was happening. "I have heard all about your little tricks—such a clever little minx," the man continued, oblivious to the fact that he was now the center of attention. "Was it Brentley who taught you? He did say that he'd school you well." He laughed again, and then, to Paul's shock, reached his hand out toward Elizabeth's backside. Elizabeth jumped.

It didn't take Paul more than three long strides to be at Elizabeth's side. "If you dare lay a hand on her or even come within her vicinity—" Paul started, pulling the man's attention away from

Elizabeth, who now seemed to be frozen in shock.

"Eh?" the man said. He looked Paul up and down with a sneer. "Listen, I don't know who you are, but you're going to have to wait your turn, my man."

Paul clenched his fists and took another menacing step toward the man, so he was practically stepping on his toes. The man tried to back up but tripped over his own feet and fell with an *oomph* onto his backside.

He sat there looking terrified while Paul wished with all his might the fellow was more of a man so he could have the pleasure of beating him to a bloody pulp. A hand pulled at his arm, however. "No, Paul, you mustn't." Elizabeth's voice filtered through the haze of fury.

Paul turned to look into Elizabeth's worried eyes. He took in a deep breath and restrained himself. He wouldn't hit the imbecile, but he also wouldn't stay quiet. "I will meet you at dawn, sir! Name your seconds."

"What?" the fellow squeaked. He scrambled to his knees and then his feet. It wasn't an easy task for he was a rather rotund man, and he was clearly wearing a corset and couldn't bend easily.

"You heard me," Paul repeated.

"No! I-I-I apologize. Truly, no offense was meant. I admit I was hoping... Well, you know her reputation. I was just hoping she might be interested. I-I've never, er, but I've heard—I suppose she's your mistress," he finished feebly.

It took all of Paul's self-control not to knock the man down again. He could feel his nails biting into the palm of his hand. "I suggest you stop right there," he said dark and low.

The fellow paled once again but wisely shut his mouth. Only his eyes shifted, taking in the fact that everyone in the room was watching their interaction. They snapped back to Paul. "Er, who are you?"

"I am Lord St. Vincent, this lady's stepson," Paul answered. "And if you ever dishonor her again—"

The man stumbled back a little but this time retained his footing. "No, no! It-it was a misunderstanding, that's all. I, er, we used to know each other, that's all. And I, er, I thought—"

"You *didn't* think, that much is clear," Paul interrupted.

"Oh, er, no, I suppose not," the fellow said. "I think, er..." He turned to Lord and Lady Sorrell who were standing nearby. Paul hadn't noticed them—or anyone since he'd seen this man had touched his step-mother. Lord Sorrell stood by, prepared to intervene should it become necessary, but Paul had regained control of himself. He gave a nod to let the man know there wouldn't be any further disruption to his party.

The man took a step toward their host. "I'll just say good evening, I believe." He gave a quick bow and left the room as quickly as he could manage.

Paul turned to Elizabeth. "Are you all right?"

She gave a nod, but he could see she was shaking. She held a hand to her stomach, and Paul worried she was going to be sick.

"I think I'll just show Lady St. Vincent to the retiring room. Perhaps she would like to sit down for a moment," Lady Sorrell said, putting an arm around her waist.

"Yes, that sounds most welcome," Elizabeth

said quietly. She leaned in toward their hostess a touch, and they walked from the room.

Talk began again, swelling quickly around Paul.

As he watched his step-mother walk from the room, he caught sight of Miss Kendrick standing a short distance away, open-mouthed. She started toward him.

"My lord, are *you* all right?" she asked quietly, putting a gentle hand on his sleeve.

Paul took in a deep breath, releasing the last of his pent-up energy. "Yes, thank you. I apologize you had to witness that, Miss Kendrick. I'm not usually a violent man."

"No, I'm sure you're not. But that man, whoever he was, acted completely inappropriately toward your step-mother," she said. He could sense the anger underneath her words and took comfort from it.

"I hope you didn't see..." he started, not quite knowing how to finish his sentence politely.

"I'm afraid I saw everything. It looked as if he might have touched her inappropriately," she said quietly.

"I believe he did. It may not be entirely possible, but I do hope you will be able to put the sight from your mind. *Gentlemen* do not behave that way, I assure you. That man was no gentleman."

She gave a little laugh. "I do believe you. And I assure you, it hasn't put me off in any way, despite how disturbing the scene." She paused and then smiled up at him. "Lady St. Vincent is very lucky to have you."

He gave a dry laugh at that. "I don't think Lady Sorrell would agree. I'm afraid I may have just ruined her soirée."

"Oh, no, in terms of making it the most talked about event of the season so far, you most certainly did just the opposite," Lady Welles said as she and Lady Blakemore joined them.

"I'm afraid she's right, my lord," Lady Blakemore said. "It will be the only thing people will talk about for days."

Paul closed his eyes momentarily. "I am so very sorry. I do hope Lady St. Vincent's reputation does not suffer because of my actions."

"It will, but not too much, I should expect. The horrified look on her face when Lord Rogan spoke to her and, er, touched her, was enough to show his advances were most decidedly not welcome," Lady Blakemore reassured him.

"Is that his name?" Paul asked. "Rogan?"

"Yes. I know him by sight but don't know him well," Lady Blakemore said.

"Certainly, it will be *his* reputation that will suffer?" Miss Kendrick asked hopefully.

Paul could only laugh at her naiveté. "Sadly, a gentleman's is not undone by such behavior. In fact, it is quite the opposite. He might very well be applauded for his daring."

"But that's horrid!" the young lady exclaimed.

"I cannot but agree with you. Sadly, that is the way of men."

Chapter Fifteen

Edward just couldn't see himself enjoying an evening of intellectual conversation at Lady Sorrell's soirée. He was pretty certain that Miss Kendrick would find it just as dull. He could have gone to another party—he'd been invited to three that evening, but after avoiding socializing for so long, he just wasn't used to it. No, he needed a quiet evening.

He'd tried sitting at home with a book, but it was too quiet, and he was certain Elizabeth would have scolded him horribly for retreating back into his own cocoon. He compromised by going to Powell's.

There were relatively few gentlemen about this early in the evening, but there were enough so that Edward wasn't entirely alone in the reading room. He settled down with a glass of rum and the newspaper.

"A quiet evening, my lord?" a friendly voice said after Edward had been there for about a quarter of an hour.

"Yes," he said, smiling up at Lord Wickford. "And you?"

The man nodded. "I always enjoy the quiet before the storm of the evening."

Edward gave a little laugh. He returned to his paper as Wickford gave him a slight bow and moved off to greet a few other men who'd just come in.

"Mind if I sit here?" another gentleman asked, indicating the chair next to him. Edward recognized him as one of St. Vincent's friends who he'd met the week before.

"Not at all," Edward said. "It's Warwick, isn't it?"

"Yes," the man said, reaching his hand out after he'd sat down.

"Right. Conway," he said, shaking his hand. "I'm afraid I'm terrible with names."

"I understand. If you meet too many all at once, it can get confusing."

"Yes."

"Decided not to partake in the evening's festivities?" Warwick asked.

"No. I'm just getting used to being back in society. I thought an evening away from it all would be a welcome respite. You?"

"Not much for parties. My wife forgives me and goes off with her friends."

"Now, that's a good wife," Edward said with a chuckle.

Warwick agreed and then picked up another paper from a nearby table and proceeded to read.

Now this was the life, Edward thought. A moment of conversation and then companionable silence.

"Hell and damnation, I need a drink!" a rotund gentleman shouted as he came into the quiet of the reading room.

"Sir, my lord, if you please," a footman said, running up to him on nearly silent, slippered feet.

"No, I damn well do *not* please! I want a drink, and I want it now! And don't even think of handing me just a glass. I want a bottle," the man demanded loudly.

"Is there a problem, Lord Rogan?" Wickford appeared and confronted the man.

"Yes, there damned well is! I want a drink," the man said, not lowering the volume of his voice.

"It sounds as if you might have already—" Wickford started gently.

"No, I haven't! I haven't had a bloody drop, and if I don't get one immediately, I'm going to let the world know what lousy service there is at this club. You're a cheat, Wickford!"

"Now, now, my lord," Wickford said, clearly trying to soothe Lord Rogan's ruffled feathers.

"Don't you dare patronize me!" The man was about to continue when the footman reappeared carrying a tray with a bottle of rum and a glass. "Now, that's more like it."

Much to Edward's chagrin, the fellow dropped into the chair on his other side and indicated that the footman fill his glass. Edward turned and shared a frown with Warwick.

"What the hell are you two so disapproving of?" Rogan said after emptying his glass in one swallow. He refilled his glass himself, this time filling it to the brim.

"We were enjoying a quiet evening until you came in," Warwick said with a disapproving look.

"Well, I was just attacked—attacked, do you hear me? And then challenged to a duel! Who in the hell duels anymore? Isn't it illegal?" the fellow asked, beginning to mellow with his drink.

"I believe in extenuating circumstances it has been known to occur despite its illegality," Warwick replied.

"What did you do to elicit the challenge?" Edward asked. It wasn't so much that he was interested in this fellow's woes, but that he knew his type. If he didn't get his complaints off his chest, he would just go on talking all night until he had, and Edward wanted nothing more than to regain the peace and quiet they'd been enjoying.

"I didn't do anything more than what the lady asked for," the fellow said in a huff.

Edward and Warwick exchanged another glance, and Edward wondered if the duke was thinking the same thing he was. If Rogan had been challenged to a duel, then clearly whether the woman had wanted his attentions or not, the man she'd been with had not approved. Rogan should, at the very least, have been more circumspect.

"And you can just wipe that look off your faces," Rogan growled. "She is known to warm a man's bed, and she's been avoiding mine for far too long. I've seen her looking at me too. That woman wants to be with me, she's just playing hard to get. All I did was give her a little tweak on the arse and issue an invitation."

Edward had to work to keep his mouth from dropping open.

"You pinched a lady's backside and propositioned her?" Warwick asked incredulously.

"I do hope she was the sort to welcome such advances?" Edward asked.

"But it sounds as if her current protector wasn't

pleased," Warwick agreed.

"I thought she didn't have a paramour. She just got back to town after an absence—husband died or some such nonsense—so naturally, I wanted to be the first to, er, welcome her back," Rogan said with a sly, knowing smile.

A cold sensation began to creep through Edward's veins. "You wouldn't be speaking of a lady of the titled variety, would you?"

"Damn right! And now that she's a widow, I wanted to be the first to claim rights," Rogan said, emptying his glass again.

Warwick moved to the edge of his chair. "Would you care to share the name of this, er, light-skirted widow among us?"

"You are *not* going to steal her out from under me!" the man bellowed.

Warwick raised his hands. "I wouldn't dream of it. I'm a happily married man."

Edward stayed quiet.

Lord Rogan gave a satisfied nod. "St. Vincent. Lady St. Vincent." He gave a smirk. "Had quite the reputation a couple of years ago. Now that she's back in town, and this time widowed, I'm looking forward to getting under her skirts. Didn't quite make it—"

He would have continued speaking only he suddenly found himself being lifted forcibly from his chair by his cravat. Edward held the man directly in front of his face. "If you ever come near my sister again, I will not wait to challenge you to a duel. I will permanently rearrange your face right then and there."

"Your...your sister? Whoever said anything

about your sister?” the man choked out. “I don’t even know who you are.”

“My name is Conway. Lady St. Vincent is my little sister. If you come near her again… if you even dare to breathe in her direction…” Edward ground out through his teeth.

“Perhaps, Lord Rogan,” Warwick said slowly while placing a calming hand on Edward’s shoulder, “you would do better to go home, preferably to your estate for the rest of the season.”

“But only if you like looking the way you do right now,” Edward added. “Because I would be more than happy to change that for you.” He released the man who fell back into his chair.

Rogan stumbled to his feet, his face pale and quivering. “You two are as crazy as that woman’s stepson. Everyone knows your sister likes to warm a man’s bed. I was just—” He wisely didn’t finish that sentence but instead bolted from the room.

~April 1~

Paul was grateful Colburne had been available the following morning for a sparring match on short notice.

“That’s the second time you’ve thanked me,” Colburne said as he followed Paul into the ring.

Paul could only shake his head. “That’s because you might not be so happy you agreed to this in a few minutes.”

Colburne put up his gloved fists. “Oh?”

“You didn’t hear what happened last night, did you?” Paul asked, taking the first swipe at his friend.

“No.” Colburne retaliated immediately, catching Paul unawares.

He gave a little smile of acknowledgement of a hit well-timed. "Someone inappropriately propositioned my step-mother, and I very nearly beat him—well, I *wanted* to beat him to a bloody pulp."

Colburne momentarily lowered his arms in shock, and Paul got in a good jab. His arms were in place again right away. "Where was this?"

"At Lady Sorrell's. Wait, you weren't there, but Lady Colburne was," Paul said.

Colburne just managed to tap him on the shoulder before he dodged away. "I had a medical issue come up—a patient I needed to see. Diana doesn't mind if I don't go with her to parties."

"That must be nice. I escorted Elizabeth."

"That was good of you. And it sounds as if it was a good thing you were there," Colburne said.

"Yes, it was. I tell you I nearly hit the man—in public!" He got in a good hit to Colburne's chest, knocking him off balance for a moment.

"Better me today than him last night," his friend said.

"True, although I still think he deserves to be taught a lesson. I offered to meet him, but he just paled and ran like a coward."

Colburne chuckled. "I wouldn't want to be on the wrong side of you when you were armed. It's hard enough when it's just fists and they're gloved."

Paul shook his head and laughed. It was impossible to stay angry when he was talking with Colburne. It was one reason why they'd been friends for so long.

They traded jabs for a few minutes in silence.

"What else is on your mind," Colburne asked,

dancing away from Paul's long reach.

He got Colburne with his other hand. "It's still Elizabeth," he admitted.

Colburne stayed on the defensive, waiting for Paul to continue both with his attack and his conversation.

"She didn't show up for breakfast as she normally does," Paul said. "And she was very quiet last night after the incident."

"Well, that's not surprising. She's probably still upset."

"Still? Even this morning?"

"Not everyone can so easily set their emotions aside. Women, especially, have a tendency to hold on to them," Colburne explained.

Paul nodded and allowed his friend to attack. Colburne did so with more enthusiasm than skill. "You don't think this will affect her reputation adversely, do you?" Paul asked, dodging a fist on its way to his face.

"That I can't speak to," Colburne admitted. "I know nothing of society and care less, I'm afraid."

Paul could only laugh and agree. "It's not so much because <I>I</I> care but because Elizabeth does."

"Naturally," Colburne said, taking another jab at Paul. "And hopefully this will be one of those things that everyone talks about for a few days and then some other on-dit will supplant it."

"Yes, hopefully," Paul said before landing a left-right switch to Colburne's abdomen.

~*~

Claire couldn't help but feel bad for Lady St. Vincent. Not only had she endured a horrible experience the night before but now was most likely the subject of every conversation throughout the *ton*. The ladies of the Wagering Whist Society were no exception.

"I was absolutely certain Lord St. Vincent was going to hit Lord Rogan," Lady Welles said, wide-eyed as she picked up the cards that had just been dealt to her.

"The man showed a great deal of restraint," Claire agreed. "But he is a gentleman, after all."

"Much more so than Lord Rogan," Mrs. Aldridge said. She finished rearranging the cards in her hand and began to pet her dog sitting in her lap.

"I sincerely hope Lady St. Vincent's reputation hasn't been irreparably damaged by this," Christianne said. She was right to be concerned. She'd had her own fear of such repercussions when she'd had an affair with Lord Ayres and subsequently had his child. Christianne had been very smart and so careful that no one, not even her own husband or Lord Ayres, had been aware of either the pregnancy nor the child until her daughter Tina had come to London the previous season.

"It will probably be all anyone can talk about for a few days and then something else will happen," Claire said, placing the first card down onto the table. The other women followed her example, and there was silence as they each concentrated on the game for a few minutes.

"I'd like your opinions on my niece, if you don't mind, ladies," Claire said after picking up the trick she'd just won and placing it next to herself. It had been the first she'd won so far this game.

"Of course," Mrs. Aldridge said immediately.

She, of course, was the least one of the ladies at the table qualified to answer her question, but Claire let that go.

"I am quite pleased that Bel has two very strong suitors," Claire began.

"Lord St. Vincent and Lord Conway," Mrs. Aldridge said with a nod.

"Yes. But I'm wondering if I should be encouraging more gentlemen to take an interest in her. Should I be doing something more, do you think?" Claire asked.

"Well, you haven't had a party for her yet. Were you planning on doing so?" Lady Welles asked.

"I've been wondering if I should. We don't have our own ballroom, and Blakemore hates big gatherings anyway. That's why I hadn't planned on hosting a ball," Claire admitted.

"You could have a smaller party," Christianne suggested.

"Does Miss Kendrick sing or play an instrument?" Mrs. Aldridge asked.

Claire turned to her as she put down the last card in her hand. "Yes! She plays the piano beautifully."

"Well, then, that's what you should do. Host a musicale. It will show off her talent and perhaps get more gentlemen interested in her," the woman said as if the decision had been made.

"It's a good idea," Christianne agreed. Even Lady Welles nodded.

"All right," Claire agreed, "I will do so. Nothing very large, but I'll invite a number of eligible gentlemen—"

"Don't forget the two who are already

interested. Perhaps seeing her at the pianoforte will help one of them decide to take action," Lady Welles said with a little giggle.

"Of course, I will invite both Lords Conway and St. Vincent and..." she paused to think of who else she should invite.

"Lord Rosebury, Mr. Hershawn," Lady Welles began ticking each gentleman on her fingers.

"I think we could easily make a list," Mrs. Aldridge said, laughing at Lady Welles.

"And perhaps Lady St. Vincent also plays? It would be lovely for her reputation to be seen in such an innocent light," Christianne suggested.

"What an excellent idea!" Claire said, liking this idea more and more.

Chapter Sixteen

~April 2~

Lord Conway picked up Bel a little after three for her promised drive in the park. She wore her pretty, new carriage dress, which Tina had chosen for her. At the time, Bee had been certain they would never need a carriage dress, and she'd suggested a morning dress instead when Bel paid morning visits. Aunt Claire had insisted, however, and now Bel was very pleased she had.

It was such a pretty pale green, which made her hazel eyes look much closer to that color than brown, and had deep green ribbons edging the décolletage and at the wrists. Her pelisse was a matching color, and her bonnet was outfitted with new green ribbons as well, making Bel feel carefree and happy.

"You are like a breath of spring," Lord Conway said, after helping her up into his phaeton.

Bel giggled. "Why, thank you, my lord. And we match!"

He was wearing a bottle-green coat, although it was a much deeper color than her ribbons. He laughed. "Yes. It is a green day, isn't it?"

"Well, shall we see who else is wearing the color today?" she asked, turning her attention forward to the park.

"Absolutely." He set the horses in motion. "I have to admit, I am exceedingly glad you insisted we go for this drive, although I'm sorry it took so long for it to happen."

"Oh, that's all right. I'm just happy it happened at all." She gave him a bright smile.

They were quiet as he maneuvered through traffic and then into the stream of carriages driving slowly through the park. They spent the next half hour waving to those who they knew and commenting on nearly everyone they saw. This lady had the loveliest hat, that gentleman absolutely should not wear a blue neckcloth with a brown coat—they laughed and chatted easily.

When Bel caught sight of her friend Lydia and her husband in a carriage going in the opposite direction, she gave a little squeal of delight. "Oh, Lord Conway, you must stop, please."

He did so with a little laugh. "As you wish."

"Lydia, how charming you look today! And good afternoon to you, Lord Welles," Bel called out.

"Good afternoon," they said in unison.

"It is a beautiful day, is it not?" Lord Conway said.

"It is. And, Bel, we received an invitation this morning to a musicale hosted by your aunt," Lydia said with a big smile on her face. "I'm so looking forward to hearing you play!"

"What is it that you play, Miss Kendrick?" her husband asked. "My wife has not shared her knowledge with me," he said with a laugh.

"Oh, I play the pianoforte. I am so glad you will be there. I'll need all the support I can get. I've never played in public without my sister beside me."

"Really? Does she play as well?" Lydia asked.

"No, but she's quite a passable singer."

Lord Conway burst out laughing. "Damned with faint praise."

"Oh no, I didn't mean it that way, truly," Bel said, feeling her face heat. She loved her sister and didn't wish to insult her at all.

"I'm sure you didn't," Lord Conway said.

"Surely, she's better than just passable," Lydia said with a laugh.

"She is. Certainly, she is. But in either case, she won't be there, so I will need all of you there to support me. You will be there too, my lord, won't you?" she asked, turning to her companion.

"I wouldn't miss it for the world!"

"Oh! That reminds me. I was going to purchase that new music by Beethoven and see if I couldn't learn at least the beginning of it for my aunt's gathering," Bel said.

"Well, then, it sounds like you are going to be quite busy for the next few days," Lord Welles said.

"I am, aren't I?" Bel agreed, widening her eyes and giggling.

"We won't keep you, then. Lovely to see you!" Lydia said as her husband pulled away.

"Would you like me to take you over to Ackerman's to see if they have the music?" Lord Conway asked.

"Would you mind, terribly?" Bel asked.

"Not at all. Shopping for music is one of my favorite things to do." He looked around to make sure the path was clear before he pulled out of the line of carriages and headed with slightly more speed toward the nearest exit.

His tiger hopped down and took control of the horses when they reached the store, allowing Lord Conway to help Bel down.

The shop was warm after the cool of the early spring day, and there were quite a few people wandering around admiring the displays. Lord Conway immediately caught the attention of one of the shop-keepers and requested the latest music from Beethoven. The man knew immediately what he wanted and went off to get a copy for them.

While they waited, they admired the artwork adorning the walls.

"Is there anything you need, my lord?" Bel asked.

He smiled down at her. "At the moment, what would make me happiest is to see you with this new music and hear you play it on Friday at your aunt's party."

How did this man always know precisely the right thing to say? Bel giggled and turned her face away so he wouldn't see her blushing. Being with Lord Conway never failed to make her happy. And now there was no doubt in Bel's mind that she would work as hard as she could to have at least some of the music ready for the musicale.

The shopkeeper came back a few minutes later with a few pieces of music in his hand. "Did you want his latest dances, Miss, or the newest piano sonata?"

"Oh! There's a new sonata?" Bel asked, very excited. She hadn't heard about that.

Lord Conway gave a little laugh at Bel's

enthusiasm. "It looks as if you've made a sale of the sonata."

Bel turned to him. "But I did promise to learn the dances, didn't I. I should take that one instead."

"Miss Kendrick, no matter what you play, I'm certain it will be a delight," Lord Conway said.

Bel felt her insides melt a little, but she did buy the sonata.

~April 3~

"Bee!" Bel called out in a loud whisper as she ran into their room the following day.

Bee could hear her all the way from where she was sitting on the floor of the dressing room.

Bel stopped just inside the door. "What in the world are you doing there?" she asked.

"The maid was just cleaning the room," Bee explained.

"Oh, and you needed to hide." Bel nodded, understanding immediately. "Well, get up. You need to get dressed quickly and go out and pay morning calls with Aunt Claire."

"Why me? Why aren't you going?" Bee asked, standing.

"Because I need to learn this music," she said, putting a hand on her hip as if Bee should have known this.

"You know you can't play the pianoforte while I'm out, don't you?"

"Of course I do!" Bel huffed. "I'm dedicated but not stupid. I'll pretend to play here." She held the music up for Bee to see. "I don't want to stop going through it. It needs to be ready by tomorrow night!"

"You don't have to learn the whole piece by then. No one will expect you—"

"I know, but I want to have the beginning perfect, at least. Now, please, hurry! Aunt Claire is waiting downstairs." She started helping Bee from her dress before she'd even had a moment to lift her hands.

"All right, all right. I'll do it, thank you. You pick out what I'm going to wear," Bee said, shooing her sister's hands away.

Bel turned to the clothes press and started muttering to herself. "I wore this yesterday. Lord St. Vincent saw me in that last week. Oh, this! Wear this. If Lord Conway is there, he hasn't seen it yet, and if Lord St. Vincent is there… Well, he probably won't remember," she said, pulling out a sprigged muslin.

Bee just laughed as Bel dropped it over her head. Together they got her buttoned up and her hair fixed to match Bel's.

"Now, do be quiet," Bee said warningly just before heading out the door.

"I will, I will. I promise," Bel whispered. She put two fingers to her lips to indicate she would be silent and stay that way.

"Whose home are we going to?" Bee asked as the carriage pulled away from the house.

Her aunt looked at her oddly. "I just told you before you went up to get changed. Lady St. Vincent is hosting an at-home today."

"Oh, yes!" She giggled. It came out more nervous than Bel-like. "How silly of me!"

Her aunt turned to sit forward again, but Bee caught her glancing her way more than once before they arrived at their destination.

Bee couldn't believe Lady St. Vincent had the

nerve to hold an at-home considering all she'd been through at, and since, Lady Sorrell's soirée. After curtsying properly to the lady and the other guests scattered around the elegant gold and blue drawing room, Bee couldn't help herself. She approached their hostess who was standing closer to the door.

It wouldn't be right to reach out to take the older lady's hands, so Bee simply clasped her own together. "My lady, how *are* you doing? I do so hope you are bearing well with all that has happened?" she asked, leaning forward a little and speaking softly so that no one else could hear her words.

Lady St. Vincent had no inhibitions on her own behavior; she took Bee's hands in hers. "Miss Kendrick, you are so good to ask. Do you know, no one has said a word or broached the topic all afternoon?" She too leaned forward to speak confidentially. "I think they're terrified of saying anything, as if I don't know that everyone is talking about it." Her smile held a tinge of sadness.

Bee gave her hands a slight squeeze. "Of course you do! You're an intelligent woman. How ridiculous. But *are* you doing all right? Are you managing to brush aside the talk?"

"I am, so far. I have St. Vincent here with me—he's been steadfast—and I've realized that the only thing for me to do is to pretend it never happened. I just have to hope society will forget it quickly as well."

"Well, if they have any sense at all, they will understand and know the truth of it. There were so many eyewitnesses, they have to realize his attentions were completely unwanted and unwarranted."

"Sadly, society has very little sense. They see what they want to see, believe what they want to believe," the lady said with a shake of her head. "I can only hope you never have cause to be the subject of their appropriation."

Bee could only look sympathetically at the lady and give her hands another squeeze. Lord St. Vincent joined them just then, and the two women dropped hands as Bee turned to greet him.

"I do hope you are doing better as well, my lord," Bee said, after curtsying to him.

He gave a little laugh. "Certainly much better than the last time you saw me."

She smiled and asked with a raise of her eyebrows, "And you've been able to put the incident behind you, as well?"

"Well… Let's just say that so long as I never see Lord Rogan again, I shall remain as even-tempered as ever."

Bee laughed. "That's not saying very much."

He gave a little shrug. "I'm afraid it's the best I can do."

She gave a nod. "Then that's what we'll have to accept."

"I am looking forward to your aunt's musicale tomorrow night," Lord St. Vincent said. His eyes filled with a warm smile that made Bee wish with all her heart that she could be there too. Of course, it would be impossible since her sister was going to be performing. Bee hid her sadness behind her smile.

"And I'm looking forward to seeing you there. And to hearing Lady St. Vincent play," she said, turning to the lady.

"Oh, well, don't expect much," the lady said with a laugh. "It is my brother who truly has all the musical talent in our family."

Before Bee could ask what talent he had, they were interrupted by Bee's aunt, who had been caught by a friend of hers the moment they'd walked into the room. She joined them now. "Lord St. Vincent, how lovely to see you today. I understand we have you to thank for the beautiful bouquet of daffodils and lavender lending their fragrance to my drawing room?"

"It was my pleasure, my lady. I'm glad you are enjoying them," he said, giving her a slight bow.

The flowers, of course, had been sent to Bel after Lady Sorrell's soirée, but her aunt had insisted that such a pretty bouquet be kept in a public room. Although Bee had told her sister everything that had happened that evening, she hadn't been there to feel the brief moment of terror and the immense relief that followed. She simply couldn't understand what Bee had experienced and, therefore, didn't feel the warmth Bee had felt when the flowers had arrived. She had wished that she'd been able to enjoy the flowers in private, but Bel had been just fine with them remaining in the drawing room.

Bee wished she could have said something to Lord St. Vincent now, but she didn't know how to express herself, how to relay feelings that she, herself, didn't understand. Just looking at the flowers melted something inside of her. Made her think of him and that, in turn, had sent even more warmth through her veins. How could she tell him this? How could she let him know that sending the sweet bouquet had somehow touched her heart?

CHAPTER SEVENTEEN

~April 4~

Bee fussed over Bel's dress even more than usual the following evening. She was wearing her best new evening gown, a cream-colored silk with a white lace overdress. It brought out the richness of her red hair without making it look garish and emphasized her peaches-and-cream complexion. Creamy strands of pearls were laced through her hair and single pearls adorned her ears. She even had a pearl pendant hanging on a pretty, slender gold chain around her neck.

Bel swatted her sister's hand away from her dress. "All right, Bee! That's enough," she snapped.

Bee stepped back in surprise. "I'm sorry, I just want to be sure you're looking your best. Lord Conway, Lord St. Vincent, and a number of other gentlemen are going to be there—all to see you."

"I know! You *don't* have to remind me."

"You're nervous!" Bee exclaimed. "I don't believe I've ever seen you nervous before a party."

"I've never been to a party where *I'm* the main attraction," Bel said, trying to keep her voice steady. Her stomach was already in knots, and her sister wasn't helping.

Bee placed her hands on Bel's shoulders and

looked her in the eye. "You are talented, charming, and lovely. Every gentleman present is going to want to woo you after tonight, if they don't already."

Bel relaxed a little. "I know exactly which one I *want* to woo me, but the whole reason you're here is to guide me in this. Who would you like to see me with?"

Bee's eyes shifted to the right as she thought about her answer. "They all have their merits."

"Of course they do, otherwise Aunt Claire wouldn't have invited them."

Bee dropped her hands back to her side and took a small step back. "To be honest, I think Lord Conway is the right one for you."

Bel's heart filled with happiness, and she threw her arms around her sister. "I'm so glad you feel that way!"

Bee giggled. "Because he's the one you like best too?"

"Yes!"

"I'm so glad we're in agreement. Lord Rosebury is very nice, and Lord St. Vincent, I think, is wonderful, but neither one of them are right for *you*. I am happy to see that Sir Reginald was *not* invited—"

"Why? He's so funny!"

"Funny? Yes. Amusing? Absolutely! An eligible husband? No!"

Bel just giggled while Annie came up and smoothed down her hair, which had gotten a little mussed when she'd hugged her sister.

"All right, now, off you go," Bee said, putting her hand on the door handle. "I'll be listening as best as I can."

Bel took in a deep breath, which wasn't entirely easy, considering how tight her new corset and gown were so she and Bee could share them.

Aunt Claire nodded with approval as Bel entered the drawing room, and her uncle turned around from where he was pouring a glass of Madeira for his wife. "My, my, you look very beautiful this evening, my dear," he said. A grin widened his face. "May I pour you a glass of wine?"

"Yes, please, Uncle. I think that would be most welcome," Bel said gratefully.

"Are you nervous or excited?" he asked as he complied.

"Both! Most definitely both," Bel said with a giggle.

"You will do very well," her aunt said, sipping from her own glass. "I have full confidence in you."

"Thank you, Aunt. That means a great deal to me," Bel said with feeling.

Her aunt gave her a comforting smile just as they heard the first knock on the front door.

Lord and Lady St. Vincent were the first to arrive, Lord Conway the last. All the ladies of the Wagering Whist Society were there as well as Tina, her husband, and Margaret. A few other eligible gentlemen had been invited as well as some other young ladies to even out the numbers. It was a much larger group than Bel had expected, probably thirty people in all.

For some reason, Aunt Claire had seated Bel in the center of the long dining table with Lord Rosebury on her right and Lord Bertram on her left. Lady St. Vincent was directly across from her giving her the oddest smiles. Bel wondered if Bee had said something to the lady that she'd forgotten to tell her. When the lady had come in, she'd grasped Bel's hands warmly and behaved as if they were the closest of friends.

Bel had become wise enough to respond likewise, but she wished Bee had told her what had transpired between them. On the other hand, now that Bel thought about it, she might have tried to do so, but Bel was too busy practicing, concentrating on her music, to listen to a word her sister had tried to say to her the previous day. The moment she and their aunt had returned from their morning calls, Bel had escaped from her room to practice and had stayed at the pianoforte until well into the night, hardly even taking a break to eat dinner.

Hopefully, all that practicing would pay off. It did not help her interact with their guests, though.

"Is there anything wrong, Miss Kendrick?" Lady St. Vincent asked after Bel had extracted her hands from the lady's.

"No! No." Bel gave a little giggle. "I'm afraid I'm just a little nervous, that's all. It's been so long since I've performed in public."

"Ah, I understand. I have to admit to being a little nervous myself," the lady said, giving her a warm smile.

"I'm sure you'll play beautifully," Bel said automatically.

"As will you."

"I don't know. I'm playing a new piece that I only just got the other day. I haven't had a great deal of time to learn it properly," Bel admitted.

"Oh, I do understand," Lady St. Vincent said. "Well, you'll do the best you can, and I'm sure it will be good enough."

It wasn't exactly what Bel wanted to hear, but it was honest.

Bel was grateful for the time between dinner—which she'd hardly touched—and the musical portion of the evening. The men took their time over their port, and Bel forced herself to sip at a cup of tea to calm her nerves.

Finally, they all gathered in the music room. Bel sat in the front row as Lady St. Vincent took her place at the pianoforte. Lady Blakemore stood next to the instrument at the front of the room and waited for everyone to get settled in their seats and turn their attention to her. To Bel, she looked like a school teacher waiting for her students to pay attention to the day's lesson. Her hands were folded across her waist, and she had only the slightest smile on her lips.

Finally, everyone quieted down.

"Ladies and gentlemen, it is my pleasure to welcome Lady St. Vincent to our humble little gathering. She will be playing for us first, and then Miss Whitely, Lady Blackglass, and finally, Miss Kendrick will entertain us with a new piece by Beethoven on which she has been working."

Bel shrank down a touch. Did she have to mention that the piece was new? Well, there was nothing for it now. Very briefly, Bel had considered not playing the Beethoven and falling back on something familiar, but now she had no choice.

Lady St. Vincent began to play. It was a rather simple piece but pretty, and it showed her to be a graceful musician, which was all that playing the pianoforte was supposed to do for a lady. The second piece she played was slightly more difficult and, sadly, she stumbled a little over some of the more difficult runs. But she kept a gentle smile on her face the entire time, providing an excellent example for Bel to follow.

The applause was polite as the lady stood and gave them a curtsy. The other two young ladies performed with some proficiency but nothing extraordinary.

Bel approached the instrument when it was finally her turn. She sat down and wrung her hands for a moment and then stood up again.

"I must apologize to you all to begin with. I'm very nervous," she admitted.

She received a number of smiles and nods.

"As my aunt mentioned, I just received a new piece of music—a Beethoven sonata. I have been working very diligently on it, but it is not yet as perfected as I would normally like before I play it in public." She wrung her hands again.

"Perhaps it would help you to relax if you were to play something you already know very well, first?" Lady St. Vincent suggested.

"That's an excellent idea, my lady. But what I know best are the songs I've always played for my sister to sing and as she's not here..." Bel let her voice trail off as she wished with all her might that Bee was allowed to show herself.

"Well, I'm certain my brother knows any songs you might wish to play," Lady St. Vincent said, turning to look at Lord Conway.

Bel's breath caught in her throat. The gentleman had mentioned to her once that he sang opera in Venice. She looked to him as well. "It would be a great honor if he were to sing for me—us. I meant us, of course." She stumbled over her words, but Lord Conway's gaze caught hers, and he knew what she'd truly meant. She wanted him to sing for her and only for her.

Still, he gave his head a little shake. "I'm sorry, but I haven't sung in months."

"Oh, come now, Conway," his sister goaded him and even gave his arm a little playful shove.

"Please, my lord?" Bel added her voice to those encouraging him.

He looked around and then gave a little shrug of his shoulders. "For you, Miss Kendrick, only so that you can relax a little."

He stood up and came to the pianoforte. Bel sat down and took in a deep breath. "Do you know Caro Mio Ben by Giordani?" she asked. It was a tune she and Bee had learned just the previous Christmas and had played again and again; they'd enjoyed it so much. It was a beautiful piece that would show off Lord Conway's voice and help Bel warm up her fingers a bit.

"Of course!" he said with a smile.

Bel nodded and began the introduction. Lord Conway began to sing, his tenor voice like the softest piece of velvet. It started out soft and gentle, then dipped and swayed with the lovely tune. He turned, making eye contact with Bel as he came to the crescendo, the highest notes, before his voice dipped down again with the melody. His deep blue eyes held hers in a soft cradle. She felt calm, protected, and nothing but joy and happiness.

Her fingers played from memory as she floated on his voice. She could look at his handsome face, listen to his amazing voice, and wallow in his gaze for a lifetime. His voice gentled into the end of the piece, and Bel's fingers gently feathered the last few notes allowing the sound to drift away on a breath.

The applause and calls of bravo caught Bel by surprise. She'd completely forgotten they weren't alone. Lord Conway started and, with a laugh, turned to bow to the audience. The smile he turned back to her was as soft and gentle as his magnificent voice had been just a moment ago. It slid over Bel, making her warm and happier than she thought she'd ever been.

"Belle," he said so softly only she could hear him. She wasn't sure if he was saying her name or calling her beautiful when he pronounced it in the Italian way. Either way, she could feel herself flush with his praise.

He cleared his throat before bowing to her. "I believe you are able to play your piece now?"

Bel gave him a nod and a smile. Indeed, she was most definitely warmed up. He sat down, and Bel turned her attention back to the instrument in front of her.

With the warmth of what she and Lord Conway had just shared still running through her, Bel hit the first chord of the piece. From there, her fingers just seemed to know what to do. The beauty of the piece, the fun little runs and trills that she had been going over again and again for the past three days, both on the pianoforte and in her mind, slipped from her fingertips. She didn't fully get lost in the music as she usually did both because the piece was still new to her, and because she was so very aware of Lord Conway watching her, but she did put her heart into the piece. With all that she had, she played for him.

~*~

"Here is to a wonderful party." Blakemore held up

his glass in salute to Claire.

She gave a little laugh and raised hers as well.

They were sitting in their room, each in their favorite chair by the fire. Claire had changed for bed as always, but Blakemore was still in his breeches and shirt, although he'd stripped off his neckcloth and kicked off his shoes and stockings the moment he'd entered the room. They were always the first to go. His coat went quickly after them.

Claire had retired to her dressing room to change with the assistance of her maid the moment she walked into their room. Now that she was comfortably attired, with her hair braided for the night, she could finally relax and analyze the evening.

"I have to say, Bel did play beautifully," she said before taking another sip of her brandy.

"She is quite talented—once she got past her nerves," her husband agreed.

"And it was very kind of Lord Conway to sing for us and help her relax."

"Do you think he'll take the plunge?" Blakemore asked, a little smile playing on his lips.

"And propose? There is certainly something there," Claire said, thinking about it.

"Well, that's obvious. But I've heard he's still mourning a lost love."

Claire lowered her glass. "Really?"

"Had a mistress living with him in Venice. Well, I don't know that she was a mistress precisely, but they weren't married. She was an opera singer like him."

"Well then, clearly she *was* a mistress."

"I suppose, but apparently he nearly married her and was quite broken up when she died. Lady St. Vincent said she wasn't certain he was entirely over her yet. She's worried it was hampering his ability to find someone here."

Claire blinked at her husband. "You seem to know a great deal about Lord Conway's private affairs."

He gave a little shrug and gave her a grin. "A little wine, a dose of charm."

"Some political wheedling," Claire added with a laugh.

"You know I can be very persuasive when I want to be."

"And I know you can get almost anyone to tell you anything," she chuckled before taking another sip of her drink.

"It's a very handy talent for a politician, don't you think?"

"And for a doting uncle. So, you used your wiles on Lady St. Vincent, did you?"

"I just wanted to know more about Conway. Make sure he was good enough for Bel," her husband said with another shrug.

Claire smiled lovingly at him. "You are good."

"I've rather taken to the chit," he admitted.

"I have to admit I have too, although—" Claire paused and tried to organize her thoughts. "There's been something odd that I just can't put my finger on. Sometimes she behaves one way, and sometimes it's almost as if she's a completely different person."

Blakemore frowned. "I can't say I've noticed, but then, I haven't been around her as much as you."

"Yes, well..." She sighed. "It could just be my imagination. Let's just hope Lord Conway comes through before too long. My sister has been writing to me almost every day wanting to know when there'll be an announcement."

"Not anxious at all is she?"

Claire laughed. "I'm sure it will work out."

CHAPTER EIGHTEEN

~April 5~

Edward followed his friend Giampiero into the ring at Gentleman Jackson's the following morning. "Thank you for meeting me, although I thought you'd said you didn't want to talk in the ring."

His friend gave a shrug and put up his fists ready to fight. "I have trouble finding sparring partners. I will risk it."

Edward gave a little laugh and threw the first punch. It missed as Giampiero dodged out of the way. "How have you been? I haven't had a chance to get to the opera yet, but I have plans to come next week."

"Ah, I did hope you would have come backstage afterward had you been there. But you have not come," Giampiero said, landing a blow on Edward's shoulder.

"I've been busy." He blocked a left-right combination and was proud of himself for not getting hit by either. Maybe he was getting the hang of this again. "But what about you?"

Giampiero shrugged and threw another punch, which Edward dodged. "It is much the same. What keeps you busy? The women?"

Edward laughed. "Yes. Well, *one* woman."

"Ah, yes. I thought so. You are too handsome and charming. They cannot resist you." His last word turned into more of an *oomph* as Edward's fist connected with his abdomen.

"I avoid most of the young ladies. They are empty idiots," Edward said, blocking another punch.

"But there is one?" Giampiero asked, immediately throwing another punch. This one landed in his solar plexus, making Edward unable answer him right away. He nodded.

"She is lovely and plays the pianoforte better than anyone I've seen in a long time." His fist glanced off Giampiero's arm.

"Ah, she is a musician," his friend said, understanding immediately.

"Such emotion!" Edward answered with a right-left combination.

"And beauty?"

"Brilliant red hair, big hazel eyes, full pink lips, and a laugh that makes you smile," Edward said, just standing still for a moment. Luckily, his friend allowed him his momentary daydream and didn't take advantage of his undefended stance.

"You are in love!" Giampiero exclaimed.

Edward started to move again. "I don't know about that." He laughed and threw another punch.

"But I can see it. I can hear it in your, *ooph,* voice."

Edward managed to land another punch to his abdomen.

"Do you mind? Do you think it wrong?" Edward asked, blocking his friend's attempts.

"It is not for me to say. You are a man. I am merely your friend."

"But you were also Angelica's friend," Edward said, lowering his fists again.

He shouldn't have because Giampiero immediately took advantage. He hit Edward in the shoulder, then in the stomach before he could even try to shift out of the way.

"I loved her like a sister, but as you, yourself, said the last time we met, she is gone. You are not. You should be happy, Eduardo."

Edward nodded and silently thanked his friend for his understanding before hitting him again.

~*~

Bel slept late the morning after the musicale, but Bee was feeling hungry, so she went down to breakfast in her sister's place.

"You are looking remarkably refreshed," Lady Blakemore said as she began to help herself to some toast and accepted a cup of tea from the footman.

"I slept very well," she said, giving her a smile. "I hope you did as well?"

"I did, thank you."

Bee buttered her toast and then slathered some jam onto it, all the while aware that her aunt was watching her closely. "Is there something wrong, my lady?"

"No, no," she said quickly. She turned back to her own breakfast. "We don't have any plans for the day."

"Oh, that's good. It will be nice to have a quiet day after all the preparation for the party last night."

"Yes. I've given half the staff the day off."

Bee gave her a smile. "That was kind of you. They've been working hard and deserve the time."

"Yes. Quite so."

There was silence for a few minutes as they each ate their breakfast, but then Lady Blakemore asked, "What did Lady St. Vincent say to you last night before we went into the music room?"

Bee widened her eyes. Bel hadn't mentioned anything to her about speaking with Lady St. Vincent. "Nothing of import," she answered, desperately hoping she was right.

Lady Blakemore narrowed her eyes at Bee for a moment. Bee attempted to avoid her aunt's gaze by turning back to her breakfast. She reached forward and picked up her teacup.

"You're left-handed."

The words caught Bee by surprise, and she started to choke on the liquid she'd been swallowing. Coughing into her napkin, she could only shake her head. She'd completely forgotten. She was indeed left-handed. Bel was right-handed. It had never occurred to her that her aunt would notice.

Before she could even regain her breath, her aunt was up and striding out of the room. Bee jumped up and hurried after her. "Aunt Claire," Bee called, following her up the stairs. The woman could move very fast when she wanted to. Bee could hardly keep up without actually running.

The lady was at Bel's bedroom door by the time Bee caught up with her. She paused there, her hand on the door handle. "Is there anything here that you don't want me to see?" she asked accusingly.

Bee couldn't say a word. Either way she would be caught.

With a nod, Lady Blakemore went into the room. She stopped just inside the door, taking in the sleeping girl in the bed. Bel's bright red head was peeking out from under the covers, but her face was hidden.

Her aunt cleared her throat loudly. When she didn't stir, her aunt said loudly, "Beatrice! Isabel!" Clearly, she didn't know who was who.

Bel bolted upright. "What?"

Bee could only stand behind their aunt, wringing her hands.

"What is the meaning of this?" Lady Blakemore said in a low, menacing voice. She turned back to Bee. "How long have you *both* been here?"

"From the beginning," Bee said quietly.

Aunt Claire's face was dangerously red as she looked from one girl to the other. "You may think this is a fun game to play, but I do not. Does your mother know?"

"No, my lady," Bee answered.

"Please don't send us away," Bel pleaded.

"We'll see about that." With that she strode out the door, slamming it behind her.

Bel just looked at Bee with wide eyes. "What happened?" she whispered.

"I'm left-handed."

"And she *noticed*?"

Bee could only nod.

Bel dropped back onto the pillows.

What were they to do?

~*~

Claire walked straight down to Blakemore's study. She walked in without knocking—something she'd never done before. Her husband was sitting at his desk, which was scattered with papers. He looked up at her entrance, his pen hanging an inch from a piece of paper.

"What is it? What's wrong?" he asked immediately as he stuffed the pen into the ink stand in front of him.

Claire slowly lowered herself onto the chair just in front of his desk and then raised her eyes to his. "They're *both* here. I was right."

Her husband shook his head. "Who are both here?"

"The girls. The twins. They've both been here *all* along."

His eyes widened. "How do you know? Are you certain?"

She nodded. "I noticed at breakfast that Bel was using her left hand to butter her toast and drink her tea. Before this, I'd noticed she was right-handed."

He gasped.

"I went up to her room with her following me...and found the other one still abed! They are *both* here!"

"And they've both been here this *whole time*?"

"For two weeks! They've duped us for two weeks!"

Blakemore sat back in his chair, astounded. "We don't know which one went where."

Claire could only shake her head.

"You knew it, though! You knew there were two of them. You said so last night. Sometimes Bel acts one way, and then she behaves completely differently another time."

"Yes," Claire said, beginning to come out of her daze. "That right! Sometimes she knows something, and other times she doesn't. The day before she asked me whose home we were going to when we went out to pay our morning calls..." Her voice trailed off. "They must have switched. One of them was...Bel, I suppose, because she'd been practicing the pianoforte and only she plays, Beatrice does not. Bel was practicing when I told her to get changed because we were going out. Beatrice must have gotten dressed and gone with me because she asked where we were going. She didn't know, even though I'd told her just a few minutes earlier."

Blakemore shook his head incredulously. "They've been switching back and forth."

"Yes. One evening it must have been Bel who went out, and the next it was Beatrice. That's why she was giggling one night yet clever the next."

"You noticed, but didn't realize—"

"It never occurred to me that they would play such a trick!"

"It was cleverly done, I have to give them that," he said.

Claire could only shake her head. "I feel like such an idiot!"

"Now, now, I'm certain they didn't do it to cause harm. There must be a very good explanation for why they've done this."

She looked up at him. "Because they both wanted to make their debut? Why else would they have done so?"

"I don't know."

"Well, I don't think I could speak with either of them with any civility just now. I am... I am livid."

She stood up. "I'm going for a walk."

It was all she could do as the anger grew inside her breast. She'd never been played for such a fool before.

~April 6~

Paul escorted Elizabeth into the party with a sigh. She turned and looked at him.

"Is everything all right? You've been very quiet."

He raised an eyebrow and gave her a small smile. "Of course." Movement in his peripheral vision caught his attention. "One of your friends is headed straight for you." He turned his smile on to the Duchess of Warwick as she approached them.

"Good evening, Lord St. Vincent, Lady St. Vincent," the young woman said, giving them both a nod.

"Duchess, you are looking very well this evening," Elizabeth said, giving her friend a smile.

"And you. And may I just say how lovely it is to see you in a color other than purple or gray?" the duchess said.

"Why, thank you," Elizabeth said.

"May I be so rude as to inquire whether your husband is here, Your Grace?" Paul asked.

The young lady laughed. "You may, and yes, he is over there speaking with Andrew and Lord Wickford."

"Andrew?" Paul asked and then laughed when he saw his friend Colburne standing with Warwick and Wickford. "Do you know, I've known the man for nearly fifteen years, and I've never called him by his given name?"

"Oh! I thought since you were such good

friends you would have," Her Grace said, turning slightly pink.

"You know school boys. We all had nicknames for each other. I always called him "Crow"–short for Crowther, his family name," Paul explained.

The young woman laughed and nodded her understanding. "That's right. And you called Warwick, Binny, didn't you? I've heard Andrew call him that once."

"Yes. His title when we were in school was Binley," Paul said.

"And what did they call you?" Elizabeth asked.

Paul chuckled. "'Saint' because that was what my title was going to be, and I most certainly *wasn't* a saint, so it was a great joke."

The two women laughed.

"Well, if you will excuse me, I'll go and join them and leave you ladies to your discussion of fashion." He gave his step-mother a smile. "You're in good hands, I know, the duchess is famed for her knowledge and talent on the subject." He gave them a nod and headed off.

A moment later, he was nodding to his friends. "Gentlemen."

"Ah! Saint, good to see you," Colburne said, clapping him lightly on the back.

"You're not too bruised now, are you?" Paul asked with a laugh.

"Not any more. A soaking in a tub of hot water made me feel much better," his friend said with a laugh.

"Did you two spar?" Warwick asked.

"Yes. I let him get a few hits in," Colburne said, giving Paul a wink.

"Uh-huh. That's why *you* needed a bath afterward," Wickford said with a chuckle.

"Is Miss Kendrick here tonight?" Warwick asked, with a suggestive twinkle in his eye.

Paul's good feelings immediately dropped to the floor. "No," he said soberly. It was ridiculous that they should do so; it wasn't as if he had feelings for the chit. "Surely you noticed the performance last night."

His friends didn't say anything but just looked at each other. They knew very well what he was talking about, but he'd spell it out just in case there was any doubt. "The song Miss Kendrick and Conway shared... Well, I quite don't know what to call it, but the way they were staring at each other like puppies. You would have had to be blind not to have noticed."

"I'm so sorry, old chap!" Warwick said, lowering his eyebrows over his deep-set eyes.

Paul gave a little shrug and a smile. "It's all right. There are plenty of other young ladies for me to choose from. I'm certain I'll find someone to marry soon enough. And if it isn't this season, there's next year as well, and the year after that. I'm not in any great hurry, truly."

"But you liked her a great deal," Colburne said.

"She has proven herself to be a rather changeable girl, so I'm certain I'm better off with someone else," Paul said with a slight lift of his shoulder.

"What do you mean?" Wickford asked.

"Well, I don't quite understand it, but one moment she's a giggly feather-brained thing like all the other girls making their debut, and the next evening she's telling me that she's reading a history of Greece and holding an intelligent conversation! I honestly don't quite know what to make of her."

"Is it possible she is both giggly and intelligent?" Warwick asked.

"Yes," Colburne backed him up, "Lady Welles is both a bit of a butterfly and highly intelligent. I've had a number of incredible conversations with her. And my own wife can be, well, I won't say light-headed exactly, but she's also quite clever."

Paul shrugged. "I suppose she could be, certainly. The point is moot, however. I'm sure Conway will be very happy, and I am safely out of the running."

What he didn't mention to his friends, of course, was the disappointment he felt at losing Miss Kendrick to Conway. It was odd, but he almost felt betrayed by her. She'd been interesting, funny, and, at times, quite clever—just the sort of girl with whom he thought he could happily live.

He paused to consider his feelings for a moment and knew, deep in his heart, that there was more to it than that. He'd felt something... something else for the girl. He didn't have a name for it because he knew that love didn't exist. Perhaps it was simply lust. Yes, that must have been it. She was a shapely, comely girl. He was certain it was just lust.

Well... It was all right. He turned and surveyed the other young ladies in the room. Surely there was another who wasn't as stupid as she seemed.

Chapter Nineteen

Bee wrung her hands together as she waited for the summons to enter her aunt's private drawing room. This was not going to be easy, and she really didn't want to do this, but she knew it was the right thing to do. It was something she *had* to do.

"Come in!" her aunt's voice called.

Bee did so but kept her eyes lowered even as she curtsied. "I was wondering if I could have a word, my lady."

"Which one are you?" her aunt's tone wasn't particularly kind, but Bee didn't blame her.

"Bee, my lady. I... I've put on my bracelet." She held up her wrist. She had on a thin gold chain with a small gold bee dangling from it.

"Let me see," her aunt said, holding out her hand.

Bee approached the sofa where she was sitting and showed her the bracelet. "Bel has one that is similar but with a little bell attached to it. They were gifts from our father on our tenth birthday before we went off to school."

"Very nice—and quite useful." The lady nodded approvingly.

"I always wear mine on my right hand and Bel wears her on her left," Bee explained. "But, um, I wanted to...to apologize."

Lady Blakemore inclined her head slightly. "Go on."

"What we did was inexcusable. However, I thought that perhaps if you understood the reasoning behind it you might not...not feel..." She floundered for a word.

"Hurt?" her aunt supplied.

"Yes." Bee swallowed. "It wasn't done with any sort of malicious intent at all, I promise. I-I'm afraid I simply wasn't thinking about you or how my actions might affect anyone. For that I am deeply and truly sorry." Bee blinked back the tears that had sprung to her eyes, keeping them lowered so her aunt wouldn't see.

Perhaps she did anyway for her tone softened. "You may sit down." She indicated the chair next to her.

"Thank you, my lady."

"Will you explain to me why you did this? Was it because you didn't want to wait until next year for your own season?"

"What?" Bee's gaze flew up to her aunt's face. "No! Of course not. I completely understand my parents couldn't afford to bring us both out at once, and I was more than happy to wait my turn."

"Then why?"

"It's because of Bel." She lowered her gaze once again to her hands, tightly clasped in her lap. "I love my sister dearly, but I'm very sorry to say she doesn't always have a great deal of sense. She, she gets an idea in her head, thinks it'll be fun, and goes off and does it without any thought to the consequences. My father always said she lived for the day—*carpe diem*. She's also not exactly the best judge of character. I wanted to be here to keep an eye on her, if at all possible, and to meet any men she might be interested in marrying to make sure they were good—not just handsome, or funny, or well-dressed."

Bee immediately realized she'd said something wrong when in her peripheral vision she saw her aunt's back straighten even more and her chin go up.

"And just what do you think I'm here for?" Lady Blakemore asked indignantly.

"You... I beg your pardon, my lady, but you are nothing like my mother. You-you stay with Bel—or me—when we're at a party. You *do* seem to be looking out for my sister."

There was silence for a moment while her aunt digested what she'd just said. "Do you mean to tell me that your mother does *not* do this?"

"No. When we go to a party or to an assembly, my mother usually leaves us to our own devices from the moment we walk in the door. She's there to see and socialize with her friends."

"She... Oh, my word! No *wonder* you risked everything to come here," her aunt whispered to herself. "She doesn't stay with you at all? She doesn't see who you are meeting or dancing with?"

"No—and I'm sorry to say this—but I've had to rescue Bel from a garden or library more than once," Bee admitted. It was horribly embarrassing that her sister had so little sense when it came to her behavior, but it was clearly something her aunt needed to know—especially if she was going to send

Bee home. "I think because you've stayed by her side when at a party, she hasn't had a chance to get herself into any trouble. Each time she's gone out, I've reminded her to stay with you and not to go off with anyone. Thank goodness, so far, she has heeded me. It is most likely a combination of my reminders and your diligence, my lady."

Lady Blakemore shook her head. "I just can't believe your mother wouldn't..." She straightened herself once again. "Well, I can assure you that I would *never* leave your sister unattended. You've risked a great deal for nothing, I'm afraid."

"Are you going to send me home?" Bee asked quietly, not really wanting to know the answer.

Her aunt pursed her lips slightly as she considered the question. "I haven't yet decided what I'm going to do." She frowned for a moment. "Where do your parents think you are?"

"At a friend's home. I've got a good friend from school who lives in Oxford. She's been forwarding letters from me to my parents, and theirs here to Bel," she explained.

"Well, it sounds as if you thought of everything." Her aunt didn't sound particularly pleased by this. "I will let you know what I've decided. In the meantime, you are to stay in your room. I have not informed the staff that you are both here, and they will understandably become confused if they see you both. We don't want them sharing this information with anyone outside."

"Yes, ma'am."

~April 7~

Claire didn't even wait until her dearest friend, Christianne, had served her tea before asking, "Are you ready?"

Christianne laughed as she poured. "Is it possible to be too ready?"

"I don't know. Do you feel as though you are?" Claire asked, accepting the cup.

"Well, I feel as if this wedding should have happened a long time ago, that's for certain," she said with a laugh.

"Of course it should have," Claire agreed. "But you were good to wait until Tina and Warwick were settled."

Christianne shook her head, but her smile lingered. "Liam and I thought it best." She put down her own teacup. "Not for a minute did we think that anything would stop their wedding, but we felt it safest to wait."

"It's understandable," Claire agreed. "And it was so lovely to be at Warwick for Christmas. Everything was beautiful, and we even had snow."

Christianne smiled fondly. "It was magical."

"And yours will be as well," Claire said quickly.

Christianne laughed. "Yes, only very, very different."

"Are all the preparations done?"

"Oh, yes. Tina and Margaret have proven to be absolute godsends when it comes to arranging things. Between the two of them, the entire wedding has been planned, the wedding breakfast, of course, *and* the ball which Tina is hosting the following night."

"It's going to be magnificent, I'm sure!" Claire said with an enthusiasm she didn't quite feel. She felt horrid, but her own problems were weighing heavily on her. After a brief pause, she asked, "Might I change the topic?"

Christianne put her cup down again after taking a sip of her tea and looked Claire in the eye. "There's something bothering you, I can tell."

Claire sighed and nodded. "I just... I don't quite know what to do."

Christianne widened her eyes. "*You* don't know? What is it, Claire? What's happened?"

Claire tried to find amusement in her friend's gentle teasing. "Do I always know what to do?"

"Nearly always." Christianne reached out and put her hand on top of Claire's. The small gesture made Claire's chest tighten with emotion.

She took a deep breath to dispel the feeling. "I learned something rather shocking the other day."

Christianne waited patiently for her to continue.

"It turns out that my nieces have been playing a trick on me and society. They are *both* here and have been for the past *two* weeks."

"What?"

Claire nodded. "Beatrice explained the entire situation to me yesterday, and I understand their reasoning, but somehow... It just didn't make it better, well, not for me, personally."

"I don't understand. Why is Beatrice here? I thought their parents had sent just the one girl because they couldn't afford to bring them both out at once. Was Beatrice overly eager? Was she jealous? What was her reasoning?"

"Those were exactly my first thoughts as well," Claire said. "But no. She told me the reason she is here is to ensure that her sister chooses the right sort of man to marry. Apparently, Bel has a history of going off with unsuitable gentlemen—of being attracted to that sort."

Christianne's mouth fell open.

"Beatrice says that her sister isn't a very good judge of character, so she came along to meet the men Bel was interested in and make sure she becomes engaged to the right man." She deliberately left out the part her niece had told her of her sister getting into inappropriate situations, thinking that would simply be too much.

"And what does she imagine you are there for?" Christianne said, her ire rising for her friend.

"I am sorry to say that my sister has been remiss in her duties as a chaperone, leaving the girls entirely on their own whenever she took them out. Beatrice expected the same of me, or rather, didn't realize that I would be so attentive and careful."

"Oh dear," Christianne whispered.

"I just… Well, I completely understand her worries. Bel is *not* the most discerning young woman. She is flighty. What touches my heart most is what Beatrice has risked by being here, by doing this."

Christianne shook her head. "They could have been discovered by anyone. It would have ruined *both* their reputations and *yours* since you would have thought to be complicit."

Claire swallowed hard. "I know."

"And now? What are you going to do?"

Claire could only shake her head. "I don't know, and that pains me almost as much as this trick does."

"You *could* send them both back to their parents," Christianne commented.

"I could," Claire agreed, "or I could send just Beatrice back."

"And if you did either one, you could also refuse to sponsor them."

"She risked *everything* for her sister," Claire said, trying her best to keep her emotions in check. "I... I *never* would have done such a thing for Susan. Never."

"Oh, Claire, I don't believe—"

"It's true, Christianne. Susan and I didn't get along. In fact, we've had the best relationship in recent years exactly *because* we haven't seen each other."

"But surely, if she needed your help, you would have been there in a moment. You are the most generous person," Christianne argued.

Claire could only shake her head. "I would have recently, certainly, but not when we were younger. No, Beatrice's behavior has put me to shame."

Christianne reached out to her once more. "And now you don't know what to do with the girl."

"No," Claire sighed. "Do I send her back? Do I allow her to stay?" She shook her head. "I just don't know." She took in a deep breath. "I've always known what the right thing was to do. I've always followed the rules to the letter, never straying. But now... Now I am tempted to let them both stay and continue on as they have. It is wrong and uncomfortable but, quite possibly, the right thing to do for the girls. I don't want to see my nieces hurt. I've grown much too attached to them. On the other hand, I would then be just as bad as they. I would be flouting society's rules—*lying*. I couldn't! I couldn't possibly..."

"I *do* know what you should, however,"

Christianne said with a smile.

Relief flooded through Claire. "I knew you would have an answer! You are the most intelligent, wonderful friend. What should I do?"

"You should ask the ladies of the Wagering Whist Society. *They* will know."

Claire widened her eyes. "Of course! Where is your score-keeping book? When is our next game finished? I'm certain I have lost. My mind has been so pre-occupied lately that I haven't been playing well at all."

Christianne gave a laugh and got up to get the book. She ran her finger down the page with their current game and gave a nod. "You are absolutely correct. You have lost. We will play one more hand, and then you can reveal your grand secret."

"Tomorrow, then?" Claire asked, beginning to feel nervous about revealing the trick that had been played on her.

"Tomorrow."

Chapter Twenty

A knock on the door startled Bel and Bee; they both jumped. With a look at each other, Bee gave a shrug and slipped into the dressing room. As far as they both knew, their aunt was out, so whoever it was wouldn't know they were both there.

As soon as the door was safely closed behind Bee, Bel answered the door. "Yes?"

A footman was there. "I beg your pardon, Miss, but the Duchess of Warwick is here."

"Oh! Thank you, I'll be right there," she said and started to leave the room.

"Er, actually, Miss, she requested to come and visit with you in your bedchamber," he said awkwardly.

"Well, that's certainly out of the usual," Bel said with a giggle.

"Yes, Miss. She says she has something special for you. May I show her up?"

"Yes, of course," Bel said. She left the door open and turned to wait for Tina at the window.

"The Duchess of Warwick," the footman announced a few minutes later.

Bel turned and found Tina clutching a brown paper package to her chest.

"I'm so sorry for my unusual request," Tina said, coming farther into the room.

"Not at all," Bel said, coming forward and giving her a little curtsy. "Please, come in." She carefully closed the door behind her friend so they could have some privacy. She imagined that was why Tina had requested to meet in this room rather than the public drawing room where anyone could come in at any time.

"Is Bee here as well?" Tina asked, her voice quieter. "Or are you Bee?" she asked with a little laugh.

Bel giggled. "No, I'm Bel, and yes, of course Bee is here too." She went and opened the dressing room door. Bee was sitting on a chair in the far corner of the little room, reading her book. She looked up, her eyes widening questioningly.

"Tina's here," Bel told her.

"Here as in here in the house or..."

"No, here as in your room," Tina said with a laugh from behind Bel. "And I've got a gift for you."

"Oh! I'm so sorry. I was so involved in my book that I didn't even hear you come in." Bee put her book down and came out to join them. "How are you?"

"I'm doing well, thank you. Here, I made this for you." She handed over the package to Bee.

"My goodness! Thank you," Bel's sister said, taking it.

Tina smiled. "Save your thanks for when you see what I've brought."

Bee shared a look with Bel, who was so eager to see what Tina had brought, she had to restrain herself from grabbing the gift from her sister and tearing it open. Bee had always been so slow about opening presents.

She placed the package on their bed and then, much too carefully, opened the package. She pulled out a beautiful cream and lace gown with pale blue ribbons.

Both girls were confused.

"I've already got a gown that looks exactly like that," Bel said, reaching out to touch the dress.

Tina laughed. "I know. This is an exact replica of yours, Bel, but made a tiny bit smaller for Bee."

Now they were really confused. Both Bee and Bel looked to Tina for an explanation.

"That's the dress you were planning on wearing to the wedding ball, isn't it?" Tina asked.

"Yes," Bel answered.

"Well, now you can *both* go," Tina said.

The twins looked at each other.

"One at a time, of course," Tina clarified. "I was thinking we could sneak Bee into my house, then at some point in the evening you two could switch. That way you could both attend."

"What a wonderful idea!" Bel exclaimed.

"How sweet," Bee said at the same time. "And thoughtful!"

"You are really too good, Tina," Bel said, stepping forward and pulling their friend into a quick hug.

"Truly," Bee said, following her sister's example.

Tina giggled. "It's really too important of an event for one of you to miss. I just couldn't let that happen."

"I was feeling awful about it, too, but I didn't see any way around it," Bel agreed.

"Well, this takes care of it," Tina said.

"I can't tell you how wonderful this is," Bee said, with a broad smile. It began to falter, however. "What about Aunt Claire?"

Tina looked blankly at them.

"She knows that we're both here and would be furious if we were to attend the party, even if it were one after the other," Bee explained.

"What she doesn't know won't hurt her," Bel said with a little shrug.

"That would be wrong, Bel," Bee said.

"I do not condone continuing to lie to your aunt, but are you willing to miss the event of the season?" Tina asked with a lift of her eyebrows.

Bel could see her sister struggling with her conscience.

"You are going to let Tina's hard work at creating this second gown go to waste?" Bel asked her sister. "You are going to sit here at home while I go to the ball and quite possibly dance with Lord St. Vincent? I can't say no if he asks."

Bee wrung her hands in frustration.

"Do I need to go on?" Bel asked.

"No, but... We promised! And not only that, but it's wrong!" Bee said.

"It *is* wrong. You are right," Bel said, turning back to Tina. "I'm so sorry, Tina. Bee won't go, but you know I will be there." She took Tina's arm and walked with her toward the window. "I've heard you have a large garden."

"Isabel Kendrick!" Bee said furiously.

For a moment Bel felt horribly guilty. She knew precisely how to manipulate her sister, but she also knew that both she and Bee would feel bad if Bee didn't attend the ball.

"So then, how are we going to do this?" Bel asked, looking from her sister to Tina and back again.

~April 8~

Never had Claire dreaded going to a Ladies' Wagering Whist Society meeting, yet today she did. It wasn't so much telling her secret as it was the humiliation that was sure to come with it. The thought that she'd been tricked was rather mortifying. The fact that her nieces had ignored the basic rules of civility with this ruse... If Claire wasn't so *very* particular about following the rules, she supposed it would make things so much easier. But she was, and this was not going to be an easy day for her.

Dearest Christianne, who knew her so well, understood immediately the moment she saw Claire's expression.

"It's going to be fine," she said softly. "Remember, you're among friends."

Claire nodded and did her best to smile.

"Ladies," Christianne said, clapping her hands to get everyone's attention, "I believe we are all here. Shall we get started?"

Everyone nodded and arranged themselves at two tables as always, mixing themselves up so that no one partnered with the same person they'd played with the last time they met.

Claire sat across from Mrs. Aldridge and her little dog, Duchess. She didn't mind the dog so much, so long as she kept her mouth off the cards—

once she'd stolen a card off the table and given it an experimental bite. They'd had to get a whole new deck to play with since that one card had been clearly marked.

Claire did her best to keep her attention on the game, but her mind kept wandering back to her nieces. How *could* those girls play such a trick on her? It was a betrayal of all her good will. They'd *lied* to her.

"The trick is yours," Mrs. Aldridge said, pulling her attention back to the game.

"What?" Claire asked. How did she know about the trick? Claire hadn't even said anything yet.

"The trick. On the table," the woman indicated the four cards that sat in the center of the table. Claire had put down the king of spades, not even looking to see what card she was playing.

"Oh! Yes, of course." She gathered the cards and placed them next to her elbow. It was the first trick she'd won all day—and would probably be the last she won all season if her nieces had any say. But it was nothing to the trick her nieces had played on her.

No. She couldn't do this. She simply couldn't wait until the hand was over as Christianne had suggested.

She set down her cards and stood up. "Ladies, I do beg your pardon, but I am in need of your help." She had to do this before her nerves truly set in. "Until this hand, I had the lowest number of points. That's not going to change, so I'm just... I am just going to reveal my secret to you now if you don't mind."

"Of course, Lady Blakemore," Lady Moreton said, putting down her cards.

"I thought you were upset about something. You've been rather distracted lately but nothing compared to today," Mrs. Aldridge said.

"I certainly don't mind if you've got something you need to speak about," the duchess said, also putting her cards down.

"I would never say no to someone who needed help," Lady Welles said.

"A few of us have already benefited from the wisdom of this group," Lady Colborne said with a warm smile.

"Indeed, we have," Christianne agreed.

"I don't believe anyone minds. What is the problem, Lady Blakemore?" Mrs. Aldridge asked, moving her dog from her lap to the floor.

Claire swallowed her nerves and reminded herself once more that these were her friends. "It seems that... Well, that I have been played for a fool." There, it was best to get the worst out there at the start.

"What?" Lady Moreton exclaimed.

"How?" Lady Sorrell asked.

They all looked at her, waiting patiently for her explanation.

"You all know that my niece, Isabel, has been here to make her come out," Claire began. The ladies all nodded. "And you know that she has an identical twin sister," she continued.

"Do not say that it has been the other twin who has been here this whole time?" Lady Welles exclaimed.

Claire felt her face heat with embarrassment. "Worse. They've *both* been here."

There were gasps of shock, although Lady

Welles giggled outright.

When Christianne glared at her, she covered her mouth. "I am sorry, but that is the funniest thing. I mean, can you not tell them apart at all?"

"They are absolutely identical. The only difference is that one is left-handed, one right. And they have differing talents and personalities, of course."

"Was that how you realized they were both here?" the duchess asked.

Claire nodded. "I noticed that my niece was using her left hand to reach for her teacup one morning."

"Oh, that's very clever of you," Lady Moreton said.

"Very observant," Mrs. Aldridge agreed.

"Do you know why the other came—I'm sorry, I don't remember her name," Lady Colborne said.

"Beatrice. She's the elder of the two," Claire said. "She is also the more practical one. She actually had an excellent reason for being here." Claire explained everything to the women over another cup of tea, which she privately wished could have been something a little stronger.

"But that is excellent reasoning," the duchess said when she'd finished.

"Yes, which is precisely my problem," Claire said. "Not only do I understand and sympathize with her, I quite admire her for risking so much to look after her sister."

"But what is Lady Blakemore to do about it?" Christianne asked the ladies, getting to the heart of the matter.

"Ah, yes, I see the problem," Mrs. Aldridge

said.

"You *shouldn't* punish a girl for looking after her sister," Lady Welles began.

"But you also can't condone such dishonesty," Lady Moreton said.

"It's true. She should have come to you from the start," Mrs. Aldridge agreed.

"But perhaps she didn't know what sort of reception such an admission would have received," Lady Colborne said.

"Such speculation isn't useful at this point," Lady Sorrell pointed out. "You want to know what we think you should do."

"Precisely," Claire said.

"I beg your pardon," Lady Moreton said, "but where do her parents think she's been for the past two weeks? I mean, surely they would have noticed her missing if she'd been at home with them."

"That's an excellent question!" Mrs. Aldridge exclaimed before turned to Claire for an answer.

"She said she was supposedly visiting a friend in Oxford," Claire said. "The girl has apparently been covering for her, forwarding any letters her parents have written and sending letters from Beatrice on."

"That's a *very* good friend," Lady Welles commented.

"In Oxford? You wouldn't happen to know the girl's name?" Lady Sorrell asked. "I grew up there. Perhaps I know her, and if so, then maybe we can enlist her help in sorting this out."

"I don't know who she is. I'm afraid I didn't ask," Claire said. "So, do you believe I *shouldn't* send Beatrice back to her parents?"

"Personally? No, I do not," Lady Sorrell said. "To me, it sounds like she's simply been caring for her sister. If there's an easy way to explain her presence here—"

"Or have her, somehow, 'join' her sister," Lady Colburne interrupted.

"Yes! If there is a way for her to 'come to town' without anyone realizing she's been here all along, that would be an excellent idea," Christianne agreed with enthusiasm.

"So, there should be no repercussions for this atrocious behavior?" Claire asked.

The ladies were all silent for a moment.

"I completely agree that her behavior has been beyond the pale," the duchess began, "but considering her reasoning for it and the risk she took, no, I *don't* believe she should be punished."

"Well, if you think about it, living in her room, with only a few hours outside of it when she went out as her sister, has probably been punishment enough," Lady Welles said.

A number of women nodded their agreement.

Claire sighed. "Very well. I will find out the name of her friend, and if you know her, Lady Sorrell, perhaps we can find some simple, believable way of 'bringing' Beatrice to town."

Claire wasn't entirely certain she agreed with the ladies' conclusion that Beatrice should go completely without punishment. On the other hand, she didn't feel it right to send her home, which was the most appropriate punishment Claire could think of. She didn't know what her sister or her husband would do when they learned of their daughter's behavior. It was entirely possible they would do nothing at all since lax parenting seemed to be their way. On the other hand, Claire didn't want to entirely ruin the girl's life either should they decide to treat her harshly.

No, perhaps this was the best solution after all.

Chapter Twenty-One

~April 9~

Edward took in a deep breath. The smell of the opera. It was like coming home. The scent of so many bodies, of the fresh cut wood and paint of the sets, the stink of the tallow candles edging the stage. It all smelled so good.

"Oh, Lord Conway, it's magnificent!" Miss Kendrick said, standing beside him in his box. He had taken to calling her Belle. She had thought it sweet, understanding immediately the Italian word for beautiful and the play on her given name, Isabel. Her giggles when he'd asked permission to address her as such had been like music to his ears. But now...

Now, there was an ache in his heart as he reacquainted himself with the opera. It had been too long since he'd set foot inside a theatre. It had been too painful. But for Belle he had to set aside the pain, set aside the memories, set aside his longing to be back on stage, singing the arias he loved so much.

He forced a smile and turned to her. "I was certain you would like it. Please, sit." He pulled the chair closest to the stage out for her. She lowered herself onto it gracefully, not looking away from all there was to see for even a moment. He turned to Lady Blakemore and indicated for her to take the chair next to her niece.

"Thank you, I'll sit just behind with Blakemore," the lady said, taking the seat closer to the rear of the box. She would still be able to see the stage but from between him and her niece. It was a strategic place for a chaperone to sit, where she could watch the stage and her charge at the same time.

Her husband gave a little chuckle and a wink to Edward as he took his seat next to his wife. He knew as well as Edward did what the lady was doing.

"I'm certain the two of you will be the only people in the house actually watching the stage," Lady Blakemore said with a little laugh.

"So, it's true that people only come to watch each other?" Belle asked, turning around in her chair.

"They couldn't give a fig what was happening on stage," her uncle responded with a laugh.

"But the music...?" Belle asked.

"They are only interested in who is sitting with whom," Edward concurred.

"What a shame," Belle said with a shake of her head. "Oh! They're beginning," she said as the curtain parted to reveal the scene carefully constructed before them.

Edward turned toward the stage and nearly jumped from his chair. A dark-haired beauty strode onto the stage singing—Angelica! But no, she was a mezzo-soprano, not a lyric soprano. Her voice was high and at times too thin, so very unlike the rich, full voice of his love. Her face was much wider than

Angelica's and her bosom much larger. No, his love had been perfect with a thin, delicate bone structure, but lungs and a voice that brought tears to men's eyes and had women's jaws dropping with jealousy.

Even as he watched the soprano on stage, he felt himself shrinking from the young lady sitting next to him. All he could think about was Angelica. She had been his love, his lover, his friend. She had supported him in so many ways when he'd been new to Venice. She'd helped him get started singing professionally, teaching him all he needed to know to become a part of a company. But more importantly, even though they'd been from two different worlds, they'd understood each other. They'd had something very special.

Yes, it had been two years since he'd nursed her until her death, but being here, in this theatre, brought back all his memories of their time together. They'd been completely devoted to each other, and here he was defiling her memory just by being with Belle.

His throat began to close with emotion. By the time Giampiero strode onto the stage, his fantastic baritone voice filling the theatre, Edward could hardly breathe.

If he could have dared walk out on his friend, he would have, but Giampiero's voice kept him rooted to his seat, as if a large rock had been placed in his lap. He couldn't have gotten up if he'd wanted. All he could do was close his eyes and listen.

~*~

Bel was enthralled with the music, with the singing, with the whole theatre. It was the most wonderful experience of her life. She sighed happily and looked next to her to share her happiness with Lord Conway but was shocked by his expression.

If tears had been running down his face, she wouldn't have been surprised. His eyes were closed and his lower lip trembled ever so slightly with emotion.

Was it the singing? It couldn't be the story, it wasn't sad—at least not yet.

What was it that was making him so emotional?

Heedless of her aunt sitting just behind her, she reached out and placed her hand on top of his as it sat on his knee. She'd hoping to soothe him, and her effort did cause a reaction, just not the one she'd wanted.

He jumped from his chair, excused himself, and fled from the box.

It was too much. He couldn't do it. He couldn't stand to be with Belle. Not now. She was so kind. So thoughtful. He was sure she'd only meant to share her excitement or perhaps to comfort him? He didn't know. All he knew was that he couldn't stand her touch. Not when Angelica was pursuing him from the grave.

He could still hear Giampiero's voice even out in the corridor. That was good. He could listen from here. He wouldn't have to sit next to Belle where he could not only smell her sweet, delicate scent but sense her confusion at his reaction. He hoped she wouldn't be too upset, but he just... He *couldn't* sit next to her.

He leaned his head against the wall feeling the music, seeing Angelica even behind his closed eyes. He could do this. He *would* get through this evening even if it felt as if his heart was being ripped from his body.

At the intermission, Belle came from the box to find him. He was grateful she hadn't done so before then, but he still had some explaining to do. Could he... Dare he tell her about Angelica? No! It was bad enough he was upset; he couldn't make her so as well.

"Lord Conway, there you are," she said, her voice gentle and soft. "Are you all right?"

"My sincere apologies, Miss Kendrick," he said, trying his best to turn his lips up into a smile and failing horribly. "You couldn't possibly understand how difficult this is for me."

"But I would like to. Are you able to tell me?"

She was so good! He didn't deserve such a sweet girl. He shook his head. "I-I can't. Please, I need you to understand."

"Of course. You're very upset." She reached out and put her hand on his arm, light as a feather and yet soothing. How could he possibly be in so much pain and yet feel calmed by this slip of a girl?

"As soon as I am able, I will explain it all to you. Please, just know that this has nothing to do with you. It is entirely me, and I must apologize for my atrocious behavior."

"No, I mean, I understand. Or, at least, I'm trying to."

"You are too good. Come, at least allow me to introduce you to my good friend, Giampiero Abelli. He is the baritone. The male lead."

"Of course, I would be honored. I just need to inform my aunt, first."

She popped back into the box, leaving Edward to wonder how he could have been so lucky to have had Angelica and now Belle. Both were amazing women. Both were so talented. Both inspired him to be a better man.

Belle was back a moment later accompanied by her aunt. "Is it all right if my aunt comes along?"

"Of course!" Now that the music had stopped, he was beginning to regain some measure of control over his wayward emotions. A few deep breaths as they made their way down to the stage level and back to the dressing rooms, and he was composed by the time they were knocking on Giampiero's door.

It was opened with a flourish, and his friend stood there in his costume and full make-up. "Ah! Eduardo, magnifico! I am so happy you have finally made it," he said, his voice still projecting loudly.

"I promised I would, did I not?"

Giampiero stood back and allowed them to enter his dressing room.

"Please allow me to introduce to you Lady Blakemore and her lovely niece, Miss Kendrick," Edward said, indicating the women.

"It is such an honor to meet you, sir," Miss Kendrick said, sounding awe-struck.

"The honor is mine, señorita," Giampiero said with a sweeping bow.

"We are enjoying your performance a great deal," Lady Blakemore said.

"I am so happy. And what of you, Eduardo? How are you doing?" Giampiero asked, turning to Edward and raising one darkened eyebrow.

"It is...difficult, as you would expect," he answered honestly.

His friend's energy level dropped immediately.

"Yes. I am not surprised."

"Your voice is so magnificent," Miss Kendrick said, clearly sensing the change in atmosphere. "And the soprano is quite lovely as well."

"Ah, but you hear the difference in our voices. I can see this," he said with a sly smile.

Miss Kendrick giggled, "Hers is very pretty but not...not as full as yours. Not as strong."

"No. She manages, but the director chose her for her"—he indicated his chest—"er, not for her voice."

"Too many opera singers are thus," Lady Blakemore agreed, losing her smile.

"Too many directors hire who they think will appeal to the gentlemen rather than the best vocalists," Giampiero agreed. "It is unfortunate."

"We should get back to our box, and you will need to return to the stage soon," Edward said, opening the door and ushering the ladies out.

"Yes, yes. Thank you so much for coming by. Thank you," Giampiero said, waving them off.

Edward paused, then turned back and gave his friend a quick hug. "You are a good man and an incredible vocalist."

Giampiero held onto his arms and looked deeply into Edward's eyes. "You miss her. I see it in your eyes. Do not. She is *here*." He placed his hand on Edward's chest.

Edward swallowed hard but something calmed inside of him. Angelica would never be forgotten. She would live on in them and in the opera forever.

As they neared the door to the box, Belle turned back to him and said quietly, "Will you be all right for the second half?"

Edward did a quick check of his emotions and gave her a nod and a little smile. "I think so. I will certainly do my best."

"Seeing your friend helped," she commented astutely.

"Yes. It did. Giampiero is a very good friend, and we have known each other for years."

"Old friends are the best of friends." With a nod, she turned and went into their box. Edward followed.

Chapter Twenty-Two

~April 12~

Bel looked around at the crowd of about fifty people, clustering at the front of the enormous St. Paul's Cathedral, and wondered what a large wedding would have looked like. This, apparently, was a very small, private affair.

Lady Norman, standing at the altar in front of the vicar, looked stunning. She was absolutely glowing in a simple deep blue silk gown with lace trimming and sleeves. Lord Ayres, her fiancé, was next to her in a matching blue coat and breeches. His waistcoat was the same blue, but with a deeper blue embroidery that mimicked the lace pattern of Lady Norman's gown.

"Lord and Lady Blakemore, Bel, welcome," Tina said, coming forward to greet them. She looked stunning as well. Her dress was a pale blue, complementing the bride's dress but much more understated so as to not outshine Lady Norman. Her smile, however, matched that of Lady Norman to a remarkable degree.

"Good morning, Tina," Bel's aunt said, taking hold of her hands. "You look lovely. Are you ready for this exciting day?"

"Oh, most definitely," Tina laughed. "I've been

ready for the longest time."

Lady Blakemore laughed. "That is precisely what Christianne said when I asked her the other day."

Tina shook her head as she continued to laugh. "I'm not at all surprised."

Lady Margaret came and joined them. Her dress was also blue, but of such a pale color it was almost hard to tell that it wasn't white. Only the white lace trimming—the same as on Lady Norman's gown—highlighted the color. "Isn't it a wonderful day?" she said, with a broad smile.

"Indeed, it is," Bel answered with a giggle. She didn't think she'd ever seen Lady Margaret so happy and at ease.

"I hear you two have been working tirelessly to make everything perfect for today and the ball tomorrow," Lord Blakemore said, looking fondly at the two young ladies.

"Well, I don't know about tirelessly, but it certainly has been a bit more of a challenge than we'd anticipated," Lady Margaret said.

"Poor Margaret shouldered most of the work," Tina said.

"Oh no, that's not true at all! We worked equally hard, I'm sure," Lady Margaret said with a shake of her head. She didn't lose her smile, though, and Bel imagined that she would have it all day long.

"In any case, I'm certain you are both happy that the day has finally come," Lady Blakemore said.

"Oh, yes!" they said in unison. They all laughed.

"And you all have similar gowns," Bel said, "or at least similar in color. I assume that was deliberate?"

"I thought it would be fun," Tina said with a little laugh.

"You designed all three?" Lady Blakemore asked.

"I did. And chose the material as well," Tina said.

"We'll probably be beginning soon, so you should find your seats," Lady Margaret said a little apologetically.

"Yes, indeed. And you have others to greet," Bel's aunt said.

Tina and Lady Margaret gave them a nod and moved farther down the aisle to do just that.

Bel had turned to see where they would sit when Lord St. Vincent walked up to them. "Good morning."

"Oh, good morning, my lord," Lady Blakemore said. Her eyes shifted to Bel.

"Lord St. Vincent, how wonderful to see you," Bel said, smiling boldly up at him. "Are you close with Lady Norman as well?"

"No. Actually, my father and Lord Ayres were very close friends. They were rather an odd pair. Lord Ayres is so bold and outgoing while my father was on the quieter side, but somehow they maintained a close friendship for most of their lives," he explained.

"Ah yes, of course. Often saw them together." Lord Blakemore nodded. "They would spend hours together at White's either talking or playing cards. If your father was in town, it was a good bet that he was in the company of Ayres."

Lord St. Vincent nodded, a small smile playing on his lips. "It is in my father's honor that I was invited. I understand it is to be a very small affair, though."

"Yes." Lady Blakemore looked around. "Most people are already here, I believe."

"Really?" her husband said in surprise. "Then it really *is* small."

"If this is small, I would almost hate to see what a big wedding would look like," Bel said, her eyes widening as she looked around at all the people.

"Well, for Lord and Lady Colburne's wedding, which was held at the Darby's estate, there were nearly two hundred," Lady Blakemore said. "It put quite a strain on all the inns and posting houses in the area, I can tell you."

"My goodness!" Bel exclaimed.

"Oh, we are being requested to sit, my dear," Lord Blakemore said, nodding to someone toward the front of the church.

They quickly filed into a pew, Lord Blakemore followed by his wife, then Bel and finally Lord St. Vincent. Bel was acutely aware of the man sitting next to her. He was so large and imposing. She couldn't imagine how Bee found him so attractive. She much preferred Lord Conway, who was more compact and not nearly so intimidating with his size.

"I, er, greatly enjoyed your performance last week at your aunt's musicale," Lord St. Vincent said politely. Was it her imagination or did he say that with a touch of anger in his voice? She couldn't imagine why.

"Thank you. I was terribly nervous," she said.

"Yes. So I understood. It was a good thing that Lord Conway was there to sing while you accompanied him. I understand that calmed your nerves?"

Ah, so that was it. He was jealous! How wonderful for Bee. Bel did her best to hide her smile at the realization. "Yes, it did. It was very good of him to sing for us. Do you sing, my lord?"

"Me? No!" he said quickly.

"Do you play an instrument?"

A voice called out from the front of the church, "Ladies and Gentlemen, dearly beloved, we are gathered here this day…"

Lord St. Vincent turned his attention toward the ceremony with a slight look of relief on his face. Bel once again resisted the urge to giggle and turned to watch the ceremony as well. Lady Norman and Lord Ayres looked so happy standing next to each other in front of the vicar. Margaret and Tina stood nearby in their support of the bride. It was funny. Tina was Lord Ayres natural daughter, but she stood with Lady Norman. They all looked so comfortable together; it was wonderful.

The vicar went through the prescribed ceremony, but before coming to the part where the bride and groom pledged their troth, he paused and looked out at the audience. "Weddings such as this always bring such happiness to my heart. I'm sure you are all well aware of the complicated relationship between these two people. Despite all they have been through, despite the fact they have had to wait for twenty-five years to see this day come, they are here today to celebrate the great endurance of true love. I am truly overjoyed to ask William Alastair Gerald Ayres, do you take this woman before you…"

Bel blinked away a few tears that threatened to fall as Lord Ayres stood taller and looked at his lovely bride, who he'd waited so patiently for. She heard a *tsk* and turned to the gentleman sitting next to her.

Lord St. Vincent was frowning and shaking his head ever so slightly. She wanted to ask him what he could possibly find objectionable in such a sight, but Lord Ayres strong, clear voice distracted her.

"With this ring, I thee wed, with my body I thee worship, and with all my worldly goods I thee endow. In the name of the Father, and of the son, and of the Holy Ghost. Amen," he said, sliding a ring onto the bride's hand.

The lady repeated her vows and even gave the gentleman a ring, which Bel was surprised to see. They were pronounced husband and wife and then went off to sign the parish registry.

Bel sighed happily. "How wonderful."

Lord St. Vincent gave a little laugh. "You ladies *do* think so, do you not?"

~*~

Miss Kendrick widened her eyes at Paul. "Of course! Don't you?"

Paul wished he could tell her the truth of his thoughts on the matter, but as he'd previously been contemplating going through this exact ritual with her, he supposed it would be best to keep his ideas to himself.

Despite all the nonsense Elizabeth spouted to him of love, he was not a believer. His father had told him that women held these fanciful notions, but it was just stuff and nonsense. A good marriage, his father had told him, was one in which the woman believed herself in love with the gentleman and, therefore, would do anything to keep him happy, and the man had a sound head on his shoulders and handled all matters of import.

There had been no love between his parents, Paul had known that from an early age. His mother and father had tolerated each other—barely. They deigned to be in each other's company when they needed to be but, aside from that, lived completely happy, separate lives with his father mostly staying in London and his mother staying at their estate. She would visit town every so often to be with friends, and he would visit the estate to handle things there, but they didn't interact much, and they liked it that way.

All this ridiculous talk of Lord Ayres and Lady Norman waiting for their true love made Paul want to laugh out loud. The fact that Miss Kendrick had not so discreetly wiped a tear away from her eyes after the vicar's silly little speech made him glad that he *hadn't* been the one to win her affections after all. He didn't want an emotional, weeping wife who would expect him to behave in an absurd manner, cooing over her or whatever other nonsense was expected of one "in love."

No, he was very glad he'd dodged the point of that blade. The woman he married would be clever, intelligent, and practical. It was odd that Miss Kendrick had displayed precisely those qualities at times, while at other times she behaved just like all the other silly girls making their come out. He supposed she changed her dress five times before deciding what to wear as well. In any case, he was just as happy for Conway to have to deal with her and not himself.

Paul gave Miss Kendrick a little smile before standing and helping her from the pew. "I am very happy for Lord and Lady Ayres, and I most sincerely hope they find happiness together for many years to come."

The smile she gave him told him it had been precisely the right thing to say. That was good enough for him.

~April 13~

Bee hated continuing to lie to her aunt, but she didn't think it would be wise to let Lady Blakemore know that she, as well as Bel, would be attending the wedding ball. Their aunt hadn't said what she was going to do about them both being there. In fact, she hadn't spoken to either of them very much at all since she'd discovered Bee's presence.

"Let's give her some time to work it out," Bee had said when Bel had proposed going and speaking with her. Bel was feeling as bad as her sister about the whole thing, but Bee thought it best to leave their aunt alone for a bit—and that included not informing her about their plans for the ball.

Bee donned Annie's cloak later the afternoon of the ball and slipped down the back stairs. Tina's carriage was waiting in the alley next to the house, and Bee managed to sneak out the back door without anyone the wiser.

The coachman let her into the back gate of Tina's home, and she paused to take in the enormous garden. From where she stood, she could admire a small kitchen garden filled with herbs and a few vegetables, but beyond that, paths led off to such a distance that she couldn't even see to the other end. She'd never even imagined a London home could have such an extensive garden. Well, that's what one got when one was a wealthy duke, she supposed with a little laugh to herself.

She'd just closed the back door when a voice made her jump.

"And just where do you think you're going?" a woman's sharp voice said from behind her.

Bee turned around but kept her gaze lowered and her hood up to hide her identity. She stayed silent.

"Don't even think about sneaking out of this house, girl. There is too much work to be done in preparation for this ball tonight," the woman said. Bee assumed she must be the housekeeper.

"Yes, ma'am," Bee mumbled.

"Now get back to wherever it is you're supposed to be—you *do* know where that is?" she asked in a harsh tone.

This time Bee just nodded and went straight to the door of the back stairs, which Tina had told her where to find. As she climbed the stairs to the upper floors, she let out a breath. "Whew, that was too close," she whispered to herself.

Bee knocked softly on the third door on the left just as she'd been instructed. Tina answered, pulling her into the room. She quickly gave Bee a hug. "I was so worried! I'd forgotten how many people would be about."

"I was caught downstairs by the housekeeper," Bee admitted. "Luckily, she thought I was sneaking out rather than coming in. I was able to quickly escape up the stairs."

"Oh, my goodness!" Tina said, her eyes going

wide. "I'm so glad I brought your dress back with me instead of having you bring it."

"Yes! If I'd been seen with that, she might have thought I was stealing something," Bee said with a sudden spike of fear lacing through her.

Tina took in a deep breath and shook her head. "Well, you're here now. Relax and later Pauline will help you dress."

Her maid, standing just behind her, gave a little curtsy. Bee nodded and smiled to her before pulling out her book and settling down in the window seat while Tina and Pauline worked on getting the duchess ready for the evening.

Chapter Twenty-Three

Bel felt so strange getting dressed without Bee there to comment on everything or help by giving a twitch here and a smooth there. She'd never thought about how much her sister participated in the process of getting her ready to go out until she wasn't there to do it.

Once more she felt grateful to her sister for risking so much to come with her to London. She didn't know what she would have done if Bee hadn't been there to see her off to each and every outing. Her touches to Bel's toilette weren't actually needed. Annie was an excellent maid, but it was that silent show of support as she did those little things that made all the difference. They gave Bel confidence and a feeling of warmth and love.

And now she didn't have that just when she was about to go off to one of the most important events of the season. She took in a deep breath and let it out slowly. She could do this. She didn't need Bee with her all the time. She'd gone off on her own plenty of times, she reminded herself. Yes, yes, she had, and she could do so again this evening.

And besides, she would be seeing Bee at Tina's.

The line of carriages approaching the duchess's home stretched around the entire square.

"My goodness," Lady Blakemore said, craning her head a little to look out the window without actually opening the glass. "How many people are coming to this dinner?"

"I thought it was just going to be a few of their closer friends and relatives," Bel said.

"That's what the duchess said," Lord Blakemore grumbled. He didn't care what anyone thought. He lowered the glass and stuck his head right out the window.

"Blakemore!" his wife scolded.

"What? I just want to see how long this is going to take us," he responded, pulling his head back in.

"It will take however long it takes," Lady Blakemore said. "And we will be patient."

He sighed and settled back against the comfortable seat. "Yes, my dear. As we have no other choice in the matter, I suppose we will."

Bel gave a little giggle and settled back as well.

When they finally reached the door, they were greeted by the duke, Tina, and Margaret. They all looked stunning, but more than that, they looked happy.

Tina gave Bel a wink as she curtsied. "You look stunning just as I knew you would," Tina said.

"Almost as if you've seen me in this gown before?" Bel asked with a giggle.

"Was Tina there when you tried it on?" her aunt asked. "I don't believe she was."

"No? Well, I certainly *feel* as if I've seen it on you. It must be that I imagined what you'd look like in it," Tina said with a laugh.

Bel understood that she'd seen her sister after she'd gotten dressed and all was well.

"Tina absolutely has the most incredible ability to know how a dress will look on someone before they've even tried it on," Margaret said.

"Ladies, this is all fascinating, I'm sure, but there is a line," the duke said gently.

"Oh! Of course, how rude of us," Lady Blakemore said.

"Margaret, may I just quickly say that you look radiant tonight?" Bel said in all honesty. She didn't know what it was that made her friend look so wonderful, but she seemed to have some sort of inner glow that Bel had never noticed before.

"Thank you, Bel," Margaret said, a little surprised. "Perhaps it's just the happiness of the evening."

Bel could only give her a quick nod before she was led away by her aunt and uncle.

Dinner was a jolly affair with laughing and a good deal of teasing of the newlyweds. Despite the large number of people—at least the fifty who'd attended the wedding, maybe more—everyone knew each other well enough to relax and celebrate the occasion. It wasn't long after they had finished that the other guests began to arrive for the ball.

Tina took hold of Bel's arm, giving her a little start as she'd approached from the back. "I do beg your pardon, my lady," Tina said to Bel's aunt, "but would you mind very much if I took your niece for a little stroll about?"

"Not at all," Lady Blakemore said. "I am more than happy to have the opportunity to chat with Lady Sorrell and Lady Moreton." The two women were just approaching them, so Tina gave a little nod and led Bel off.

Before Bel realized what she was doing, Tina

led her straight out into the garden. "I'm sorry for this, but I think it's the only way for us to get upstairs to see your sister," she said quietly.

"Oh! Yes, of course. How clever of you," Bel responded immediately. She'd been wondering how Bee was doing. Now was a perfect time to check on her.

They went back into the house, through the back door, and up the servants' stair.

Her sister was happy to see them. "How was dinner?"

"It was a lot of fun," Bel said.

"I was so sorry you couldn't have joined us," Tina added.

"It's all right. Pauline brought up a tray for me. It was delicious," Bee said. She turned to look at Bel. "But if you don't mind, I think we should switch places now rather than later."

"Oh?" Bel had been hoping to make this visit short so she could go and find Lord Conway. She was beyond eager to see him again; it felt like ages since their evening at the opera. She wanted so desperately to know he was all right. She'd been worried about him ever since that evening when he'd been so sad and upset.

She didn't quite know what it was about being at the theatre that had disturbed him, but she imagined it was merely all the memories he had of singing and being a part of something so incredible. Still, she wished he'd come to call on her after that evening to talk to her. He hadn't, and all she could do was hope to have a word or, at the very least, a dance with him this evening. Perhaps she could ask him to call on her, or would that be too forward? She might very well do so anyway because she truly wanted to know that he was all right and—this she would admit only to herself—intensely curious about his response to the opera.

"If we switch now," Bee said, reclaiming Bel's attention, "then I can sneak back to Aunt Claire's while everyone is here and occupied. If I go to the party later, then you're going to have to be the one to sneak back home while I attend the ball."

"Oh, yes, I see," Bel said. "It would be much easier if you snuck back. You know what you're doing, and I've never done it before. Very well." She dropped down onto Tina's bed, trying hard not to show her disappointment.

Bee came to her. "If you truly prefer—"

"No, no. It's all right. I'm just eager to see Lord Conway, that's all."

"He usually shows up late, if that's any consolation," Tina said.

"That's true, he does!" Bel said, perking up immediately.

Bee laughed. "That worked."

"But she's right," Bel argued.

"Yes, she is, but that doesn't mean you're not very amusing." Bee shook her head and turned to Tina.

"We should probably go then, before we're missed," Tina said.

"My book is there if you want to read," Bee said before walking out the door with the duchess.

~*~

As they entered the ballroom from the garden, Bee couldn't help but look around to see if Lord Conway *was* anywhere in sight. Happily, Tina was right, and he didn't seem to have arrived yet.

"Ah, there you are," Aunt Claire said, approaching them with Lord Blakemore.

"We just went out for a breath of air," Tina said quickly.

"It's a lovely evening," Bee added. "Unusually warm."

"It must be for you to go without your shawl," her aunt said.

Bee pulled at the tops of her gloves which extended all the way up her arms, past her elbows.

"I'm afraid that's my fault, my lady. I completely forgot," Tina said quickly.

"Well, as long as you weren't cold," Lady Blakemore said.

"Miss Kendrick, may I be so bold as to say you look incredible this evening. You have truly proven to be a diamond of the first water," Sir Reggie said, while executing a beautiful leg before her, sweeping his hand down as he bowed over his outstretched limb. Bee hadn't even seen the man approach.

She would have frowned at his silliness, but then she quickly remembered she was supposed to be her sister, so instead she giggled and curtsied. "You are doing it too brown, sir."

"Not at all. Your gown brings out the fantastic color of your hair, the lovely green of your eyes, and the sweet pink of your cheeks," he said gazing down at her.

"La, sir, one would think you were wooing the girl with such talk," Lady Blakemore said. She did so with a smile that didn't quite reach her eyes, Bee noted. Not only were they *not* smiling, they were looking harshly at the man.

He understood her unspoken message

immediately much to Bee's relief. "I would not dare to overstep, my lady. I just speak the truth, for how can one not when faced with—"

"Thank you, sir, we understand your meaning," the lady said quickly before he could begin to spout his nonsense once more.

"I say, Sir Reggie, do you know if there's a card room about?" Lord Blakemore asked, putting his hand on the man's shoulder. He efficiently turned Sir Reggie around and guided him off.

"Lord Blakemore is a very useful gentleman to have around," his wife said with an approving nod. "I do hope he doesn't get lost in that card room for the entire evening."

Bee gave a true laugh and followed her aunt farther into the room.

They didn't get very far before Mr. Hershawn and Lord Rosebury joined them. "Ladies," Lord Rosebury bowed.

"It's a pleasure to see you," Mr. Hershawn said, doing likewise.

Lady Blakemore's smile was real as she nodded to the two gentlemen. Bee had the feeling she liked the men and wondered if her aunt wished Bee and her sister had taken to them as well. "I have seen neither one of you dance this evening," Lady Blakemore said, looking from one to the other.

"But, my lady, the night is still young," Mr. Hershawn objected.

"There has only been one dance performed as yet, and in fact, it is still going on," Lord Rosebury agreed, looking out onto the floor where the dancers were maneuvering in front and behind each other.

"I find it impossible to believe that neither of you could find a partner for it," the lady persisted.

"Well…" Lord Rosebury hedged.

"We *might* have been otherwise occupied," Mr. Hershawn said.

Bee couldn't help but laugh at the two men. "And what was it that had you so occupied you would sit out a dance? I was certain you both preferred dancing above all else."

"Only if it was with you, Miss Kendrick," Mr. Hershawn said, turning a bright smile on to her.

She laughed and shook her head. "That is not an answer, sir."

"I have a suspicion they don't want us to know what they were doing," Lady Blakemore said with a laugh of her own.

"Well, this is the celebration of a wedding," Mr. Hershawn said.

"Yes," Bee prompted.

"So, it does put ideas into one's mind," Lord Rosebury continued.

"Don't tell me one or both of you were proposing to a young lady?" Bee blurted out.

"What?" Mr. Hershawn was clearly shocked by the idea.

"Absolutely not!" Lord Rosebury concurred.

"Then?" Lady Blakemore asked.

"Have you noticed that Lady Margaret keeps looking over toward the wall by the door?" the Duchess of Kendell said, coming to join them. "Oh, good evening, gentlemen," she added belatedly.

"I *had* noticed that, actually," Lady Blakemore said.

They all turned to watch Margaret, who was laughing at something her dancing partner had said. Her eyes, however, were straying toward the wall, just as the duchess had said.

"That's very odd," Bee said. "Who is standing there? I see Lady Blackglass and Lord Bertram in the vicinity. There is a footman and two young ladies who look like they're trying to blend into the wall."

Lord Rosebury and Mr. Hershawn both laughed. "They do look that way, don't they?" Mr. Hershawn said.

The duchess *tsked* her tongue. "There is no one there for her to be looking at."

"It is rather odd," Lady Blakemore agreed.

"Well, if you will excuse us," Lord Rosebury said.

"But you haven't told us what you were doing when you should have been soliciting young ladies' hands for the dance," Bee protested.

"Oh, er, speaking with some other ladies," Mr. Hershawn said.

"Yes. Lady St. Vincent and then Lady Shipton, but neither were interested in, er, dancing," Lord Rosebury said.

The duchess gasped and then glared at them.

"Good evening," Lord Rosebury said. The two men gave a quick bow and went off.

"I have the feeling I'm missing something," Bee said, looking at the two older ladies who were giving each other a significant look.

"Nothing for you to worry about, Miss Kendrick," the duchess said, letting Bee know she was indeed missing something, but that perhaps it was better that way.

She turned and saw Lord St. Vincent strolling past on his own. "Good evening, my lord," she called out, effectively stopping him.

He turned and gave her and the ladies with her a polite smile. "Ladies." He bowed.

"Did you enjoy the wedding yesterday, Lord St. Vincent?" the duchess asked.

His smile began to falter.

"My lord, we had been discussing travel last week," Bee said, recapturing his attention. His smile returned as he turned back to her, making heat rush through her. She prayed she wasn't blushing, but she pressed on anyway. "I was wondering if you've had a chance to speak with Lady Colburne. I understand she lived abroad for a good part of her life."

"Really?" he asked, looking quite interested.

"If you will excuse me, I believe Margaret is looking for me," the duchess said and went off in search of her charge.

Bee bobbed her a curtsy, but she wasn't looking, so she turned back to Lord St. Vincent. "Yes, she was telling me that she lived in France and then Germany. It was apparently quite fascinating. She had learned some French before she moved there, then became quite proficient in the language. As soon as she'd done so, her father moved them to Germany and she had to start all over again with a completely new and very different language. Do you speak either French or German, my lord?"

"I am quite knowledgeable in French, although I have to admit my Latin and Greek are much better when it comes to reading the language," he said.

"But I know nothing of German. How about you, Miss Kendrick? Have you a talent with languages?"

She sighed. "Like you, I can speak French well enough, but I don't know German. I asked for tuition in Greek, so that I could read Sophocles in the original, but the school I attended had no facility to teach me. I was extremely disappointed. Instead, they wanted me to learn to embroider or paint."

"Which are appropriate fields of study for a proper young lady," her aunt agreed.

"While Greek is not?" Bee asked.

"No, it is not. Perhaps you and I should have a word about such things later, *Bee*," her aunt said, frowning at her.

Chapter Twenty-Four

Bee's eyes widened as she realized she'd given herself away. Her stomach began to churn from the anger in the lady's eyes. She turned back to Lord St. Vincent and was somewhat mollified. He was looking at her with undisguised admiration, which immediately thawed the ice that could have been coating her skin from the look her aunt was giving her. On the one hand, she'd earned respect from the gentleman she most wanted to impress; on the other, she was now in serious trouble.

"Would you care to dance, Miss Kendrick," Lord St. Vincent asked.

"Thank you, my lord, I would enjoy that a great deal," she said, smiling up at him and trying to hold back the relief washing through her. That was exactly what she needed—to get away from Lady Blakemore's fury before it erupted.

She took his arm as he led her out onto the floor. Instead of taking up a position just in front of her aunt, however, he walked her toward the front of the room and then paused. "Or would you prefer to take a walk outside on the balcony?" he asked, turning toward her with a sly little smile on his lips.

"My lord, did you do that on purpose—ask me to dance so you could take me for an unescorted walk outside?" Bee asked, a little shocked and very pleased at the same time.

"I do beg your pardon, but yes, that is precisely what I did. I don't quite understand what happened, but suddenly your aunt became extremely angry with you, putting you in an awkward situation."

"And you removed me from the situation, so I wouldn't have to both be polite to you and deal with my aunt's anger, which would have been extremely difficult," she said in wonder.

He just smiled.

"Thank you." The words came straight from her heart.

"It is my pleasure," he said with a nod of his head. "Now, which would you prefer—to dance or to get a breath of fresh air?"

"Oh, the fresh air, most definitely!" she said with enthusiasm.

"I was hoping you'd choose that one," he said with a laugh.

They made it out the French doors to the balcony without being seen by her aunt just as the music was beginning.

The evening wasn't too chilly as they strolled along the balcony. "I got a small glimpse of the gardens earlier," Bee admitted. "They look to be quite extensive."

"Really? I admit, I've never seen them," Lord St. Vincent said.

"Shall we explore a little? Would you mind?" Bee asked. She was certain it was very wrong to descend into the garden alone with a gentleman, but she wanted to see the gardens and spend more time with Lord St. Vincent.

"I wouldn't mind at all," he said, smiling and offering his arm to her.

She took it, feeling her cheeks heat again.

"I have to admit, you surprise and confuse me, Miss Kendrick," he said as they strolled along the pretty path in between the flower beds.

"Oh?"

"One evening you tell me that you have no interest in history, and the next you tell me how you are reading a history of Greece. One day you are looking with blatant interest at Lord Conway, the next you ask that I escort you into a dark garden. I don't quite know what to think."

"I appreciate your honesty, my lord," Bee said as she tried to figure out how to explain, without explaining, that she was actually two very different people. What was she to do? What *could* she say? For it certainly wasn't the truth, despite the fact that he was being so wonderfully honest with her. How she wished she could be so with him!

"That's all well and good, but *do* you have an explanation to offer?" he asked, pausing to look at her.

"I'm afraid I don't. All I can tell you is that I am who I am. And, although I may have had a...a moment with Lord Conway, I would *much* rather it had been with you." Her face burned with embarrassment. She couldn't believe how bold she was being, how daring! Now she truly was behaving more like her sister than herself.

"I can't tell you how gratifying it is to hear that," he said, his voice going soft and deep. He stared down at her, and she realized that, somehow, he'd gotten very close to her. Very, very close.

She swallowed and looked up into his eyes. Was it her imagination or were they getting even closer? Her gaze switched to his lips. No, he was definitely... He was going to kiss her!

It was the lightest of touches. Bee's eyes fluttered closed as his lips brushed against her own. They didn't move away, but instead lingered there, giving her soft little kisses again and again until she responded likewise. His hands grasped onto her shoulders, and she was grateful for his steadying hold on her. Her knees went weak, and she felt like would have fallen right into him, or melted, he felt so good.

His kiss became stronger, more confident as she began to kiss him back. She could feel warmth radiating off him, smell the scent of his soap, taste a sweetness which she could only imagine was simply him. With a suddenness that nearly toppled her, he pulled away.

"I... I beg your pardon," he whispered.

"Don't."

He chuckled. "All right, then, I don't. Kissing you is wonderful, but I shouldn't."

"Oh," she said, hearing the disappointment in her own voice. "No, I suppose not."

"We should return. The dance may already be over."

After they returned to the ballroom, before Lord St. Vincent could escort her back to Lady Blakemore, Tina intercepted them. "I do beg your pardon, but I'm afraid I need a word with you, Miss Kendrick."

"Oh, of course. If you would excuse me, my lord?" Bee asked.

Lord St. Vincent merely bowed and walked away leaving the two girls.

"I'm sorry, Bee, but I'm sure your sister is eager to come down and join the party," Tina said.

"My goodness, has it been so long already? I've completely lost track of the time."

"I'm not surprised. It's very easy to do so in the garden," Tina said with a mischievous look in her eyes.

"I will go to her immediately, and then I should return home," Bee said, looking about and wondering how to arrange for her return.

"The coach is waiting for you in the alley next to the house," Tina said. She'd already arranged everything, Bee realized gratefully.

"Thank you. Thank you for everything, Tina. I can't tell you—"

"No need. Just seeing you so happy made it all worthwhile," Tina said, giving her a quick hug.

Bee just smiled at her and then went back out into the garden. This time she went back toward the kitchens and the back entrance to the house. Up in Tina's room, she found Bel pacing furiously.

"What has taken you so long?" her sister said the moment she walked in the door.

"Lord St. Vincent kissed me," Bee said quietly.

Her sister's mouth dropped open. "What?"

"In the garden. Not a quarter of an hour ago."

Bel grabbed onto Bee's arms. "I would hug you, but then my hair would get mussed. Oh, my goodness, Bee, I'm so happy for you!"

"Well, he didn't propose! He just—"

"Kissed you!" Bel whispered loudly and

dramatically.

"Yes," Bee breathed. She shook herself free from her happy dream. "But you need to go down. Oh, and Aunt Claire knows it was me with her before that. I was speaking with Lord St. Vincent about travel and languages, and she realized who I was. She was *not* happy."

"Oh, no! What are we to do?"

"I don't know, but you should probably identify yourself when you rejoin her, and somehow tell her that I've gone home."

Bel gave a mirthless laugh. "And how am I to do that?"

"Very quietly?" Bee asked with a shrug.

Her sister just frowned at her before walking out the door.

~*~

"Where have you been?" Lady Blakemore asked as Bel approached her back in the ballroom.

"In Tina's room, seeing Bee off. She's on her way home," Bel answered honestly.

Her aunt's face lost all its color.

"It's all right. No one saw her, and if they did, they would just think she was me—we're wearing the same dress."

"At the same time?" her aunt asked. She clearly wasn't thinking straight.

"We have two identical dresses," Bel explained.

"Oh, yes, of course," her aunt shook her head, realizing she wasn't making sense.

"Good evening, Lady Blakemore, Miss Kendrick."

Bee turned to see Lord Conway smiling at her

and couldn't help the rush of good feelings that coursed through her. "Good evening, my lord."

"Would you care to go for a promenade, Miss Kendrick? I assure you, we won't go far," he added, looking at Aunt Claire.

"I would be delighted. Aunt, if that's all right with you?" Bel asked, turning to look to Lady Blakemore. The lady just pursed her lips together, but nodded her assent.

Bel took Lord Conway's arm and walked off with him.

"Are you feeling better this evening?" she asked, looking up at him.

He gave her a warm smile. "I am, thank you for asking. I'm still horribly embarrassed by my behavior the other night. It was quite inexcusable."

"No, no it wasn't," she protested immediately. "I just wish you could have explained what upset you so much."

He nodded as he led her outside onto the balcony.

~*~

"Claire, are you all right?" Christianne asked, coming up to her, accompanied by Lady Sorrell and Lady Welles.

"What? Yes. Why do you ask?" Claire turned to her friends.

"Because I have never seen you so derelict in your chaperonage duties before. This is the second time I've seen Miss Kendrick walk out onto the balcony this evening," Christianne said.

"And with a different gentleman each time," Lady Welles said with a little giggle.

"What?" Claire turned to look toward the

French doors. "Lord Conway just said that they were going to go for a promenade."

"And the first time?" Lady Sorrell asked.

"Who was she with the first time? When was that?" Claire asked, realizing how awful it sounded.

"She was with Lord St. Vincent, and it was about half an hour ago," Christianne said, drawing her eyebrows down as she looked at Claire closely.

Claire scowled. "He invited her to dance. I didn't notice them go outside."

"But why is she going outside with two different gentlemen? She wouldn't be playing one off the other, would she?" Christianne asked.

"I can't believe Bel would be so cunning," Lady Welles said.

"Trying to get one of them jealous perhaps?" Lady Sorrell suggested.

"No." Claire sighed. "The first one was Beatrice with Lord St. Vincent, it's Isabel with Lord Conway."

Christianne and Lady Sorrell both gasped. Lady Welles began to laugh. "Oh my! I so wish I'd known that. I wonder if I've met them both? I honestly don't know *who* I've met."

Claire could only wince and shake her head. "It's horribly embarrassing. I can't control this. I can't..." Never in her life had Claire been in such a predicament and never in such a public way. She just wanted to go home and curl up in her room with a very large glass of wine. She could feel the pinprick of tears in her eyes and quickly blinked them away.

"They switched without you knowing?" Lady Sorrell asked, clearly surprised.

Christianne put her hand on Claire's arm. "No, you cannot control them. They are determined—"

"—to embarrass me!" Claire finished for her.

"No," Christianne said with patience. "To make the most of an opportunity. I'm almost surprised that it was Beatrice who went out with Lord St. Vincent and Isabel with Lord Conway. I would have expected that Beatrice would want to spend some more time with Lord Conway to ensure he's the right one for her sister."

"We hadn't seen him yet, but Lord St. Vincent had come to speak with us," Claire explained.

"He only just arrived a short time ago. He certainly wasn't here half an hour ago," Lady Welles said.

"Well that explains that," Lady Sorrell said.

"Perhaps Beatrice wanted to be sure of Lord St. Vincent," Lady Welles offered.

"Perhaps. I have no idea what is going on anymore," Claire said.

"It's all right. We'll get everything straightened out. Don't you worry," Christianne said, giving Claire's arm another pat.

"Thank you. Thank you to all of you for being so good and understanding. I can't tell you..." Claire couldn't continue. Her throat felt thick and tight. She swallowed.

"It's all right, Lady Blakemore, we understand," Lady Welles said.

"Truly we do," Lady Sorrell echoed.

"But now I do believe you *should* return to your duties," Christianne said gently.

"Ugh! Yes," Claire said and headed off toward the balcony.

~*~

"I've truly been worried about you," Belle said, looking up at Edward. She was so beautiful. So sweet. After the way he'd treated her, he didn't deserve her.

"You needn't. I'm fine, and I apologize once more for my behavior," he said.

"It's all right. I just want you to be happy. Your friend Mr. Abelli seems to be a very kind man, and my goodness, it was fantastic listening to him sing," she said with a little giggle.

Very sweet! He smiled at her. "Yes, he is both a good friend and a talented baritone."

"Do you know the soprano who sang that evening?" Belle asked.

"No. She's a member of this English company. I know Giampiero from Venice where we sang together," Edward explained.

"Ah. Then you won't mind if I admit to you that I didn't like her very much?"

Edward burst out laughing. "No, I won't mind at all. I have to admit, I didn't like her either. Her voice—"

"Was too thin," Belle said, interrupting him.

He smiled. "Yes. She isn't a lyric soprano, and to be honest, I don't think she's trained very much."

"Yes, that must be it. That must be what I heard." She smiled up at him in the most beguiling way. Edward could feel himself being drawn to her. He wanted to kiss her, to hold her, to laugh with her.

"And what I heard was you were going for a promenade, not a walk on the balcony alone," Lady Blakemore said, interrupting them.

Edward looked up at the lady frowning fiercely at him.

"I... I beg your pardon, my lady. It was too warm inside," he said.

"And it is too alone outside," she retorted.

"Er, yes. Yes, I suppose it is," he agreed reluctantly.

Chapter Twenty-Five

~April 14~

The following morning, the girls were woken by their aunt glaring down at them in their bed.

"Aunt Claire!" Bee said, sitting up. She nudged her sister.

"What?" Bel whined.

"Aunt Claire is here, and I believe she would like a word," Bee said, not taking her eyes from their aunt.

"Indeed, I would," the lady said without cracking a smile or softening her voice in any way.

Bel sat up, suddenly awake. "Good morning, Aunt," she said, blinking.

"It is *not* a good morning, I'm sorry to say. And it's not going to be a good day, nor a good week."

"What's happened?" Bel asked.

"What has happened is that your little antics last night were noticed. They were noticed by at least three people and quite likely many more," their aunt said, putting her hands on her hips.

Bee swallowed hard. "Who saw?"

"What did they see?" Bel asked.

"They saw Miss Kendrick go outside into the

garden with Lord St. Vincent," she said, looking at Bee. "And then a little later, they saw her go outside onto the balcony with Lord Conway," she continued, turning to look at Bel. "They want to know what sort of game she is playing. Is she trying to play one gentleman off the other? Wanting to make them jealous to bring one of them up to scratch, or is she just the sort of girl who spreads her favors around to multiple gentlemen at a time?"

Both girls gasped.

"They wouldn't think—" Bee started.

"Oh, yes they would!" her aunt said, interrupting her.

Bel looked to Bee. "What are we to do?"

"What you are going to do is this—you, Beatrice, are not to leave this room. Ever. At all. For the rest of your time here, unless I know for certain that Isabel is in it. One of you will be in this room at all times. If I find you have both left this room at one time, you will *both* be returned to your parents and will *never* enter this house ever again. Do I make myself clear?"

"Yes, my lady," they said in unison.

"Good. Now, Isabel, get dressed and prepared for the day," she commanded.

Bel threw back the covers. "Are we going to pay morning calls?"

"No. We have been invited to a garden party and you are going. You will show society that you are a sweet and well-behaved girl and will go off with *no one*. You"—she pointed to Bee—"are staying here and will not be leaving the room."

Bee nodded. "I will be here all day."

~*~

A few hours later, Bel walked into Lady Hartfell's lovely garden with her aunt. There were a number of people standing around talking, enjoying cakes and tea.

"Good afternoon, Lady Blakemore, Miss Kendrick," the lady herself greeted them.

"Good afternoon, my lady. How wonderful this is, and such an incredible, warm day you've chosen to have your party," Bel said, giving her a curtsy.

"Yes, indeed," the woman beamed with happiness. "We are very lucky that the weather is good today. Only once in the past five years that I've been hosting this party have we had to move indoors."

"How wonderful," Lady Blakemore said, giving her a smile.

The lady nodded and moved on to greet some more guests. Bel did her best to stay by her aunt's side and be polite to everyone they met. She was determined to be a model young lady. She had nearly made it all the way through two hours of chatting, smiling, and being polite without a misstep and was feeling very proud of herself.

She'd been speaking with Lord Conway, giggling over a story he'd been telling her, when she noticed that her aunt had her back to her and was speaking with someone else.

"Oh, I do beg your pardon, my lord," she said, as he finished his tale, "but it looks like my aunt has moved. I promised her I would stay by her side all day."

"Oh? Is there some problem?" he asked with a worried raise of his eyebrows.

"It's just that she wasn't happy we'd gone out on to the balcony last evening," she admitted.

"Ah, yes. She did make that clear, didn't she? I do hope you didn't get in too much trouble?"

"Only a little bit. But I'm hoping that if I'm good all day today, her anger will abate enough that I won't be held on such a tight rein," she said, leaning toward him and speaking more confidentially. She felt as if her aunt had her on a leading string, and she was already chaffing at it.

He gave a little chuckle. "It's an admirable goal. I will do my best to help you achieve it by leaving you now."

"Thank you. You are very kind."

"Ah, Miss Kendrick!" Sir Reggie said, intercepting her the moment she took a step in her aunt's direction. "A word if you will."

"Yes, sir, of course," Bel said. She just could not be impolite, not even to this jolly man.

"I wanted to ask if you might be interested in a little evening of fun and mystery," he said more quietly.

Bel was immediately intrigued. She took a quick glance at her aunt. She was still nearby, if not within hearing range.

"This is not exactly something you would want to request permission for," he said even more quietly.

"Sir Reggie, I'm shocked," she said with a giggle.

"Indeed," he agreed with a wiggle of his eyebrows.

"What is it that you have in mind?" She knew she shouldn't ask. She was trying hard to be good, but this... This sounded positively delicious.

"A masquerade at Vauxhall," he whispered.

Bel gasped. "A masquerade?"

He nodded with a smile.

"At Vauxhall? I've heard about that place. It's a pleasure garden, isn't it?"

"It is. I could pick you up from your house at midnight Thursday. I would, however, strongly recommend you not mention it to anyone."

Bel's mouth nearly dropped open. "At midnight?"

"*That* is when it begins," he said with a sly smile.

She cast another quick glance toward her aunt, who was just beginning to turn around to look for her. "I'll see you then," she said quickly before moving toward her aunt. "Aunt Claire, I do apologize," Bel said in a normal voice. "I didn't see you move away."

"You need to pay more attention, Isabel," her aunt scolded her gently.

"Yes, my lady. I assure you, I will do so." And she did... For the rest of the day, she didn't leave her aunt's side. It was a difficult day.

~*~

Elizabeth was sitting quietly with a book in her drawing room when Edward was shown in by the footman. She stood, smiling broadly when his name was announced.

"Edward! What a wonderful surprise!" she said, coming forward.

He gave her a kiss on her cheek. "I hope I didn't catch you at an awkward time."

"No, not at all. Come in. Sit down. Can I offer you tea?"

"Something stronger?" he asked with a little

smile.

"It's eleven o'clock in the morning. How about some tea?" she asked with a laugh and rang for the maid.

Edward made small talk until their tea was served and then got straight to the matter as his sister handed him a cup. "I need your advice."

"Of course! Anything," she said, sitting back with her own tea.

"I'm certain you've noticed I've been paying marked attention to one particular young lady," he started. He needed to go no further because his sister's grin covered her face.

"I might have noticed," she said with a laugh.

"Yes, well, I took her to the opera last week," he started again.

Elizabeth's eyes widened. "You did?"

He nodded and then winced. "I didn't even make it through the first act before I had to walk out of the box. I couldn't..." He took in a deep breath. "The soprano looked so like her."

"Oh, Edward, I am sorry."

He shook his head. "It was terrible. Luckily, she sounded nothing like Angelica but just seeing her... I couldn't even watch." He took in another breath. "If I am to have a life with Belle, I should tell her, shouldn't I? I need to be honest. Completely honest."

"Belle? You mean Miss Kendrick?" Elizabeth clarified.

He nodded.

"Well, yes. You *will* need to tell her everything. Can you do that?" she asked.

He stared off into the distance, not really focusing on anything. Just thinking about it made all his muscles tense and his heart pound in his chest. "I don't know."

"As you say, though, if you want to spend the rest of your life with her then you need to tell her. You need to tell her *before* you propose."

Edward put down his teacup, having not even taken a sip. "But how?"

"What do you mean, how? Just say it. Tell her you lived in Venice."

"Tell her I lived with a woman and loved her so much it hurt?" he asked. Thoughts of Angelica, remembering how they'd lived, what they'd shared…all the pain at her passing, all the love he had for her. It all came back, all those feelings. His heart swelled with emotion—both the good and the bad.

"Tell her that you were in love and she died," Elizabeth said, interrupting his thoughts.

"Can I admit to Belle that I'm still madly in love with Angelica?" he asked.

"No! Are you?" his sister asked, tilting her head a little.

Edward had to think about it—and that in itself was shocking to him. A month ago, perhaps even two weeks ago, he wouldn't have had to think; it would have been obvious and immediate. Of course, he loved Angelica. He loved her with all his heart, all his soul.

But now? Did he still love her?

"I *do* still love her," he said slowly. "But now… Is it horrible that I believe my love for Belle is beginning to replace my love for Angelica? It *is* horrible, isn't it?"

"No! It's not and I don't think that love can be replaced. You'll always love Angelica. It's just that now you also love Miss Kendrick."

He looked at his little sister. She was so wise and clever. She knew these things. It was why he'd come to her.

"And because you love Miss Kendrick, you need to tell her about Angelica, then tell her that you love *her* and want to spend the rest of your life with her," Elizabeth said.

She was right. He knew she was right. He'd known it when he walked in, but he needed to hear it.

~April 15~

"What am I going to do with those girls?" Claire cried with frustration. Thank goodness, she wasn't actually crying, but all the women of the Wagering Whist Society could surely feel how annoyed she was.

"You need to keep your patience for just a little while longer," Lady Moreton said. She was sitting across from Claire at the card table where the cards had just been dealt for their first hand of whist.

"Until when?" Claire asked, rearranging the cards in her hand.

"Did you find out who she was supposed to be visiting in Oxford?" Lady Sorrell asked.

"Yes! I asked Bee yesterday," Claire said, lowering her cards. "It is a young lady named Cassia Benton. Do you know her?"

Lady Sorrell's eyes widened. "*Cassia*?"

"*Do* you know her?" Mrs. Aldridge asked, looking across at the woman.

"I know her very well. She's my sister!"

"What?" Lady Moreton said, turning toward her.

Lady Blakemore gasped. "I didn't even put the names together. Of course! Your father's name is Benton, isn't it? I'd completely forgotten."

"But that makes things so much easier!" Mrs. Aldridge said. Her excitement was somehow conveyed to her dog, Duchess, who'd been laying down next to her mistress's chair. The pup now sat up and gave a bark.

"It does, indeed!" Lady Sorrell agreed.

"What? What is it?" Christianne called from the other table, earning herself a frown from the Duchess of Kendell who was sitting across from her. The lady hated it when they spoke between tables. Claire completely agreed it was horribly impolite, but since it was just the eight of them there, she didn't think it was a terrible *faux pas.*

"The girl Beatrice is supposed to be staying with is Lady Sorrell's sister," Claire explained, raising her voice a little so Christianne and the other women at her table could hear.

The dog barked again in the excitement, clearly understanding that something momentous was happening.

"But that's wonderful! Lady Sorrell, can you write to your sister?" Christianne asked.

"Of course," Lady Sorrell said.

"But what is she going to say? How are we going to resolve this?" Lady Welles asked.

"It's very easy," Lady Sorrell explained. "I will go and visit my sister and return with Beatrice, bringing her quite publicly into London. I'm thinking I could even mention this is the reason I'm going for a visit."

"I don't know you should go that far," Lady Welles said. "But you could certainly mention you are going to see your sister for a couple of days."

"I don't want to be 'gone' for too long," Lady Sorrell commented.

"No. You could probably just disappear for two or three days," Lady Colburne said. "I don't know how long it actually takes to get to Oxford, but if the journey can be done in a day, you only need to have time to go and come back."

"It takes two days to get there," Lady Sorrell said with little enthusiasm.

"Perhaps she could meet you half way?" Lady Colburne offered.

"Yes, she could certainly do that. Or we could say that she is," Lady Sorrell said.

"You will need to actually write to your sister and tell her that you're doing this," Mrs. Aldridge put in.

"Oh, of course. I will," Lady Sorrell agreed.

"And I should write to *my* sister and tell her that Bee is coming to visit me," Claire added.

"I'm certain they both will be most surprised," the duchess agreed.

"I'm going to have to lie," Claire said unhappily. "I dislike that intensely."

"But it is *her* fault Beatrice came in the first place," Lady Welles said.

"Indeed. If your sister had kept a closer eye on her daughters, they wouldn't have felt the need for Beatrice to be here to look after Isobel," Christianne agreed.

"So, then, it's decided. I will 'go' this afternoon to fetch Beatrice from my sister and return…when?" Lady Sorrell asked everyone.

"Sunday when everyone is out riding in the park. You can drive by the park in an open carriage, if you have one, with Beatrice beside you," Lady Welles proposed.

"That's not too soon? It would actually take me two days to get there and two days back. Sunday is just four days away," Lady Sorrell pointed out.

"No one is going to question it so closely, I'm sure," Christianne pointed.

"They wouldn't dare," the duchess agreed.

"Lady Findlater might," Lady Welles commented more quietly.

"I don't believe Lady Findlater could do the math," the duchess said roundly.

There were horrified giggles, but no one contradicted her.

"I will take Bel riding with me and Lydia in the park on Sunday afternoon, so she is seen out and about," Lady Colburne said.

"Yes, that is an excellent idea," Mrs. Aldridge agreed. "Everyone will see the two of them are here."

Claire nodded. "All right. Lady Sorrell will bring Beatrice to London on Sunday, then this problem will be solved once and for all." She could breathe again.

CHAPTER TWENTY-SIX

~April 16~

Bel was unusually quiet all Thursday afternoon, Bee noticed. It was true that they hadn't seen a great deal of each other that day, but still, when Bee had seen her sister, she'd hardly said a word and had seemed preoccupied.

After dinner, Bel came up to their room and actually laid down on their bed. Bee came right over. "Are you unwell?" She put a hand on her sister's forehead.

Bel lifted it off with a laugh. "I'm perfectly fine, I assure you. No need to worry. I just want to take a little nap before the festivities of the evening, that's all."

"What festivities are those? Aunt Claire said we were going to have some quiet evenings for the rest of this week until it's time for me to 'arrive' in town with Lady Sorrell."

"Yes, I know," Bel said. She closed her eyes and settled in for a nap as if what she'd said had answered Bee's question. It most definitely hadn't, and she wanted an answer. There was a horrid chill running down her spine as if something were about to happen, and she didn't like it.

"Bel, what festivities are you talking about?

What are you planning?"

"Don't worry about it, Bee."

"Now I'm really nervous!" Bee sat down at the edge of the bed, shoving her sister toward the center. "What are you planning, Isobel?"

"Nothing you need to worry about. Didn't I just say so?"

"Yes, you did, which is why I'm worrying. Tell me. Now!"

Bel sighed heavily but sat up. "Sir Reggie asked if he could escort me to Vauxhall this evening, that's all."

"Vauxhall? The pleasure garden?"

"Yes. See? Nothing to worry about."

"You aren't thinking of going without Lady Blakemore, are you?"

"Of course, I am! That's the whole point! I need to go out and have some fun. If Lady Blakemore were to come, it wouldn't be fun at all. Sir Reggie is extremely amusing, and he knows how to enjoy himself. I want that! I've been tied to Aunt Claire's side for days now, and I just want to go out and—"

"Have fun," Bee finished for her. "In other words, get into trouble."

"I won't," Bel argued.

"What if someone sees you? You most definitely will get into trouble!"

"I will be masked," Bel explained not so patiently. "It's a masquerade!" She tried to hide her smile, but it peeped out anyway.

Bee thought about it. A masquerade was most definitely fun. It was also anonymous, so long as her sister kept her mask on. She would also be completely alone with a man, and Bee didn't like that part of it one bit. Not only that, but the man in question was Sir Reggie. If it were Lord Conway, it would be another matter entirely. Bee trusted him. She didn't trust Sir Reggie any farther than she could throw him—and then she remembered something.

"If what you want is a masquerade, isn't Lord Wickford hosting one soon?"

Bel's smile grew. "Yes! I can't wait. It's going to be magnificent. A Venetian Ball with everyone in those incredibly beautiful Venetian masks and fabulous gowns. Aunt Claire and I were discussing it yesterday with Lydia, Diana, and Margaret. They're all looking forward to it. Tina is helping everyone design their costumes, of course. Margaret said she was having the time of her life doing do so. Aunt Claire is going to ask her to design something for me as well."

Bee swallowed down her jealousy, then remembered this ball would be after she had officially been brought to town. "If she's going to design a gown for you, perhaps she'll design one for me as well. What do you think? Would that be too much to ask?"

"No, of course not! I'm sure she'd be delighted. Of course, Aunt Claire and I couldn't say as much in front of Margaret because she doesn't know you're here, but I'm certain you won't be forgotten." Bel put a consoling hand on Bee's arm. She did feel better.

"Well, then, with the Venetian Ball coming up, why do you need to attend this masquerade at Vauxhall?" Bee asked, getting back to the point.

Bel shrugged and smiled. "Because it's fun and

because Aunt Claire won't be there!" She laid back down. "Now let me rest."

"No! That is precisely why you *shouldn't* go. Bel, honestly, I forbid it."

Her sister cracked open one eye and then closed it again. "Uh-huh."

"That is not the right answer," Bee protested. "Tell me you won't go."

"Bee..." Bel paused. "All right. If I tell you I won't go, will you finally leave me alone?"

Bee thought about it for a second. "Yes."

"Then I'm telling you I won't go." Bel closed her eyes again.

Bee didn't believe her sister for a minute. In fact, she was certain Bel had just told her that she was, in fact, going, but right now there was nothing Bee could about. Well, she would wait, and if her sister tried to sneak out, Bee would stop her. She would physically restrain her if need be.

After keeping a close eye on her sister all night, Bee finally succumbed to the weight of her eyelids. They closed before she was even aware of it. As soon as she realized what had happened, she did her best to pry them open again, only to find they closed again immediately.

~*~

At the stroke of midnight, Bel closed the front door to her aunt's house with a quiet click. The street was empty but for a coach coming toward her. She walked forward, her heartbeat kicking up a notch, but the coach didn't even slow as it went past her.

She stepped back in disappointment. Silence greeted her as she looked up and down the street. There was no one about at this bewitching hour. A man turned the corner and came stumbling down the street, singing quietly to himself. Bel shrank back closer to house, but just then another coach approached. This time it slowed and pulled right up to her.

The door swung open, but the interior of the coach was completely dark.

"Sir Reggie?" Bel asked, approaching the door.

A man's giggle wafted out to her, and Bel couldn't help but giggle right back.

"Come, Miss Kendrick, don't dawdle now," his voice beckoned.

She hopped up, and within moments, the vehicle was back in motion, causing Bel to fall right into Sir Reggie's lap. His hands encircled her waist, and she found herself being shifted off to the seat.

His face appeared as if from nowhere.

"Sorry, I'm just pulling on my domino," he said with a laugh. "Yours is on the opposite seat along with our masks."

Bel reached across for the bright red piece of material. It took her a minute, but she finally discerned how to pull the garment over her head and dress.

The masks he had brought were wonderful confections. His was a brilliant blue material with matching feathers dangling from the lower part of the mask, hiding his face. Hers was black lace with bright red feathers bobbing gently above. The sight of the two of them in their masks—for Sir Reggie had been clever enough to bring a hand mirror so she could see—made Bel burst into full-fledged laughter. After that, her giggles hardly let up between Sir Reggie's absurd comments and her own nervousness.

She gasped with delight as he hailed the boat that would take them across the river to the pleasure gardens.

"My lady—for so will I address you from now on, so no one will know who you are," he said, handing her into the boat.

"Oh, sir, this is so much fun!" Bel said, giggling some more. She felt positively drunk on happiness already, and they hadn't even reached the gardens.

They disembarked at large wrought iron gates where Sir Reggie paid their admission.

The gardens themselves were absolutely magical. Twinkling lights were everywhere, and yet, the entire atmosphere was dark and mysterious. Black and red-clad waifs floated about, or so it seemed, although Bel knew they were just other guests like themselves.

They walked down a tree-lined path from the river, the sound of music pulling them forward. And then suddenly, the magnificence of Vauxhall opened up before them. There was a large open area for dancing. At the building on the other side of the clearing were boxes where people sat laughing, talking, eating, and drinking. An orchestra played from a balcony above, and the center was filled with people either dancing, sometimes stumbling, and giggling their way through the steps. But there was one thing everyone present had in common—they were all happy.

Bel was in heaven.

"What do you think?" he asked, standing next to her, taking it all in as well.

"It's magnificent!" She turned and threw her arms around him in her exuberance. "Thank you, oh, thank you, sir, for bringing me."

He laughed and hugged her back. "You are most welcome, and if this is the thanks I get, I will happily bring you here again and again."

Bel just laughed. "Can we dance? Or do we go for a promenade? Or what do we do? Tell me."

Sir Reggie just chuckled at her enthusiasm. "All of the above. Whatever you want to do."

"All right. Let's promenade first since the dance is already in progress, then when the next set begins, we'll dance. Does that sound all right?"

"Your wish is my command, my lady," he said, making a grand leg to her.

~*~

When Bee next pulled her eyes open, the candle by her bedside had been extinguished. Frantically, she felt the bed next to her.

Empty! Bel was gone.

"No!" Bee cried in an anguished whisper. She jumped out of bed and began to pace back and forth, trying to decide what to do.

She couldn't go to the pleasure gardens herself; she had no idea where they were or how to get there. She couldn't send Annie, who would be in the same predicament.

No, she needed someone who would know what to do, where to go, and how to find her sister. Her mind very briefly flitted past her aunt and uncle. There was absolutely no way she could involve them. This was precisely the sort of thing that would get both her and her sister thrown out of this house for good.

Oh, she just wanted to scream... or pummel her silly sister. How could Bel have done this to her? How could she be so irresponsible? Especially after

Bee had told her *not* to go. She had warned Bel that this was a bad idea. But no, she didn't listen. She *never* did. One of these days...but no. This would not be the day that Bel would pay for her stupidity. If she did, then Bee would as well, and she was not willing to throw away everything—

Lord St. Vincent.

Of course! He was the one who could save her sister.

Bee started toward her bedroom door but then stopped. *She* couldn't go and ask him to save Bel. He didn't know she existed. She made a sharp turn and headed into the dressing room.

"Annie," she whispered, shaking the maid. "Annie, I need you to get up."

"What? What is it, Miss?" her maid sat up with a start.

"Miss Bel is missing. I know exactly where she is, but I can't go and get her. I need you to go to Lord St. Vincent's home and ask him to rescue her. Please," Bee explained quickly.

Annie's mouth dropped open for a moment, but she was used to her mistress by now. Almost nothing fazed the girl. She was up and throwing on her dress in a moment, much to Bee's relief.

"Thank you, Annie. I honestly don't know what we would do without you."

"No, I don't think you would," she agreed with a little laugh. She pulled on her cloak and then turned to Bee. "All right, where is she?"

Bee explained everything to her and saw her on her way. All Bee could do now was wait, which would certainly be the hardest part of this entire evening.

~*~

Paul was enjoying a quiet evening. It was exactly the sort of night he loved most—sitting in his favorite chair, a good book in his lap, and a bottle of good port by his side. He'd considered spending it at Powell's, but it was too likely he would be called upon to actually speak with others if he were there, and he really wasn't in the mood to be social just now. No, a quiet evening at home, alone, was exactly what he—

"I beg your pardon, my lord," his footman said after a brief knock on the door.

Paul looked up at the man who dared to disturb him.

"There's a maid here who says she's in desperate need of your assistance. Something about Miss Kendrick."

Paul jumped to his feet, his book dropping to the floor. "Miss Kendrick? Is she all right?"

"I wouldn't know, my lord. Would you speak with her maid?"

"Yes, yes, of course! Send her in." Paul's heart began to race. If anything had happened to that sweet, gentle girl...

"I do beg your pardon, my lord," said a young woman in a mob cap and dark cloak after being shown into his library. She curtsied low.

"What is it? What's happened to Miss Kendrick?"

"She's gone off to Vauxhall with Sir Reginald, my lord. I-I'm terribly worried. I begged her not to go, but the moment I fell asleep, she must have slipped out of the house," the girl said, wringing her hands in front of her.

"Vauxhall? What the hell does Sir Reginald think he's playing at? That's no place for such a delicate, well-bred girl!" Paul nearly exploded.

"No, my lord. I tried to warn her..."

"She doesn't realize, I'm certain. No, how could she?" He headed toward the door. "Have no fear, I'll fetch her back safely."

"Oh, thank you, my lord, thank you," the girl nearly cried as he strode past her.

He didn't even wait for his horse or phaeton to be called up from the stables but strode right out to find himself a hack to take him to the river.

Forty minutes later, he was paying the entrance fee and practically running down the boulevard into the gardens.

Chapter Twenty-Seven

Bel was laughing hard at the ridiculous antics of two drunk men as they tried to take part in the dance. They had no partners, so one of the men was trying to take the lady's part, but he didn't exactly know the steps from the lady's side of things. Besides that, he was too drunk to particularly care whether he was doing it right. He and his friend were laughing and talking above the music even as they attempted to execute the moves.

The men finally gave up, leaving Bel and Sir Reggie without the other couple they needed for the quadrille.

Sir Reggie took Bel's hand and led her from the floor as well. "Perhaps now would be a good time for you to get me a drink. Would you mind very much, sir?" Bel asked sweetly.

"Of course," Sir Reggie said with a bow. "It would be my pleasure. You wait here, and I'll return momentarily."

She watched him go off and then wondered if maybe she shouldn't have gone with him. The two drunk men were standing nearby, eyeing her in the most disturbing way.

"Hah," one of the men said, coming closer. "Finally got rid of him. Well done, my sweet. Now we can finally have some real fun, eh?"

"Most defi-defi-definitely," his friend attempted to say, slurring his words together.

"He'll be right back," Bel said, moving away from the men. "Truly. You don't want to have fun with me. I'm no fun at all." Her heart began to pound so hard she could hear it above the music.

"It'll take him a while to get you that drink you so cleverly sent him off to find. Clever puss," the first man said, tapping her nose with his finger—at least, that's what he'd tried to do. He missed and tapped her cheek instead. He gave a laugh as if she'd sent Sir Reggie off just so she could be alone with these men.

"No, no," Bel protested. "You misunderstand."

"Oh, do we?" the second man asked, coming to her other side and leaning against the wall she had been standing against.

Bel looked between the men. She was trapped. There was a man on either side, and in front were the dancers hopping and skipping around with a carefree *joie de vivre*. Sir Reggie was nowhere in sight.

"Yes, truly, you do." Her last word ended up a screech as one of the men reached behind her and pinched her bottom. "Sir Reggie!" Bel called out, heedless of everyone around her. The second man only laughed as if her cry for help was amusing him. He reached toward her chest, but before his hand could touch her, a dark figure emerged from between the dancers and grabbed it, twisting his fingers cruelly.

~*~

Paul had looked around frantically at the crowd of dancers filling the space in front the pagoda. How was he going to find one girl, probably masked, amongst all these revelers?

He ran his hands through his hair, wanting to pull it from his scalp in frustration.

He wound his way through the dancers. He didn't dare call out her name for fear someone was here who would know her. That would be a sure way to ruin her reputation, if it wasn't ruined already.

He'd just about made it to the other side when he heard a screech, then a woman call out for Sir Reginald. He advanced toward a girl in a bright red domino and feathered mask. Two men surrounded the girl. They were laughing, but she most definitely was not. Even as Paul watched, one reached out and pinched her bottom, making her jump forward. The other took advantage of her move and started to reach toward the girl's bosom. He didn't make it before Paul grabbed hold of his fingers and twisted.

"You *don't* want to touch her," he growled, directing all his fury at the man and his companion, who clearly had the girl in the perfect position to take what they wanted. He hated men who did this, no matter who they were or who the hapless woman was between them. Two against one was wrong; two men against one woman infuriated him. Two drunken idiots against the woman he loved, and he was livid.

"Hey!" the first man protested even as the second one screamed in pain. "We saw her first. She's ours—" He didn't quite finish the last word because Paul's fist flew, sending the fellow backwards onto his ass.

Miss Kendrick screeched and pressed herself back against the wall of the pagoda.

Paul pulled the second man away and shoved him off as hard as he could.

"Hey, watch it, there!" Sir Reggie's voice cried. "Oh, now look what you did." He stood looking at the two glasses of wine that had been knocked from his hand and now lay on the ground.

"Just what the hell do you think you were doing bringing her here?" Paul asked, advancing on the twit.

"What? St. Vincent, what are you doing here?" Sir Reggie asked.

"I am saving her from these two ruffians who thought she was open game since you kindly left her alone," Paul ground out, just barely able to keep himself from sending Reggie flying as well.

"What?" Sir Reggie squeaked. He looked around and noticed for the first time the two men on the ground, obviously in pain, and Miss Kendrick, trembling against the wall.

"Oh, er, I, I didn't realize..." Sir Reggie began.

"You didn't *think*!" Paul finished for him.

"Er, no, I guess... I guess I didn't," Reggie said slowly.

"I am taking her home." He turned toward Miss Kendrick who ran to his outstretched arm. He pulled the trembling girl close.

"It's all right now," he said gently. "It's all right."

Strangely, despite the incredible kiss that they'd shared the other night, she didn't feel the same to him. She didn't feel as comfortable, as right. It must have been his anger, which still lingered.

~April 17~

Bel wouldn't even leave their room the following day. She was still upset about the previous evening. She'd cried in Bee's arms for nearly half an hour after Lord St. Vincent had left her with Annie, who'd been waiting outside for them to return. The maid had escorted the silent girl up to her room and then stood aside as she'd fallen against Bee's shoulder.

Of course, there was no way they could tell their aunt what had happened, so they simply told her that Bel was feeling under the weather. Bee would be taking her place for the day.

The woman didn't care, so long as both girls didn't leave the room at the same time. She did stop in to check on her and make sure Bel wasn't seriously ill, but other than that, she left the girl alone and went down to host her weekly at-home.

Lord St. Vincent was the very first guest to arrive. Bee greeted him with a big smile but did her best to temper it, knowing he thought her to be Bel, who had just gone through a horrific ordeal the previous night.

"Miss Kendrick, may I just say how happy I am to see you looking so well," he said, coming forward.

"Thank you, my lord. Thank you for *everything*," she said meaningfully.

He smiled and nodded his head in acknowledgement.

"Would you care to have a seat?" she asked, indicating the sofa at the farther end of the room. "And some tea?"

"Thank you." He took the seat she'd proposed and accepted the cup of tea, but it was the smile he gave her when she sat right next to him that truly warmed her heart.

"I am so glad to see you suffer no ill effects from your adventures of last night," he said softly enough so only she could hear him. Still, she had to lean closer to make out his words.

"I have to admit I slept a great deal later this morning than I normally do," Bee said, knowing she had to make something up or else he would realize that she, herself, hadn't been the girl he'd rescued.

"But you are clearly made of sterner stuff than I realized. I was sure I would be hearing from your aunt that you were indisposed." He gave her a warm smile. "I can't tell you how glad I am to see that you aren't."

Bee felt a heavy twinge of guilt at lying to this man who had been so wonderful. She ducked her head down under the pretense of taking a sip of her tea.

"Please, if we could not speak of it, I would greatly appreciate it. It-it's painful," she whispered, keeping her eyes lowered.

He drew his eyebrows down for a moment. "Of course. How thoughtless of me. Tell me how your study of ancient Greece goes."

She looked up and gave him a grateful smile.

~*~

Edward had been hoping to arrive just as Lady Blakemore opened her home to visitors, so he could get Belle alone to speak with her. His plans were ruined by the fact that he wanted to do this the correct way—speak first with her uncle, get his permission to address her, and then go and speak with the girl herself.

He arrived early at Lord Blakemore's home only to find the gentleman himself had gone out. Edward followed the footman's suggestion and went to Powell's to find the man.

"Is Lord Blakemore here?" he asked the footman at the door.

"I believe he's in the reading room, my lord."

Edward nodded and head in that direction.

"Ah, Conway, haven't seen you in some time," Lord Wickford said, meeting him just inside the door.

"I've been a bit busy," Edward said, trying to discreetly look over his friend's shoulder.

"Not too busy that you might think of missing my ball next week?"

"What? Ball? Oh, the Venetian thing? No, no, of course not. It's already the talk of the town. The next big event," Edward said, giving Wickford a smile.

"Well, that's the hope anyway. I see you're eager to find someone. Perhaps I can help," he said, turning to survey the room.

"I do beg your pardon, Wickford. It's just... I'm here to speak with Lord Blakemore about his niece," Edward admitted.

"Oh ho! Are congratulations in order, then?" Wickford gave a laugh.

Edward responded with a nervous smile and a chuckle. "I don't know yet. First, I have to speak with the gentleman and then the young lady herself. I'll let you know."

Wickford laughed and gave him a clap on the back. "Well, then, you'll want to explore in that far corner over there. That's where the gentleman can usually be found."

"Thank you!"

Edward headed off in the direction Wickford had indicated and indeed found the gentleman hiding behind a newspaper. "Excuse me, my lord," he said. "Might I have a word?"

"Eh?" Lord Blakemore appeared from behind his paper. "Oh, Conway. Of course, of course. Have a seat. Would you like a drink?"

"No, thank you, sir. I think I want to be as sharp as possible for this," Edward said with a little laugh.

"Ah... Have a question you'd like to ask me, son?"

"Yes, sir, that's it precisely," Edward said, grateful the man understood immediately.

"Yes, yes. Well then, I'm not the person you should be speaking with, you know."

Edward sat back, a little surprised. "Do I need to write to her father?"

"What? No, no. You need to speak with *her*. Yes, yes, that would be best. Off you go, then."

"But..." Edward started to argue.

"No, no. There's no sense in speaking with me." The man shook his head and then quickly ducked back down behind his paper, clearly dismissing him.

Edward didn't quite know what to do. What did he mean he had to speak with her first? It was always proper to speak with her guardian before asking the girl. How odd.

Edward frowned, but it was useless glaring at the man's newspaper. He had no choice but to head back to the Blakemore's home.

When he got there, however, there were already a number of people in attendance. Edward stood just inside the door for a good minute trying to locate Belle. Finally, he found her.

She was sitting on a sofa with St. Vincent. In fact, she was sitting very close to the man. In fact, she was sitting with her head so close to his, they were practically touching.

Edward's heart froze.

She giggled at something St. Vincent said. Oh, yes, the man was looking quite pleased with himself, very pleased—as well he should, making the girl Edward loved giggle and flirt. His stomach tightened.

"My lord," Lady Blakemore approached him. She paused, turning to see what he was looking at. She frowned, as well she should.

"If you will excuse me, my lady. I believe I came at a bad time." He turned on his heel and left, unable to even look in Belle's direction for a moment longer. He could hear Lady Blakemore sighing as he walked out the door.

Chapter Twenty-Eight

For once, Paul truly felt as if he was in the right place with the right person. Sadly, politeness dictated he leave the beautiful, funny, and intelligent Miss Kendrick. He didn't want to. He could have gone on chatting and laughing with her probably for hours, but there were other guests she needed to speak with, and her aunt was glaring at her from where she stood by the door.

"I believe your aunt is trying to get your attention," Paul said reluctantly. Miss Kendrick had her back to the lady, but he couldn't allow her to ignore the look her aunt was giving her. If he did, Miss Kendrick would probably get into trouble later.

"Oh! Goodness, she's not looking very happy, is she?" Miss Kendrick said after turning around to take a glance at her aunt.

"No, which is why I said something."

She smiled at him so warmly, he could feel the heat of it straight through to his soul. "I am truly sorry, my lord, I believe I need to attend to our other guests."

"Yes. It is wrong of me to monopolize you in this way. I'll be off then. I am very glad you're not feeling any worse for last night's adventure."

"It was so kind of you to check up on me, and thank you once again for coming out to—"

He held up his hand. "It was my pleasure. Any time you need me, you know I will be there."

She nodded, blinking a few times. Goodness, what emotional creatures women were. He bowed to her and walked out into the beautiful sunshine of the spring day.

Looking around, he debated whether he wanted to simply go for a ride in the park... But no, it would probably be crowded with members of the *ton* seeing who was out with whom. What he wanted, he decided, was a little exercise. He headed off to the Gentleman Jackson's Boxing Saloon. He was sure he would find someone to spar with, perhaps even Gentleman Jackson himself.

Strangely, he found Conway at one of the bags, hitting it for all it was worth.

"Conway," Paul nodded to him as he began to strip down to his shirt.

The man stopped what he was doing for a moment, looked at him, and then went at the bag again with even more gusto. Just as Paul had pulled on a pair of gloves, Conway walked up and tapped him on the shoulder.

"Care to have a go?" he asked, pointing to the empty ring.

"My pleasure. You're not exactly in my weight class, so I'll go easy on you," he said, meaning it to be a joke. They actually probably weighed about the same, but Paul was much taller while Conway was broader.

"What do you say we make it a wager, then?"

Paul stopped on his way into the ring and

turned his shoulder so he could look at Conway.

"First man to his knees goes to concede to Miss Kendrick, telling her she should marry the other."

Paul turned all the way around. "You want to fight for the privilege of marrying Miss Kendrick?"

"Yes. I saw you there today at Lady Blakemore's. You were sitting with Belle on the sofa, your heads so close they were almost touching, but she is *mine*. While you were sitting there giggling with her, I went to her uncle and asked for his permission to address her," Conway informed him.

Paul anger spiked. "But you haven't asked her yet."

"No, because *you* were there turning her head."

He contemplated telling Conway about the kiss he'd shared with the girl. He thought about telling him how he'd saved her life the night before. But saying all this would not reflect well on either him or Miss Kendrick, and he would never impugn her reputation in any way.

But did he want to fight Conway for her hand?

Yes. Yes, he did. The answer came to him without a moment's hesitation. "All right," Paul said. "We fight for Miss Kendrick. The loser bows out of the race for her hand and tells her the winner is the right man for her." He proceeded into the ring.

He was about to stretch and warm himself up a little when Conway took his first shot, hitting him just below the ribs on his side.

"All right, if that's the way you want to play it," he growled and shot back, getting the man in his shoulder. He would have to aim lower. Sometimes it was almost a disadvantage being tall.

~*~

Edward was not going to let this giant get the best of him. He knew himself to be stronger, and he'd been practicing a great deal recently with Giampiero. He had never seen St. Vincent here. The man probably had no technique, no skill. All he had was his height and his brute strength, but Edward had knowledge and speed on his side, in addition to his weight and muscle. He would put the man down easily.

They sparred pretty evenly for five minutes or so, but that vision of him with his head so close to Belle's infuriated him. The man had *no* right to impinge on his girl. It had taken Edward sometime to realize just how important she was to him, and he wasn't about to give her up now.

"You're not so bad at this," St. Vincent said with a little laugh. He sounded slightly winded.

Edward smiled. "I've been practicing. Sparring with a good friend of mine," he admitted.

St. Vincent nodded and shot his fist out, which Edward easily blocked.

"But I have a great deal of incentive," St. Vincent said.

"Oh, really? I don't see how. You haven't spent nearly as much time with Belle as I have. You don't share a passion for music as we do," Edward admitted, landing another shot to St. Vincent's abdomen.

"No, but we have an intellectual connection that you wouldn't understand," the man said, getting in another shot to Edward's shoulder.

"I wouldn't understand? Did you just call me stupid?" he asked, throwing a jab that was effectively blocked.

"I wouldn't call you stupid, no, but Bel has a quickness of mind. She's a very clever girl," he said, dancing to the side to avoid another hit from Edward.

"She is clever, I will grant you that, but even more so, she has passion, beauty, and talent. I admire all of that in her."

"Traits that will not last you a lifetime with her. What *we* share will endure for years to come," St. Vincent said, landing a blow to Edward's stomach.

"What do you know of marriage? What do you know of lasting love? I know..." Edward said, feeling his heart swell with emotion even as he swung out again at St. Vincent. "I know of love and devotion. I have loved and lost, and now that I have risked my heart again, you speak of an *intellectual* connection? Well, I'll tell you that is nothing. It will not drive her into your arms and keep her happy for the rest of her days. I can and *will* make her happy. I will make her laugh and dance. Our love will *sing*." In his passion and his anger at this man, who dared to try to take away his love, he extended himself, putting the whole length of his arm and body into his next punch. It landed a strong blow right to St. Vincent's chin.

The other man's head was thrown violently to the side, and he was knocked off his feet.

Edward stood over him, horrified at what he'd just done. He'd hit the man in the face. One didn't do that. It was one of the unspoken rules—a gentleman didn't mark another man's face—along with Jackson's spoken rules of not holding a fellow by his hair to keep him in place and only using your fists. St. Vincent would, without a doubt, be sporting quite a bruise the following day.

St. Vincent held up his gloved hands, panting and a little out of breath. "You won," he conceded, rubbing his jaw with his gloved hand.

"No, that wasn't gentlemanly. Come, let's have another go—"

"No." St. Vincent got to his feet and pulled off his gloves. "No, you knocked me down. I shall… I shall go and have a word with Miss Kendrick." His voice was quieter, and he was clearly upset by the turn of events, but he stayed true to his word. The man was most definitely a gentleman while Edward just stood there feeling like a cad.

After they'd dressed, St. Vincent pulled out his watch and consulted it. "I'm certain all the guests have left Lady Blakemore's. What say you, we go now?"

Edward gave a nod of assent and they headed out together.

~*~

Bee and her aunt had finally said goodbye to the last of their callers, and sat down to enjoy a little quiet, when the footman came into the drawing room once again.

"I beg your pardon, my lady, but Lord St. Vincent and Lord Conway are here and requesting a moment of Miss Kendrick's time."

"Again? But they were both here earlier," Aunt Claire said.

"Lord Conway was here? I didn't see him," Bee said, turning to her aunt.

Lady Blakemore frowned at her. "That's because you and Lord St. Vincent had your heads together and were giggling away. The man took one look at the two of you, turned around, and left."

"Oh dear!"

"You may show them in, Thomas," Aunt Claire told the footman.

Bee was shocked when the two men came in, both looking sheepish. Lord St. Vincent's chin was beginning to look decidedly bruised. She stopped mid-curtsy. "Have you two been fighting?"

They looked at each other and then back at her.

"Miss Kendrick, I wish to say—" Lord St. Vincent started.

"No, you don't. *I* am here to tell you that you have found a very good man in St. Vincent," Lord Conway said, interrupting him.

"But that wasn't... No, Conway here is the one for you." Lord St. Vincent started again.

"Wait! Wait a moment, both of you," Bee said, holding up her hands to stop this ridiculousness. Her heart began to beat a little faster in her chest. "You two *fought* over who would get to propose to me?" she asked, making sure that she understood the truth of the matter.

The two men were silent. Conway found the floor to be very interesting, and St. Vincent couldn't quite meet her gaze with his own.

Bee looked at her aunt, who just gave her a nod. She knew what Bee was thinking, and she agreed.

"If you would please excuse me for a moment," she said and ran out the door.

Never in her life had she run up the stairs. Never had her heart beat so in her ears. She could hear it pounding, driving her forward—who cared about propriety when there were men *fighting* over her and her sister!

Thank goodness Bel was awake and dressed. She was sitting by the window, staring out into the garden, when Bee ran into the room.

"Come," Bee said, grabbing her hand.

"What? Why? What's happening?" Bel asked as Bee started to drag her from the room. "Wait, Bee, we can't…"

"Yes, we can. We have permission, and Lords Conway and St. Vincent have been fighting—*fighting!*—over who got to propose to us because they think we are one person," Bee explained.

"Oh no! Are they hurt?" Bel asked, no longer needing to be dragged, but leading the way down stairs.

"Lord St. Vincent has a horrible bruise on his chin, but other than that—" Bee stopped talking because they'd reached the drawing room. They both paused, looked at each other, and took in a deep breath before opening the door and going in.

The two men had sat down next to each other on the sofa, but both rose as one when the girls walked in.

One of them gasped as they took in the two girls.

"My lords, I believe there is something my nieces wish to tell you," Aunt Claire said from where she was sitting across from the men.

"But…" Lord Conway began looking from one girl to the other. "There are *two* of you?"

Chapter Twenty-Nine

"Twins?" Lord St. Vincent asked.

The girls nodded. Bee took in a deep breath to try to still her heart.

"How long...? Why...?" Lord Conway stopped to gather his thoughts. "Why did you not tell anyone that there were two of you? Why the ruse?"

"Only one of us is supposed to be here," Bee explained.

"It's actually supposed to be *my* season," Bel said, "but Bee came to keep an eye on me."

"Was that *you* last night?" Lord St. Vincent asked.

Bel nodded.

"I sent the maid to fetch you after I woke up and found her gone," Bee said.

"What happened?" Lord Conway asked, turning from Lord St. Vincent to Bee and then to Bel.

"Miss..." he paused.

"Bel," Bee supplied. "I'm actually the elder, but you can call me Bee. It's short for Beatrice."

Lord St. Vincent nodded and smiled at her. "Paul. My given name is Paul."

A rush of warmth flowed through her at the knowledge.

He cleared his throat and continued his explanation. "Miss Bel had a little unintended adventure last night when Sir Reggie took her to the Vauxhall masquerade—"

"What?" Aunt Claire interrupted him with the most unladylike shout Bee had ever heard come from their aunt.

"I..." Bel began, her cheeks turning bright pink.

"Didn't listen to me," Bee added, giving her sister a frown.

Bel wisely kept her eyes lowered and her mouth shut.

"I tried to stay awake to keep an eye on her but fell asleep," Bee told her aunt. "When I woke up, she was gone."

"I am beginning to understand the concerns you voiced to me," Aunt Claire told Bee. "But I am not happy, as you can well imagine."

"*You* sent your maid, I suppose?" Paul asked. At Bee's nod, he continued, "I went and extricated...Miss Bel from the situation and saw her home safely."

"I am quite appalled that you didn't come to see me when you discovered come to me when you discovered your sister missing," Aunt Claire said. "But I thank you, my lord, for handling the situation so discreetly."

He gave her a nod, but he was clearly still thinking about something. "That's why you felt different to me," he said. "Because you *were* different. You aren't the one I was with the other night at the duchess's ball."

Bel smiled. "Yes. That was Bee who you were with."

"The girls switched places a couple of times throughout the evening," Lady Blakemore said, frowning at the two girls.

"Only once…well, twice," Bel said. "I went to the dinner before the ball, then Bee attended the first part of the ball, and I attended the second."

"So, who was I with on the balcony?" Lord Conway asked.

"That was me," Bel said, turning a pretty pink.

"And you've been doing this regularly? Both of you attending a party and then switching places?" Paul asked.

"Oh no," Bee said. "Usually only one of us went to a party, but the duchess's ball was a special event, and she invited both of us."

"She actually made a second, identical dress to one I already owned just so that we could both attend," Bel explained.

"She did? She *knows*?" Lady Blakemore asked.

"Yes. She figured it out early on when she measured me for a dress and then Bel went for the fitting. We're slightly different sizes," Bee explained.

"Well, this certainly explains a great deal," Paul said, turning to Lord Conway. "It looks as if I owe you an apology."

"What? No, no! It is I who owe *you* an apology!" Lord Conway said, looking slightly embarrassed.

"I think we should just call it all even since it was a misunderstanding all around," Bel said with a little giggle as she looked from one man to the other.

"But it was entirely our fault, and for that, we

most sincerely apologize," Bee added.

"Yes, absolutely," Bel agreed, becoming serious again.

"Gentlemen, I don't think it needs to be said, but this is not information that can be shared...with anyone," Lady Blakemore said. "We are going to make a show of Bee coming into town a few days hence, but until then, no one can know she's here nor that she has *been* here. I do hope you both understand that."

Both gentlemen nodded.

"Of course," Lord Conway said immediately.

"I completely understand," Paul said. He looked at Conway for a moment and then turned back to Lady Blakemore. "Perhaps... My lady, would you mind if I took Bee for a stroll in your garden?"

Bee's breath caught in her throat.

"I wouldn't mind at all, my lord," the lady said, giving Bee a smile.

Out of the corner of her eye, Bee saw Bel give Lord Conway a hopeful look. She didn't have time to see how he reacted or what he did as Paul offered Bee his arm, and they left the room to seek the garden.

~*~

They walked in silence for a bit, strolling along slowly. Finally, Paul said, "I knew there had to be something unusual going on."

Bee looked up at him, waiting for him to continue.

"Sometimes you were sweet and intelligent, sometimes you were amusing and giggly," he said. "Please don't misunderstand me, your sister is... I like her, but…"

"She's not me," Bee offered when he seemed to be floundering for words.

"No. She is most definitely not you. I get the feeling that you are two very different people."

Bee had to laugh at that. "Yes, indeed we are. She hates history, for example," she said with a sly smile up at him.

He burst out laughing. "Yes! But you are the one reading the history of Greece, are you not?"

She giggled. "Yes, I am. I love history. Poor Bel. I've dragged her to all the ruins in Lincolnshire again and again, as well as to the cathedral, lecturing her all the while. It's not surprising she hates it so."

He laughed and shook his head. He then paused his steps and turned to look at her. Taking her hands in his, he said, "Beatrice, I believe we are very much alike. You are an intelligent young woman with a good, clear head on your shoulders. I can see us having a very contented life together. Would you do me the honor of marrying me?"

When he began, when he took her hands and looked her in the eye, Bee's heart had sped up. It had become a little hard to breathe, but then as he spoke, her heart slowed again, and it felt as if a rock was slowly forming in the pit of her stomach. "A clear head? A contented life?" she repeated.

He nodded, smiling at her.

She looked up into his eyes, searching for some emotion. She thought she saw some, but she couldn't be sure. Oh, perhaps she was being silly. Perhaps she was expecting too much of him, but where was the talk of love? Where was any display of affection? Yes, they'd kissed that one time in the garden at Tina's, and she'd reveled in his unrestrained show of emotion, but where was that now? He was proposing marriage to her, and he couldn't bring forth *any* emotion?

She swallowed. Perhaps he didn't feel it. Perhaps he had no love for her and just wanted a convenient wife with whom he could get along. Could she live with that?

Strangely enough, for all her practicality and intelligence, she didn't think she could. No, when it came to marriage, there needed to be more than mutual respect. There needed to be love, and Bee just didn't know if Paul felt any for her.

She shook her head, feeling her throat tighten. "I'm sorry, my lord, but I'm not certain we *would* suit. Thank you for asking, however." She turned and left him standing in the garden, taking deep breaths as she went. She was not going to embarrass herself in front of him.

~*~

Bel and Aunt Claire were still sitting in the drawing room when Bee came back inside. Bel seemed to be dabbing at her eyes with a handkerchief. Bee ran to her. "Bel, what's happened? Why are you crying?"

"Lord Conway left," Aunt Claire explained.

"What do you mean?" Bee asked, turning to her aunt.

"He left right after you and Lord St. Vincent went into the garden. He made some excuse and just left without saying another word," Bel said, before dissolving into tears again.

Bee grabbed her sister and pulled her close. "Oh, Bel, I'm so sorry."

Bel sniffed and pulled away. "Well, I suppose it's a good thing one of us will be getting married after all this. Congratulations." She couldn't have said it in a sadder tone of voice, but Bee didn't begrudge her that at all, especially since no congratulations were in order.

Blinking back her own tears, she shook her head. "He proposed, but I turned him down."

"What?" Bel grabbed Bee's arm.

"I expect you had a very good reason for doing that," Aunt Claire said sternly.

Bee shrugged. "He said he thought we would get along tolerably well, and he admired my intelligence. I'm afraid I want to marry someone who *loves* me, not someone willing to *settle* for me because we'd get along."

"I can't believe..." Bel started. She stopped and shook her head. "But he *does* love you. I'm sure of it!"

"Maybe he does and just doesn't realize it yet," their aunt suggested.

"Well, if that's the case, then when he figures it out, I hope I'm still available because I am not going to settle for anything less," she said with a great deal more conviction than she actually had.

"And so you shouldn't!" Bel said vehemently.

"And I'm certain that once Lord Conway digests what he's learned today, he'll be back to propose. Just you wait and see," Bee said encouragingly to her sister.

"I hope you're right!" Bel said with feeling.

~*~

"Ladies, we have a problem," Claire said upon entering Christianne's home that evening after dinner.

The women of the Ladies' Wagering Whist

Society had gathered to plan their annual whist party to raise money for the poor of the Rookeries. The previous year, they'd taken time from their regular meeting to plan the party, but this year it was requested the planning be done separately so as not to interfere with their game.

Most of the women had gathered by the time Claire had come in. It seemed as if only the Duchess of Kendell and Lady Welles were missing.

"What is it?" Christianne asked.

"Lord St. Vincent has botched it."

"Oh dear, what did he do?" Lady Sorrell asked.

Claire told them the whole story of the fight, which led to the girls divulging their secret to the two men. "Lord St. Vincent then asked Bee to go for a walk with him in the garden."

"How wonderful!" Lady Colburne said.

"Yes. Lord Conway, sadly, did not have the presence of mind to do the same with Bel, but that's another issue, I believe," Claire said.

"He didn't? He didn't propose?" Lady Moreton asked.

"No. He simply left, sending Bel into a fit of tears," Claire explained.

"Well, that's completely understandable!" Mrs. Aldridge said, nodding her head.

"But Lord St. Vincent was able to turn right around and propose to Bee?" Lady Sorrell asked. "I have always believed him to be a highly intelligent man."

"Yes, he did propose, but he did such a ham-handed job of it that she said no," Claire said.

Lady Colburne and a couple other ladies gasped. "Oh, no! What did he say?" Lady Colburne asked.

"He told Bee that he admired her intellect and thought they would get along tolerably well," Claire said with a frown.

"Oh dear," Mrs. Aldridge said just as Lady Welles and the duchess both walked into the room.

"What's 'oh dear'?" Lady Welles asked.

The whole thing had to be explained once again, but by the time Claire was finished, Christianne had pulled forward a piece of paper and was dipping her pen into the pot of ink sitting in front of her.

"I am writing to him immediately," she said.

"To what end?" Claire asked.

Her friend paused, pen hovering above the paper. "To insist that he come here, this evening. We'll straighten him out," she said. She then looked down at her paper and said, "Ugh, it now has ink drips on it. Oh well, it can't be helped."

She finished writing her note and then rolled her ink blotter over it before folding it up.

"Do you think he'll come? We don't know him very well," Lady Moreton said.

"You may not, but he certainly knows some of us," Lady Sorrell said.

"And he won't disregard a direct request," Christianne said, getting up to ring for her footman.

"And just what are we going to say to him?" Claire asked.

"We are going to tell him the truth—that he made a mistake which he needs to correct," Christianne stated. She turned to hand the letter to the footman and give him directions.

"I hope Bee isn't too upset with us for getting involved," Lady Welles said, looking amongst the ladies.

"It is for her own good," the duchess said with a shrug.

~*~

Paul couldn't stand his own company after the fiasco that had been that day. And he couldn't share it with Elizabeth. Lady Blakemore had made it clear the fact that Bel had a twin sister with her was information they didn't want to get out.

He shook his head in disbelief at the fact that they had shared this secret with him and Conway at all. On the other hand, the two men hadn't exactly given them much choice. It was very odd, but never in his life had he fought over a girl, nor ever believed that he would do so. It was absolutely unlike him.

No, this day needed a good deal of digesting, and a good deal of alcohol to assist with the process. He headed out to Powell's immediately following dinner.

"Colburne, Warwick, I'm surprised to see you both here," he said, after discovering his two closest friends in the reading room of the club. They were sitting in the corner, holding a quiet conversation when Paul joined them.

"Ha! Saint, what are you doing here?" Warwick said, looking up at him.

"Not out wooing Miss Kendrick at some gathering this evening?" Colburne asked with a broad smile.

"No," Paul said with a sigh and sat down to join them. "It is because of her that I am here and in desperate need of a drink."

"Uh-oh. Is all not well in that quarter?" Warwick asked, drawing his eyebrows down and looking concerned.

Paul shook his head. "Give me a few drinks and I'll tell you about it." Although not everything, he reminded himself. Hmmm... He would have to keep at least some of his wits about him to ensure he didn't spill the girl's secret by accident. The thought did not make him happy.

The men sat in silence for a moment while Paul downed his first glass of excellent rum, and he appreciated it a great deal—both the silence and the drink. Finally, he said, "Proposed today. She turned me down."

"What?" Colburne sat forward.

"I can't believe she said no. It wouldn't be because of Conway, would it?" Warwick asked.

"Did I just hear my name?" Conway asked, strolling up to join them.

"Oh, er, evening Conway," Warwick said a little awkwardly.

"Good evening. May I join you?" Conway asked.

"Yes, of course," Paul said, indicating he take the last chair in the circle. He turned back to Warwick, "And no, it has nothing to do with him." He turned to Conway and said, "I was just telling Warwick and Colburne that I proposed to Miss Kendrick this afternoon, but for some reason that I honestly cannot fathom, she turned me down."

Conway started. "What? I can't believe it. Did she say why?"

"She said that she didn't think we would suit," Paul said, shaking his head. "I just don't understand it."

"Neither do I," Conway agreed. "I was certain..."

"As was I!"

"Perhaps it's how you phrased your proposal?" Warwick asked. "I learned the hard way that it's all in phrasing."

Paul was about to tell them what he'd said when a footman walked up, holding forward a salver. "I beg your pardon, Lord St. Vincent, this has just arrived for you." He offered the tray, with a note on it.

He took it and read it quickly, but it confused him.

"Is everything all right?" Colburne asked.

"I am being asked to join the ladies of the Wagering Whist Society. Immediately," he added, "at Lady Ayres' home."

Warwick and Colburne shared a look. "You'd better get going, then," Colburne said.

Paul looked at him curiously. "What do you know of this? What does it mean?"

"It means that the ladies have become involved. Whatever it was you said to Miss Kendrick this afternoon has been shared—probably by the lady to her aunt and her aunt to the rest of the whist society," Warwick explained.

"And if the ladies of the Whist Society are involved, I'm certain we'll be wishing you happy before too long," Colburne said with a laugh.

Warwick began to chuckle as well. "Oh, yes, no doubt."

"Better get a move on, Saint. You don't want to keep the ladies waiting."

Chapter Thirty

"Normally, Lord St. Vincent, you tell a girl's chaperone or father that you think you would suit," Lady Ayres said as soon as Paul walked into her drawing room.

"Good evening, ladies," he bowed. It looked rather like he was on trial with the eight women facing him. He felt distinctly nervous.

The younger women stood and curtsied; most of the elder ladies simply nodded to acknowledge his bow.

"I don't believe I know everyone. Lady Blakemore, would you be so kind?" he asked, turning a smile onto that lady.

"Of course. You know Lady Ayres, of course, and Lady Sorrell." She then went around the room, indicating each lady and saying their name. He knew almost everyone, although Mrs. Aldridge was new to him, and he'd never officially been introduced to the duchess before.

He bowed to them all once again and then turned to Lady Ayres. "As to your statement when I walked in, my lady, I would have spoken with Lord Blakemore, but I must admit I took advantage of an opportunity presented to me. I had the full intention of speaking with him after I had received

Miss Kendrick's acceptance of my proposal."

"What Lady Ayres was implying, my lord," Lady Welles said with a little smile, "is that you don't tell the *girl* that you think you would suit. That is something you tell her father."

He looked at her blankly for a moment. "Why not say so to the lady directly?"

"Young ladies need a more compelling reason than that to accept a gentleman's proposal," Lady Colburne said.

"What more could she want?" he asked, beginning to feel a little stupid.

"Love," Lady Moreton said quietly.

"Love?" Paul scoffed. "Love is a fantasy made up by novelists and poets to sell books, my lady, nothing more."

Gasps were heard all around the room, but Lady Ayres just burst out laughing. "And who told you that faradiddle?" she asked.

Paul straightened his spine. Of course, they didn't believe him. They were probably all avid readers of such nonsense. "My father told me, and my parents demonstrated it to me every day of my childhood," he told them straight out.

"Well, I am very sorry you had to suffer so, but I can assure you that love is very real," Lady Ayres said.

"You may believe so, my lady, because you were just married but—"

"I believe so because it is the truth. This is not my first marriage, my lord, but Lord Ayres is most definitely my first love. I was married for too many years to Lord Norman, and I most definitely did not love him," she explained.

"I also believe in love. I was married to the man I loved for nearly thirty years," Mrs. Aldridge said.

"I loved my husband most sincerely," the duchess said, "and he loved me."

"You see, my lord. Most of us in this room..." Lady Moreton paused and looked around. "No, I believe everyone in this room has been or is currently in love."

"Or since you love history so much," Lady Blakemore said, "think of Eleanor of Aquitaine."

"Or Paris and Helena," Lady Sorrell added.

"Or Romeo and Juliet," Lady Welles put in.

"They are fictional," Lady Moreton said, "but what about William Wallace and... what was her name?"

"Marion Braidfute," the duchess answered.

"Yes, thank you," Lady Moreton gave her a smile.

"And all the stories in both Greek and Roman mythology. Yes, they're fictional, but the ideas had to come from somewhere," Lady Welles said.

A number of the ladies nodded their agreement. Paul just frowned.

"You may scoff all you like at a bunch of women, Lord St. Vincent, but I dare you to go and speak with my husband about it," Lady Colburne said. "Andrew told me you went to school together. Surely you would believe him if he were to tell you that *he* was in love?"

"I just left him with Warwick and Conway at Powell's," Paul said, beginning to waver ever so slightly in his conviction.

"Then return there and confer with those men. I don't know about Conway, but I do know for certain that Lord Colburne and Warwick are both very much in love with their wives," the duchess said.

"And once you realize that love most definitely *does* exist," Lady Sorrell said, "then examine your own heart. If you still feel that you and Bee would merely suit, find someone else with whom you can comfortably live for the rest of your life."

"But if you discover that you are truly in love with her," Lady Welles continued, "then go back and tell her so."

"And then you'll see what she says to your proposal," Mrs. Aldridge finished.

Paul was dumbfounded—and dismissed. The ladies all said their goodbyes and then turned back to whatever it was they were working on.

Paul walked out of the house in a bit of a daze. He was strangely confused by what had just happened and decided that going back to Powell's for a drink would indeed be the best thing he could do right now. And if he happened to ask his friends about this love business... Well, maybe they would have something to say.

~*~

Paul's friends were exactly where he'd left them an hour ago, and there was another man with them whom he'd not met before. As he approached them, Warwick looked up and began to laugh. Colburne and the other fellow quickly joined in. Conway, who Paul was beginning to like more and more, just looked at the three men in a confused manner—like him, he had no idea what they found so amusing.

"I do hope you're going to share the joke," he said, sitting down and pouring himself a drink.

"Did they lay into you?" Warwick asked.

"Did they lecture or just look at you expectantly?" Colburne asked, beginning to chuckle again.

Paul started to laugh. "Clearly you have had some experience with these ladies."

When Warwick could stop laughing, he indicated the other man and said, "Have you met Welles?"

"No," Paul said, reaching out a hand.

The man gripped his. "John Welles," he said.

"Ah, Lady Welles' husband?"

"Yes. I take it you've just been speaking with her and the other ladies of the Whist Society?" he asked, smiling broadly at Paul.

"Indeed." He paused to take a healthy sip of his rum. "They spouted female nonsense at me and then sent me packing."

"Oh ho! What nonsense was this?" Colburne asked.

Paul took a theatrical pose with his head thrown back and a hand to his heart. "Love!"

Warwick cocked his head to the side. "What about it?"

Paul chuckled. "They claim that such a thing not only exists, but that you two—perhaps three," he said, turning to Welles, "are caught in its throws."

Colburne shrugged but strangely wasn't laughing any more. "<I>I</I> most certainly am. Welles?"

He sighed. "Deeply."

Warwick nodded. "Most definitely. Tina is an incredible woman."

"I'm in love as well, and have been before," Conway said, joining in. "Are you telling us that you *don't* love Miss Kendrick?"

Paul frowned at his friends. "My parents taught me from a young age that love was a fairytale. My father explicitly told me so."

"What?" Colburne exclaimed and began to laugh.

Conway just frowned at Paul. "I can assure you that love is most definitely real. It's wonderful, and painful, and incredible. I count myself extremely blessed for having loved and been loved by my Angelica, and now I'm hoping that… Well, that the person of my affections returns the sentiment," he said, glancing at the other men. Paul, of course, knew exactly who he meant but knew he couldn't say. This was going to get very complicated and awkward, but it was too much for him to think about just now. One thing at a time, he told himself.

"I concur," Welles said. "Definitely both wonderful *and* painful." He smiled as he took a sip of his drink. "Happily, we've moved from the painful part to the wonderful."

"I'm sorry your parents didn't have any love for each other," Colburne said. "It happens all too frequently in our society, but I can assure you, love *does* exist. It can sneak up on you before you entirely realize it, but it most definitely is there."

"So that's what went wrong with your proposal," Warwick said. "I assume the ladies informed you that you should try again and do so the correct way the next time?"

Paul nodded. "Actually, it was your wife, Welles, among others, who told me if I loved Miss Kendrick, I should tell her so."

The men all nodded in agreement.

"I had thought she was more practical than that," he said quietly more to himself than the others.

"Love can be practical," Warwick said. "My dearest wife is a business woman and was a damned good one, but when it came to love and marriage, she would accept nothing less than a full and complete commitment from me. Because of my feelings for her, I was happy to give it and did so in front of all the ladies of the Wagering Whist Society."

Paul sat forward. "I need to do this *publicly*?"

"No, no. I decided it would be best if I did so, but no, you can make your declarations in private. Just be sure to do so with honesty," Warwick said.

"And with your heart," Welles added.

"Yes, truly. Speak from your heart, Saint, and she'll know it," Colburne agreed.

It looked like Paul had some emotions to examine and think about. Love. It *was* real. Well, that perhaps explained some things.

~April 19~

Bel woke up Sunday morning to the quiet sound of cloth rustling. She sat up and found her sister pulling on Annie's cloak. "Are you leaving so early?"

"Yes," her sister said, turning around to face her. "Lady Sorrell is picking me up in about ten minutes. She wanted to leave town early before anyone else would be out so we wouldn't be seen."

"Ah, right, of course," Bel said. She gave her sister a smile. "It'll be really nice having you here openly."

Bee gave a little laugh. "Yes! I'll see you later."

She slipped out of the room, and Bel settled back down in her bed to sleep a little more.

When she woke up again, it was to the sound of thunder. She jumped out of bed and pulled back the curtains. It was pouring!

"Oh no!" All their plans for Bee to come into town at the height of the promenade… What were they going to do?

Bel got dressed as quickly as she could and ran down to find her aunt.

Lady Blakemore was sitting in her drawing room, staring out the window with a book in her lap.

"What are we to do?" Bel asked, not even giving her a proper greeting.

Her aunt just shook her head. "Lady Sorrell will just bring Bee back, I suppose. We'll have to find another occasion where the two of you can be unveiled. At least, she'll be here officially after today and won't have to continue to hide in your room."

Bel sat down on the sofa facing the window. "Yes, I suppose so." There was clearly nothing else they could do.

Bel went to practice the pianoforte and hope the rain let up. Hours later, it hadn't. Lydia and Diana arrived a little before three as they had planned. Bel was certain they would cancel but was very happy to see them all the same.

"I don't think we're going for our ride," Diana said after coming in.

"No, but I appreciate you came anyway," Bel said, welcoming them in.

"We couldn't very well let you wait by yourself,"

Lydia said.

"I have to say, I think this day has lasted forever," Bel said with a laugh.

They talked for some time until finally a commotion at the front door drew their attention, and very soon, Bee appeared in the drawing-room doorway.

It took almost no artifice on her part for Bel to jump up and run to her sister. Despite the fact they had actually seen each other that morning, Bel was so thrilled to be able to see her openly, she threw her arms around Bee and could honestly say she'd missed her terribly.

Bee looked at her a little funny but laughed. "I've missed you too! And I am so, so very happy to be here." She looked to Lady Sorrell. "Thank you so much, my lady, for bringing me to my sister."

The lady smiled and nodded. "It was my pleasure."

"No one else is here, only those who already know your secret," Lady Blakemore said.

"So Bel's show of welcoming me was unnecessary," Bee said with a laugh.

"It wasn't entirely a show, I *am* happy to see you. I'm even happier I can do so outside of our room," Bel said.

"I'm sure Bee being here openly is going to make life much easier for all of you," Lady Sorrell said.

"Yes, but since Bee couldn't come into town and be seen doing so, what are we going to do?" Bel asked.

"I've been thinking about that," Aunt Claire said. "Something you said this morning put an idea in my head."

They all looked to her.

"You said something about unveiling her," Lady Blakemore continued. She looked around with a big smile on her face, "What about if we do exactly that—at Lord Wickford's Venetian Ball."

There were gasps, and Bel couldn't contain her excitement. She clapped and giggled. "Yes! Oh, my goodness, Aunt, you are absolutely brilliant!"

The lady laughed and acknowledged the tribute.

"That is truly an excellent idea," Lydia agreed. "They can both go, masked, and then at midnight won't everyone be shocked when they unmask and there are two of them!"

They all laughed.

"It's perfect!" Bee agreed.

CHAPTER THIRTY-ONE

~April 21~

Bee was singing as Bel played the piano the following afternoon when the footman came in to inform them that Lord Conway wished to have a word.

"Please send him in," Bee requested. "And I will leave," she added after he'd gone.

Bel giggled.

"Good afternoon," the gentleman said, coming into the music room. He shook his head and laughed. "I think it will take some time to get used to seeing you two together. It's like seeing double."

Even Bee laughed at that one and then said, "Well, I'll make this easier for you and leave you two alone." She paused and then said with a sly little smile, "I am correct in assuming that you'd like a little privacy?"

"Yes, if you don't mind," Lord Conway said, giving her a big smile.

"You won't tell Aunt Claire?" Bel asked, just to be sure.

"Not for at least twenty minutes," Bee said with a laugh.

"I think that's about as much as we can ask,"

his lordship said.

Bee left the door mostly closed, but Lord Conway closed it all the way after she'd gone.

"What were you playing?" he asked, coming closer.

"Just some songs we enjoy." Bel played a little piece of *Robin Adair.*

"But now thou'rt cold to me, Robin Adair.

But now thou'rt cold to me, Robin Adair.

Yet he I lov'd so well, still in my heart shall dwell;

Oh, I can ne'er forget Robin Adair," Lord Conway sang.

She finished the song with a flourish and a laugh.

"I have to admit I was worried for a moment when you revealed your sister to me, that it was she who had the talent on the pianoforte," he admitted, leaning over the instrument toward her. "But then I thought of the song we shared that evening during your aunt's musicale, and I knew without a doubt that it had been *you* playing."

Bel's face heated with his words. She kept her gaze on the keys in front of her, fingering them but not pressing hard enough to create a sound. "It was, indeed, me that evening. Bee doesn't play an instrument, but she sings beautifully."

"You complement each other," he said.

She looked up. "Yes."

"As we do," he added more quietly.

She just smiled at him.

"And while I do love to compliment you," he said, playing with words, "I'd rather tell you how much I love you."

"But that is a compliment because being loved by you is a wonderful thing," she said, leaning forward toward him. If she didn't love the pianoforte so much, she would have cursed the instrument that separated them. "I love you too, my lord."

"Edward," he said. "You should call me by my name when you say such wonderful things to me." He chuckled.

She laughed and nodded. "Edward."

"It does sound lovely on your lips." He leaned closer over the edge of the instrument and gently placed his lips on hers. They were warm and spiced with a flavor that was entirely Edward's. He smelled wonderful. He felt wonderful. And Bel was now grateful she had stayed seated because she wasn't sure her legs would have held her if she had been standing. Everything within her seemed to melt with the heat of his lips.

His kiss was so sweet and wonderful, but their position was a little awkward. He moved away much sooner than she would have liked and then became much too serious.

Bel's breath caught in her throat, sure that he was about to ask for her hand. She was all ready to say "yes" when he said, "Belle, there is something I must tell you."

"Y-y-yes?" she asked, quickly changing the tone of her voice into a question.

He studied the top of the pianoforte for a moment. "You are not the first woman I have loved."

"Oh." She paused and then gave a little giggle. "Well, I imagine most young men have loved any number of women."

He gave her a little smile. "Those are probably closer to infatuations, and yes, I've had my share of those. But no, I'm talking about a true love. A deep love."

"Oh." Bel could feel her throat close up.

"In Venice. I, erm, I lived with a woman by the name of Angelica. We were friends for some time, and then we realized we loved each other. She moved in with me, and we lived as husband and wife, even though our union was never blessed by the church."

"Oh." Bel's throat became tighter. There had to be a reason he was telling her this. Was this Angelica going to one day come and find him? Why had he left her? Where was she now? The questions ran amok through her mind, but she didn't voice them, merely waiting for him to reveal the rest of his tale.

He cleared his throat. "Two years ago, she died of cancer. It was a slow and horrid death. I... I stayed with her the entire time, but there was nothing more I—or anyone—could do but watch her die and try what we could to relieve the pain."

Bel tried to blink back the burning tears in her eyes. "I'm so sorry," she whispered, her voice not quite working right. How horrid to watch someone you loved with all your heart die in such a way. She couldn't even imagine how painful that would be. No, she didn't even want to try!

He looked up then and managed to give her a tremulous little smile. He reached out and wiped a tear that was making its way slowly down the side of her face. "You cry, and yet you never even knew her."

"She was close to you, and she died in pain. I feel... I'm so sorry," Bel said again, unable to put her feelings into proper words.

He nodded. "I was in pain as well, as you can imagine. Emotional pain because I loved her dearly." He took in a deep breath. "But it was two years ago that she passed. I decided with the new year, I would no longer wallow in what *was* but move forward with my life. I moved back here to England, determined to try to find someone with whom I could be happy."

"You found me?" she asked quietly, hoping.

"I did, but more than that, I discovered I hadn't lost the ability to love. I discovered I could love again, yet not completely lose the feelings I had for Angelica. I still love her. But I love you as well."

Tears slipped from Bel's eyes once again. This time she wiped them away herself.

"I wanted to tell you. I felt you deserved to know."

Suddenly his behavior at the opera made sense. She gasped with the realization. "Was Angelica a lyric soprano?"

His gaze shot to hers, his eyes widening. It took him a moment, but he nodded. "Yes. Yes, she was."

"I understand, then, what you were going through at the opera."

"Yes." She couldn't believe it, but his eyes became glassy with tears as well. She couldn't stand to see him cry. She jumped up and threw herself into his arms.

"It's all right, Edward. It's all right. You can love your Angelica. I would never ask you do otherwise," she said, pressing her cheek to his chest.

His arms tightened around her. "You are too good, Belle. *My* belle. I am, indeed, the luckiest man in the world."

She pulled away a little so she could look up at him. He wasn't much taller than her, just the right height for her to reach his lips with hers while raising herself up just a touch. This time he didn't pull away but deepened their kiss, sending shooting stars racing through her body.

After a few minutes, a discreet cough made Bel jump away.

"May I assume that I am to wish you happy?" Aunt Claire said with a lift of her eyebrows and a smile slightly playing on her lips.

Bel giggled.

"Yes, my lady, I am exceedingly pleased to say that you assume correctly," Edward said with a laugh.

~April 23~

Their private family celebration of Bel's engagement to Lord Conway lasted straight through dinner that evening, to which his lordship was invited. They were just ending the very pleasant evening when the footman came in with a note.

"I beg your pardon, Miss Bee," he said, turning first toward Bee and then to Bel, "but there is a letter for you."

"For me?" Bee asked, looking to her aunt who gave her a nod of permission.

The footman turned back and handed it to her with a slight look of relief. Clearly, he hadn't known which twin was which.

Bee opened it and then read it out loud, "I would be honored if you would join me for an outing to visit the ancient Roman walls that can still be found in the vicinity of the city of London. Please let me know if you are free on Thursday afternoon. Yours, etc, St. Vincent." She lowered the note with a mix of excitement and apprehension. "What do you think, Aunt Claire?"

"I think it is an excellent idea for you to go on this outing," her aunt said.

"It sounds as if he put a lot of thought into where he would take you. You are quite enamored with history, are you not?" her uncle put in.

"I am," Bee agreed.

"I have noticed a number of the histories in my library have gone missing. I assume it is you who are borrowing them?" he asked with a chuckle.

"I read the History of Greece last week and am now on to a History of Ancient Rome," Bee said with a nod.

"So, an outing to see Roman walls would be perfect," her aunt said.

"Sounds horrendously dull, but I'm sure you and Lord St. Vincent will enjoy it immensely," Bel said with a laugh.

"I have to agree it's not something one would have ever considered doing with a young lady," Lord Conway agreed.

"It does sound perfect to me," Bee said with a giggle. She immediately got up to respond and thank Paul for his invitation.

~*~

The reins in Paul's hands slipped a touch, forcing him to hold on to them more tightly.

Surreptitiously, he wiped one hand and then the other on his thighs. How utterly ridiculous. Why were his palms sweaty? He knew precisely what he was going to say to Bee. He knew exactly where he would say it. But even more importantly, he now understood what that odd feeling in his chest and stomach were—love.

Oh, how his father would have laughed. He would have had a field day with the idea that his son was in love. How many times had he told Paul that it was all rubbish? And yet now, all Paul could think of was how sorry he felt for his father who had never known love, who had never felt this.

It wasn't the most comfortable feeling, he had to admit. And yet, it was, at the same time, the most wonderful. And he could only now pray that Bee felt the same way.

He looked over at her, sitting next to him on the bench of his phaeton. She was eagerly looking out for the wall he had told her about.

"I've heard that the Romans had a city here, but I don't know very much about it," she said. She seemed to be examining each building they passed as if the wall would just suddenly appear.

"I'm afraid no one does, but we do know that there are walls still in existence which show where it was," he commented. "Don't worry, I won't let you miss it. It's a little farther away."

She laughed and turned back to him, her beautiful face bright with color and excitement. Paul was almost annoyed that he had to turn his attention away from her and watch where he was going.

They drove for about half an hour.

"We'll start near the Tower of London. I hope

that doesn't disturb you," he asked.

"Oh no, only, I *would* prefer not to go in. I hear there is a menagerie, but I'm afraid I'm not one for unusual animals," Bee said apologetically.

"That's perfectly fine. I hadn't intended that we do so," he reassured her.

He did have to stop quite close to the Tower because that was where the piece of the wall for them to visit was located.

Bee spotted it immediately. "Is that it?" she asked, pointing to the wall made of white stone.

"Yes. Shall we get down and walk?"

She nodded, and he leapt down and then reached up to help her. He couldn't help himself, though. He suddenly felt the overwhelming desire to hold her close, so instead of simply handing her down, he lifted her, setting her gently on the ground just next to him.

They were as close to embracing as they could be in public. Her cheeks flushed and her beautiful hazel eyes glittered with a happiness that filled Paul's heart in a way he would never have imagined possible. He was hard pressed not to bend down and...

Out of the corner of his eye, he caught the movement of his phaeton. He started toward his horse, but then stopped when he noticed Nate, his liveried tiger, had the horse well in hand.

He laughed in relief, gave the boy a nod, and then held out his arm for Bee to take so they could walk closer to the wall.

"It is quite formidable," Bee said, looking up at it.

"Indeed. It was truly meant to keep invaders

out and the Roman people safe," he agreed. He turned toward her as they strolled slowly. Looking at her, feeling the warmth inside of him mix with a slight nervousness, he wondered how he could have ever thought love didn't exist. "I think it would be a wonderful thing to keep you safe," he said, speaking directly from his heart.

"Well, you've already saved my sister once," Bee pointed out.

He chuckled. "Yes, although, may I be awful and admit I wished it had been you that evening? Not that I would ever want you to be in any harm," he added quickly.

She laughed. "No, of course not. But I'm afraid I'm much too practical and staid to have ever done such a thing as go to Vauxhall for a masquerade."

"I'm *very* happy to hear that."

"Do you have such strong walls at your estate?" she asked, turning back toward the Roman wall.

"Nothing to compare to this," he said, looking up at it as well. He turned to her. "I do hope you will have the opportunity to see my home."

"If you invite me," she said with a teasing little smile that made him want to laugh and pull her to him once again.

But he was here not just to make love to her—although that was wonderful too—but he had a wrong to right. He took in a deep breath and prepared himself to bare his soul because she deserved nothing less. "I would like to do more than that. Beatrice, I made a hash out of my proposal the other day. I was stupid and naïve, and I hope you will give me another chance."

Bee bent her head to look up at the wall towering above them before looking back to Paul. "I would like it above all else if you would."

He nearly sighed in relief. This time he would do it right. He lowered himself to one knee before her, for all who were walking by to see, and said, "Miss Beatrice Kendrick, I have learned a great many things in these past few weeks, but the one lesson I've learned best is that love is an incredible thing. It lives beyond romance novels and possibly even dwells among the pages of history. I love you, and I would be honored if you would agree to be my wife."

Bee's smile couldn't have gotten any wider. "I love you, Paul, and I would be honored to spend my life exploring old ruins with you."

"Until I become one myself?" he asked with a laugh.

She giggled. "Until we *both* do."

Chapter Thirty-Two

~April 25~

Never had Bel and Bee had so much fun just getting dressed as they did for the Venetian Masquerade. They giggled and laughed, oohed and aahed over their dresses and hair, then the final piece—their masks!

They had decided to play one last trick on society. Tonight, they would be wearing identical masks and clothing. To everyone they would look like the same person and agreed to never be in the same place at the same time.

Bee was going to go a little earlier with their uncle; Bel would follow with their aunt. Yes, even their relations would be in on the trick this time, just to see everyone's expressions when they discovered there were two of them. Aunt Claire thought that doing it this way would underscore the idea that only one of them had been here until now, otherwise she was afraid that people would wonder just how long Bee had been in town. If they played this trick now, hopefully, no one would realize they'd been playing it all along.

They were dressed in identical white dresses with layers of lace and simple gold edging matching their simple white masks, which also had gold around the eyes. The masks covered their whole face so all anyone could see would be their eyes rimmed in black. They both had on white hats of tulle and lace to cover their hair, which was styled identically. It would be impossible for the casual observer to tell who was who, however just for their friends and relations ease Bee had a red rose pinned to her right shoulder and Bel had one pinned to her left.

The two girls giggled all the way downstairs, eager to see their aunt and uncle in their finery as well. Their uncle had opted for a rather simple half-mask. It was black with the eyes outlined in silver. His waistcoat was a matching black with silver embroidery. Lady Blakemore was stunning in a purple half-mask highlighted with gold paint. Purple feathers ornamented her hair, and her gown was a matching color with gold braid.

"My, don't you both look beautiful," their aunt said as they came down the stairs. They curtsied, still giggling away.

"You both look very elegant," Bee said.

"Indeed! This is definitely going to be the highlight of the season!" Bel said, still giggling.

"Well, let us be off then," their uncle said, ushering them all out the door to their waiting carriage. They would all be traveling together, but Lord Blakemore and Bee would get down first, the carriage would go around the square and when it returned to the door, Bel and Lady Blakemore would descend.

"Come along, Beatrice," Lord Blakemore said, ushering the last one out of their house.

"I'm Bel," she giggled.

"Ah! Yes, well, it is impossible to tell in your

finery."

She reminded him of their roses, but he just shook his head. Bel laughed, certain he would never get them straight.

The ballroom Lord Wickford had rented for the evening was already filled with bedecked, bedazzled, and naturally, masked party-goers.

"I see Bee over there speaking with..." Bel laughed. "Well, I honestly don't know who she's speaking with—two ladies. Perhaps Diana and Lydia?"

Lady Blakemore laughed as well. "That is the fun of a masquerade. You don't know who anyone is. If Beatrice is over there, then we should go this way," she said, heading in the opposite direction.

Bel laughed at how quickly her aunt got into the spirit of the trick they were playing. "You seem to be enjoying this as much as we always have," she commented to her aunt.

Lady Blakemore paused and turned toward Bel. "You know, I am. It's very odd. I've always been one for rules and practicality like your sister, but this... This is a little naughty and a great deal of fun. I suppose because I know you will both be revealed later on tonight."

Bel gave a little shrug. "We usually enjoy the hoax, too, just so long as no one is harmed."

Her aunt gave a decisive nod. "Precisely. Oh look, that's got to be the Duke and Duchess of Warwick."

They'd been told that Tina would be dressed as the moon, so it was easy to identify her, and obviously, the man next to her had to be her husband.

Her mask was pure white with silver outlining the eyes and a halo of silver above it. Her gown was simply a pure white froth of flowing silk. The duke was all in brown with gold shot through, not only his waistcoat but his outer coat as well, and his mask was just pure gold-colored.

"Is that Margaret next to him, do you think?" Lady Blakemore asked.

"It must be," Bel said.

The girl was in a pale pink velvet gown that almost looked to be more lace than gown. Her full mask was a beautiful creamy face with pouting red lips and pink swirls decorating the cheeks and around the eyes. Finally, she had on a pink velvet triangular hat trimmed with yet more lace and white feathers.

"Your Grace, you look so very elegant," Bel said, curtsying to him, Tina, and Margaret.

"Thank you, as do you, Miss..." he said, fishing for her name.

"Ah-ah," she laughed. "I'm not going to be giving my identity away so easily."

He sighed dramatically. "Well, I know you are in some way associated with the Ladies' Wagering Whist Society." He turned to her aunt and squinted at her. "You must be Lady Blakemore."

The lady laughed. "Well done, Your Grace."

"So that means you are Miss Kendrick," he deduced.

"Perhaps," she said with a giggle. "It's definitely going to be a challenging evening not being able to call each other by name."

"Indeed. But it's still lovely to see you this evening. And that dress looks as beautiful as I thought it would," Tina said, moving her whole head to look at Bel in all her splendor from the eye slits in her mask.

"And it is thanks to you," Bel said, reaching out to squeeze Tina's hand.

"So, *you* know who's who because you made so many of their dresses," her husband said, sounding a little miffed.

"I *designed* most of their dressed," Tina corrected him. "Thank goodness, I didn't have to make them all. I would never have finished in time!"

"Good evening," a man in a green and blue costume said, joining them.

"Lord—" Bel began. Her new fiancé had told her what he'd be wearing so she could identify him, and she had shared with him the trick she and Bee were playing.

"Ah, ah," he said, wagging a finger. "No names this evening, but yes, it is I." He made a grand leg which looked very funny because his right leg was a different color than his left. His sleeves were the opposite colors as his legs, and his mask switched again.

"This is going to be deuced confusing!" the duke complained again.

"It is Lord Conway, Your Grace," Bel whispered loudly to him.

"Thank you," he whispered back.

"Oh now, that's not quite fair, is it?" Lord Conway complained.

"Well, you know who he is, so I thought it *would* be quite fair," Bel said.

"All right, yes, I do," Lord Conway laughed.

They were soon joined by a gentleman in a long green velvet cloak. His mask was all swirls of gold and green, and his head was covered by his hood so his hair couldn't be seen. He was, however, the tallest man around, although the duke came quite close. Still, it was his height that gave him away as Lord St. Vincent.

"Good evening, my lord," Bel said with a giggle. "You look wonderful."

"And you look quite stunning," he said, with a bow. "Are you the one I'm looking for?" he asked since he too had been let in on their little secret.

"No, she's on the other side of the room," Bel said.

He laughed. "Naturally. Well, then, if you'll excuse me." He bowed to everyone and then walked off to find Bee.

"What was that about?" Margaret asked, watching his back.

"Oh, nothing. He was looking for someone, and I told him where to find them, that's all," Bel said as innocently as she could.

"But who was that?" Tina asked.

"I really can't say," Bel said with a giggle.

A woman nearby gave a loud laugh and then a little screech followed by more laughter.

"I have a feeling there's going to be quite a bit of that going on as well," Lady Blakemore said.

"What is that?" Margaret asked.

"Behavior just on the edge of propriety," her brother explained.

"Or fallen off the edge," Lady Blakemore added.

"Oh, dear." Tina turned to look in the direction of the laughter.

"Gentlemen, I suggest you keep a close eye on those you care about. This is a masquerade. People feel a great deal more emboldened when no one can see your face," Lady Blakemore said.

The sounds of the orchestra preparing for the first dance drew their attention.

"I beg your pardon, my lady, may I have the honor of this dance?" a gentleman said, coming forward and holding out his hand to Margaret.

He was dressed similarly to Lord St. Vincent, only his cloak was pinned back on one side, revealing a very fine black suit. He had neither gold nor silver embellishing his clothes, only a thin band of lace along the edges of his cloak and at his wrists and neck. His mask was white with black dripping eyes and black lips.

"Oh! Er, may I, W... er, brother?" Margaret said with a giggle.

"I suppose so, although I have to say it is very disconcerting not knowing who it is you will be dancing with," the duke said with a smile for the gentleman, perhaps hoping he would reveal his identity.

The man just bowed and held out his hand to Margaret. She laughed again as she took it and allowed him to lead her out and join the dance.

"Who do you suppose that was?" Tina asked, following them with her eyes.

"I have no idea. His voice didn't sound familiar either," Lady Blakemore said, also watching them. "And I have to agree with you, Your Grace, not knowing who's who is very disconcerting. I'm grateful to have identified Lord Conway."

"Well, speaking of dancing," Lord Conway said, turning to Bel. "Would you care to do so?"

"I would love to," Bel said, with a curtsy.

She allowed him to lead her out and then proceeded to have to best time of it. She was in the same vicinity as Margaret, and she was rather surprised to see the girl laugh and talk as if she knew the gentleman with whom she was dancing. Bel wondered if secretly she did.

The evening sped by in a blur of giggles and mystery.

Sir Reggie was easy to spot, wearing bright red and green. Lord Rosebury and Mr. Hershawn were terrible at keeping their identities secret. They went about introducing themselves to everyone.

They approached Bel as she was enjoying a glass of lemonade after the first dance.

"Didn't we just see you over on the other side of the room?" Lord Rosebury asked, looking very confused.

"I don't know, did you?" Bel asked with a giggle.

"I could have sworn we did," Mr. Hershawn agreed.

"Then perhaps you did," Bel agreed. She curtsied to them and went off in the opposite direction.

For the second dance that would bring them up to midnight, Bee and Bel had agreed in advance with their respective fiancés that Bel would dance at the front of the line and Bee toward the back. At midnight, they would find each other in the center for the unveiling.

Bel took up her position across from Lord

Conway but turned to see a woman staring at her.

"Is there something wrong?" Bel asked.

"N-no, it's just that I thought I saw you at the other end. You must have passed me somehow," the woman said.

"Perhaps I did," Bel said.

"Or could someone else have exactly the same costume? I wouldn't think that likely."

The music began, so Bel was spared from having to answer her.

The dance progressed with couples changing places after each repetition of the dance, each end working its way toward the center. The dance would finish when the people who'd begun at either end reached the middle, and it worked out perfectly.

There were laughs and odd comments as Bee and Bel reached each other and began to turn about hand in hand as the dance prescribed, but the musicians hadn't timed themselves quite as well. The clock began to strike twelve just before the dance ended.

Bel was almost too preoccupied with her sister to notice that just as the clock began to strike, the man dancing with Margaret abandoned her. It was the oddest thing, but he simply gave her a quick bow and disappeared into the crowd before the dance had even ended.

Poor Margaret was left standing alone on the floor with Bee and Bel on either side of her. She looked devastated, not even noticing the two identical girls.

"Ladies and gentlemen!" Lord Wickford's voice boomed out from the balcony where the orchestra was seated. They had stopped playing the moment the clock began to strike the hour. "Ladies and gentlemen," their host called out again.

"The time has come,
the bell has pealed,
No matter where from
Your fate is sealed
The fun's just begun…
now all be revealed!"

He threw out his arms, then reached up and took off his own mask and hat, revealing the identity everyone already knew.

There was laughter and applause.

Bel and Bee looked at each other and laughed. As one, they each pulled off their hats and masks, as others were doing as well.

Margaret suddenly gave a screech as she noticed Bee and Bel. "There are two of you!" A number of other people turned their way as well and gasped as they took in the twins.

"What is this? What's going on?" Lord Wickford's loud voice could be heard coming toward them.

The girls both turned toward him as people parted to let him through.

He stopped short a few feet away and burst out laughing. "Twins! Miss Kendrick, you did not tell us you were a twin!"

Bel giggled and Bee laughed out loud.

"But wait, which one of you is the Miss Kendrick we know?" Lord Wickford asked, coming closer.

"I am the one who has been here for the past month," Bel said. "Beatrice and I are mirror twins—

we look identical but are opposites."

"Well, this is a wonderful surprise. Welcome, Miss Beatrice. We have thoroughly been enjoying the company of your sister this season. Clearly, now we will all have double the fun," he said and then burst out laughing. "What a wonderful trick. A trick of mirrors."

About the Author

Meredith Bond's books straddle that beautiful line between historical romance and fantasy. An award-winning author, she writes fun traditional Regency romances, medieval Arthurian romances, and Regency romances with a touch of magic. Known for her characters "who slip readily into one's heart," Meredith's heart belongs to her husband and two children.

Meredith loves connecting with readers. Sign up for her monthly newsletter at http://meredithbond. com/blog/newsletter-sign-up/ to receive free short stories and get all her news before anyone else. And don't forget to find her on-line:

Website: http://www.meredithbond.com

Facebook: https://www.facebook.com/meredithbondauthor

Amazon: http://www.amazon.com/Meredith-Bond/e/B001KI1SNE

Instagram: https://www.instagram.com/meredith_bond/

Bookbub: https://www.bookbub.com/authors/meredith-bond

Newsletter: http://meredithbond.com/subscribe/

Please don't forget to leave a review wherever you buy books.

Follow all of the women of the Ladies' Wagering Whist Society

1806 Season
A Hand for the Duke
Featuring Christianne Norman, Lady Norman
The Jack of Diamonds
Featuring Miss Lydia Sheffield
The Games She Played
Featuring Miss Diana Hemshawe

1807 Season
A Trick of Mirrors
Featuring Claire Tyne, Lady Blakemore
A Bid for Romance
Featuring Alys Russell, Duchess of Kendell
An Affair of Hearts
Featuring Mrs. Penelope Aldridge

1808 Season
Love in Spades
Featuring Cynthia Montley, Lady Sorrell
coming: Spring, 2021
A Token of Love
Featuring Ellen Aston, Lady Moreton
coming: Spring, 2021
Bonus
The King of Clubs
Featuring Joshua Powell, Lord Wickford
coming: Spring, 2021

Other Books By Meredith Bond

The Merry Men Series
An Exotic Heir
A Merry Marquis
A Rake's Reward
A Dandy in Disguise
My Lord Ghost
My Gentleman Thief
Under the Mango Tree
A Spanish Dilemma
When Hearts Rebel

The Storm Series
Storm on the Horizon
Bridging the Storm
Magic in the Storm
Through the Storm

The Children of Avalon Trilogy
Air: Merlin's Chalice
Water: The Return of Excalibur
Fire: Nimuë's Destiny

Falling
Falling for a Pirate

*Chapter One: A Fast, Fun Way to Write
Fiction*
Self-Publishing: Easy as ABC
*"In A Beginning", a short story featuring
Lilith*

9 781737 208624